(Don't you) Forget about Me

ALSO BY
KATE KARYUS QUINN

Another Little Piece

KATE KARYUS QUINN

(Don't You) Forget About Me

HARPER TEEN

An Imprint of HarperCollinsPublishers

HarperTeen is an imprint of HarperCollins Publishers.

(Don't You) Forget About Me
www.epicreads.com

Library of Congress Control Number: 2013958345
ISBN 978-0-06-213596-4 (trade bdg.)

Typography by Torborg Davern
14 15 16 17 18   LP/RRDH   10 9 8 7 6 5 4 3 2 1
❖
First Edition

To:
My guy, Jamie
and
My sunshine, Zoe

We dance round in a ring and suppose,
But the Secret sits in the middle and knows.
—ROBERT FROST

(Don't you) Forget About Me

TOTAL ECLIPSE OF THE HEART

Four Years Ago

IT WAS A BIZARRE MAY DAY PARADE AT MIDNIGHT instead of midday. There were no floats, no firefighters dressed in full gear tossing out bubble gum while their single siren blared, no horns tooting in time to the beat of the drums. The golden girls did not prance and smile with their silver batons spinning figure eights. Little kids with faces red and sticky from Popsicles and candy apples didn't shove and shout or cry when the balloon they'd forgotten they were holding escaped into the sky.

Your parade lacked those simple joys and sorrows, and yet four years later it still marches on inside me, advancing toward its inevitable ending.

Officially the parade was canceled that year. It's canceled every fourth year. Any excitement—even the gentle excitement of an old-fashioned parade—is enough to trigger disaster during a fourth year. No one complains when events are canceled; instead they remind each other of the many ways in which fourth years have stolen the best and the brightest of our young people away.

The February 4th when sweet little Danny Marker turned five people into statues just by shaking their hands. Or the August 19th when identical twins Olive and Olivia Snow had a disagreement over whether that day's matching outfits would be plaid or polka-dot. Neither would give way, and the argument escalated until in the same breath they each wished the other to the ends of the earth. Before they could inhale again, both girls blinked out of existence. Then there was the May 1st when the earth opened up right where Main and State cross. The convertible with the May Queen was swallowed so quickly that she kept waving and smiling even as she fell through the split blacktop and into the dark below.

People will tell you that this is just the way things go around here when someone is taken with the madness. Sometimes that means losing the May Queen and her convertible too.

On your night, Piper, there was no May Queen. Only you in your red cowgirl boots leading the way across the intersection of State and Main. Your spurs sparked as they struck against the memorial plaque set into the road. Behind you trailed nearly half the high school. Shirtless boys in boxers, girls with long tangled hair and traces of Clearasil on their chins or cheekbones. Stumbling from their homes in bare feet, their eyes wide open yet unfocused, they formed a single-file line that wound through town and followed wherever you led. All the different cliques and groups were equally represented. It was easy to identify status in the high school pecking order when walking through the cafeteria, but under the moonlight, the jocks, geeks, princesses, and freaks all seemed similarly fragile.

The parade took a turn down State Street. Usually the blooms of the dogwood trees lining State had come and gone by May. But winter had lingered that year, and the trees had only budded and flowered within the past two weeks. As if having a change of mind, the wicked wind that had kept the long line of sleepy feet shuffling forward suddenly began to shake the blossoms from the trees and shoot them high into the sky. They didn't fall fast and heavy like the wet snowfalls that had plagued early April, but danced through the air, tickling at the noses of the half-asleep as if trying to rouse them from this doomed dream.

It was no use, though. The parade turned again, down Spring Street and toward the trestle bridge, leaving the trampled blossoms in its wake.

Going out onto the trestle bridge is forbidden, and it isn't a law that needs a whole lot of enforcing. There is enough danger in this town that nobody goes looking for it. Except you, Piper. You were the exception.

Are the exception. Are.

So I was not surprised when we ended up at the bridge.

You stopped and the parade behind you instantly halted as well, swaying in place to the gentle gurgle and shush of the Salt Spring. I'd followed you this whole way, only a step behind the same way our dog Chance eagerly followed me, not caring where you went, just glad to come along. But that simple show of devotion wasn't enough for you, Piper. As always, you needed more.

"Do you believe in destiny?" you asked me for the second time that evening.

I hadn't answered the first time. You'd just woken me from a sound sleep and I was too busy feeling grumpy about having been pulled from my warm bed. That moment when you first asked the question and I'd failed to answer seemed like an opportunity lost forever.

"No," I finally answered, even though I knew it was too late. You smiled at me, not even hearing, too far in the grip of whatever it is that claims the teens of Gardnerville during a fourth year.

"One and the same," you said, prompting me.

No. That's what I wanted to say. But the time for rebellion was past, and who knew when I would see you again.

"One and the same." I repeated the phrase that bound us tighter than other sisters, making us more like Siamese twins despite our four-year age difference.

You gave me another brilliant Piper smile in response, then blew a kiss before skipping away down the trestle bridge.

I didn't go with you. Instead I stood on solid land and tried to keep the sleepwalkers from following you. I shook them and shouted in their faces, while Chance barked and nipped at their heels. It didn't work. They were deep into dreams where the world was soft and warm and full of perfect first kisses. Eventually I stopped trying and let them pass.

The trestle bridge was over a mile long, which meant that by the time you and your followers reached the midpoint, you'd all shrunk to the size of plastic play figurines. I folded my hands together in a way that felt vaguely prayerful, and hoped that it would be enough to bring God into this and keep the train out. But there would be a train. I knew this the same way I knew that if you were the type to carry a gun, it would always be loaded. My body tensed, waiting for the telltale whistle and then for whatever would happen after that, when a man appeared beside me.

"Piper," he said, grabbing hold of my arm.

"No, Mr. Elton, it's me. Skylar," I corrected him, pulling away.

His appearance was another surprise that was not a surprise at all. He was a teacher at the high school. New that year and too young and too handsome to be a teacher. Of course, all the girls fell in love with him. You loved him too. Maybe he loved you back. But not enough. I don't know if anyone could ever love you enough, but he'd fallen so short that it had brought us all here to this fateful night.

"Piper left me a note," he said. He handed a folded piece of paper to me, as if I'd demanded evidence. I opened it. Inside was a lock of Piper's hair, a mixture of golden brown and red, exactly like my own.

"Where is she?" he asked. Then he looked past me, his eyes following the long line of the bridge stretched out before us, until his gaze stopped, caught upon the vision of your silent parade. He took a step forward and then turned back to me. "What the hell?"

It wasn't a question that needed an answer, but it was answered anyway by the train whistle finally blowing, a long angry wail. A moment later, the glow of the train's light appeared on the distant horizon.

"Shit," Elton said, stunned.

The whistle screamed again and the vibration of the train rumbled against my soles.

"Go." I mouthed the word at the same time that you shouted it, your voice somehow cutting through the noise.

The light grew, Piper, spotlighting the sleepwalkers as you touched each of their shoulders, setting them in motion, giving them orders to fly. One after another, like dominoes set up and knocked back down, they climbed on top of the bridge railing, balanced, and jumped.

No, they didn't jump. *Jump* implies an understanding of gravity and a knowledge that up is only temporary. With spring-loaded legs and arms outstretched like Superman, those young men and women didn't jump. They launched.

You could see the exact moment they woke from the dream. Midair, seconds from the icy water below, their limbs pedaled wildly, seeking something solid, but there was only the full moon, and even though it was slung low in the sky, it was still too far out of reach.

The last sleepwalker jumped, leaving only the train, and in front of it—you. Your red cowgirl boots thumped against the wooden boards while your arms pumped and your mouth stretched in a wide grin that was still not big enough to convey all the joy you felt at that instant.

There were screams from the woken sleepwalkers in the water below, and I wondered if I should help them somehow, but I couldn't swim and it didn't matter anyway because I couldn't take my eyes away from you.

You wouldn't jump. I saw that clearly. You were determined to outrun that train or let it grind you beneath its steel wheels.

Elton bolted past me, onto the tracks, toward you and the train at your heels. If I froze that moment, and cut the train from the picture, you might be long-separated lovers, running toward each other, arms outstretched, everything forgiven, and only seconds away from a happy ending.

But this was a fourth year in Gardnerville, and there were no happy endings.

ONE

Four Years Later

WILLS CROUCHES IN A DUSTY CORNER OF THE TRAIN station intent on the poor cockroach he's discovered there. He gives it an experimental poke, then plucks it from the ground and, seeing an opportunity, quickly turns it into a caboose for his wooden engine. "Choo, choo," he calls in his husky little-boy voice while the doomed roach twitches, trying to escape. Luckily, Wills's fat little four-year-old fingers are unwittingly merciful. The roach is dead long before its legs give way to the friction of being dragged across the floor.

"Wills, put that down," Mom calls to him. Normally, she'd already be at his side, wiping his hands with the bottle of hand sanitizer she always keeps in her purse. With Piper and me, Mom followed the old "if you love something, set it free" model of parenting. That didn't go so well. Now she has a second chance with Wills and is taking a completely opposite approach. Attachment parenting, I think they call it. She begged the doctor not to cut the umbilical cord. That didn't work, so she just pretended like it was still there. I don't think she and Wills have ever spent more than half a day without being an arm's reach away from each other.

"Your mother and Piper only know how to go to extremes." That's something Dad used to say. He would say it now if he saw Mom and Wills together. But he never met Wills. Mom was still pregnant when he went to an extreme of his own, flying to San Francisco to jump off their big fancy bridge when the one here would've done him just as well.

Today, though, Mom is distracted. Wills knows it too. Instead of obeying, he turns so that his roach train is hidden behind the curve of his back. Mom shifts on the hard wooden bench, like she's going to stand, but a moment later she folds her hands in her lap and turns her gaze to the double doors between us and the empty train platform.

I step in front of her, purposely blocking her view, and press my nose against the glass. The air conditioner wheezing in the corner has chilled the room enough so that my breath fogs the pane, slowly obscuring what little there is to see. Just a concrete slab with the empty train tracks below. No one is waiting to get on the train. Despite everything, not many people leave this town. The train station doesn't even have a ticket booth. It's free to leave. The only people this town makes pay are those who decide to stay.

"Skylar, please sit down."

Mom's reprimand to me is as soft as the one Wills received. If she'd yelled, I could've ignored her and gone back to pacing the ten-by-ten station. But her voice quavers just slightly, and it is enough to make me stop. I don't sit though. That is an unreasonable request. It is all I can do to stand still, swallowing my scream of frustration at being here.

Most days I wouldn't care that much. I could put up with the discomfort of one morning spent at the train station if I had one of my precious forget-me-not pills at home waiting to make it dissolve. But I'm out of pills today, and with no more being sold until tomorrow, it's a good bet that most other notters are out too. A few of them might have been clever enough to hoard a pill or two away, and if I'd gotten an early start like I'd planned, I might've tracked one of them down. With every minute that passes, the odds of this plan working out become increasingly dim.

I sigh. Loudly. Ignoring me, Mom reaches for the pile of papers next to her on the bench and flips through them. She's done this at least a half dozen times in the fifteen minutes we've been waiting. Her lips move as she reads each person's name, committing it to memory along with their personal tales of woe that have driven them here.

"How many?" I ask the question even though I don't want to know.

Mom shuffles through the papers again, stalling.

"They keep packing the newcomers in. Every single month, the train's been delivering a fresh batch of them." My voice, too loud and confrontational, fills the room. Wills looks up, his eyes wide and worried. "There must be a lot this time. Though why they'd send them now, during a fourth year that has already stretched into August, is beyond me."

"Well, you have to admit that the last few years have been mild." Mom doesn't look at me, but instead straightens the papers, tapping them against the bench beside her. "I think Mr. Elton's impulse-control programs are really starting to make a difference. Maybe this town is finally changing for the better. Isn't that what you always wanted?"

I bark out a noise that some might characterize as a laugh except that it is bitter and angry and should be accompanied by a belch of black smoke instead of a smile. Of course Mom wants to join the rest of the town in singing "happy days are here again." Never mind that Piper's gone. Maybe I'd once dreamed of a perfect Gardnerville too, but I'm older now and if there's one thing I've learned, it's that there's always a price to be paid.

Always.

As if reading my mind, Mom says, "How about trying to look on the bright side? Would that hurt?"

The thing is, Mom doesn't read minds, but I do. And I can see that she's every bit as afraid as me that none of this will end well. I can hear her mulling over the idea of leaving this town and taking me and Wills with her, but her imagination never goes beyond us stepping onto the train. She never thinks about where we'd sit, if she'd hold Wills close or let him press his nose against the glass and watch the only home he's ever known turn into a memory. She never imagines the way our bodies would jerk as the train began to move, or the moment when the train would be swallowed by the tunnel and every last bit of daylight would disappear. And because none of that is in her head, I feel fairly safe in predicting that we won't be leaving Gardnerville anytime soon.

"Skylar, I'm sorry. Let's not fight." Of course, she's apologizing. Dad taught her well. If I was a better person, I'd tell her there's nothing to be sorry about; maybe I'd even mumble an apology of my own. Instead, I say nothing, and watch as she hunches forward into a defensive position. Toward the end with Dad, she often looked like this, a turtle that had lost its shell but was still desperately trying to hide.

My father was a bully. A genial, smiling bully. I hate when people say we're alike. They mean it kindly. Everyone loved him, and to be compared to him is considered a great compliment. It's one I don't often receive. Piper was always more like Dad. Bright and charming and dangerous. I don't have any of those traits except that last one. I can be just as mean as my father was on his worst day but, unlike him, I never learned to hide it behind a smile.

"I should go," I say, seeing the escape route I've been wanting ever since Mom caught me on the way out the door.

"You promised you'd come with me," she had said, blocking the doorway.

"Oh, was that today?" I'd bluffed, pretending to know what she was talking about. Pretending to remember a conversation that might've occurred at any time in the past few weeks while I'd been wrapped in the haze of one purple pill after another. The tail end of one pill muffled a conversation, and the next one blotted it out entirely.

Of course, there was also the possibility that Mom was playing me and I'd never promised her anything. Mom may be a neglectful parent, but even she couldn't have missed the number of times in the past four years when I've stood directly in front of her and had to admit that she looked familiar but I couldn't exactly recall where we'd met.

In the end, though, it didn't matter if I'd promised or not. A train was coming with new residents and we had to be there to welcome them. Of course, the welcome mostly consisted of bubble bursting. Someone had to tell the poor schmucks that there was a downside to living in this magical town.

Mom inherited the job after Dad died. Although she's only a Gardner by marriage, she takes it a million times more seriously than he ever did. He never dragged any of us kids along and he was never on time either. Sometimes he'd leave the newcomers waiting in the station for hours after the train had chugged back out of town.

Mom always insists on us being early. Maybe because she remembers being one of those newcomers, sitting on that very same bench. Before arriving here, she'd spent the previous three years of her life in various hospitals, as her parents sought second, third, and fourth opinions. Then a recruiter approached them with stories of a magical place they could send their daughter . . . for a small fee, of course. The only problem was Mom's age. She'd just turned eighteen, which meant leaving everything and everyone she'd ever known behind. Her parents didn't hesitate, though. They sent her to Gardnerville, knowing that her good health would be guaranteed only as long as she remained here, and that no visitors were ever allowed.

I am brought back to the present when the papers flutter from Mom's hands, hitting my feet in surrender. Only then do I realize that instead of stomping away, I am still standing in the exact same place. Which means that I am here to see the pathetic lost look on Mom's face. And the tears. Always the tears. They fill her eyes, turning them into green swimming pools, and then they flow silently down her cheeks.

"It's just something in my eye," she used to say when I was little, but I don't think I was ever little enough to actually believe it.

"I'll stay," I say, breaking as I always do, and, as if in response, the train's whistle howls in the distance.

It sounds nothing like Wills's soft and husky "choo choo."

Our small town is quiet with no airplanes flying overhead and few cars on the street. Even at the farthest edges of Gardnerville, where the trailer park gives way to the slippery ravines, you can hear the train's shriek as it is forced through the narrow mountain passage. At first it's perceived as an angry echo. From the edge of the water, it sounds like a dozen different trains are pushing their way through that long and skinny tunnel. Then the train bursts out onto the trestle bridge, and the whole town seems to sway just slightly in a way that makes people miss a step when going down the stairs or spill a hot cup of coffee onto their lap.

Now I put a hand to the wall. As it trembles beneath my fingertips, I can almost sense exactly where the train is and when it will screech to a stop in front of us. Wills drops his toy train and clambers to his feet, ready to run out to the platform, but Mom springs up and pushes the door closed before he's even opened it an inch. She keeps one hand against the glass barricade while the other grips the back of Wills's shirt. She has already lost one child to this train; I guess she doesn't want to risk another.

We all take several involuntary steps backward when the train pulls into view, as if we need to give it space. But when it comes to a full stop, it seems to shrink and becomes just a machine, no more noteworthy or frightening than a blender.

The passenger-train door opens, and a long moment passes before the first person exits. Then there is a flood of them, crowding the small platform. Putting on her Gardner face, Mom finally releases Wills as she steps out onto the platform and smiles like a hostess welcoming guests to a party.

"Hello, welcome to Gardnerville, please come in! This way, please."

They are uncertain and blinking in the too-bright sun. Mom lures them inside with her pasted-on smile and gently waving hand. I count them as they fill the corners and edges of the room. The last two, a father carrying a pale girl in his arms, are numbers twenty-three and twenty-four. I look past them to see if anyone else is coming and catch sight of a lone passenger walking in the other direction.

I push past the father and sickly kid, and as I do a prickle of something secret and terrible crawls up my spine to nibble at my skull. I flick it away but not quickly enough. Secrets are already spilling into me in that loud whispery way they always have. Secrets are stupid things. They hate being contained and like nothing better than to be told everywhere and to everyone, even though this is what kills them, downgrading them to plain old common knowledge.

The father's secret will keep for now. "Hey," I call after the newcomer, as I run across the platform. There's no acknowledgment of my words; he just continues walking.

I hustle down the stairs, to the gravel path running parallel to the tracks. My feet crunch loudly as I gain on him, until I am close enough to grab his arm.

But I don't touch him. I never touch anyone if I can avoid it.

"Hey," I repeat instead. "You're supposed to go into the station for the welcome to . . ."

At last, he turns to face me. I recognize him instantly. He's a newcomer, but not one from this batch; he climbed off the train and heard the welcome speech three months ago.

"What the hell, Foote?" I ask, angry for no good reason except that Foote's annoyed me since the day he arrived and almost instantly became Elton's favorite guy. "You weren't on the train, were you?"

I eye him, taking in the jeans, white T-shirt, and old-fashioned fedora. He should look silly, but instead he has this knack for appearing different in a way that makes you think "cool" instead of "weirdo." There's only one problem with his usual look—today the front of his shirt is caked in blood. The edges of it are dry and crusty, but at the center of his chest there are three dark spots where the blood is still wet and shimmery and the T-shirt is torn away so that I can see the red skin beneath.

"It looks worse than it is," Foote says as I turn green. "But I figured it would be best to clean up instead of going through orientation again." His voice is deep and strong. It doesn't sound like the voice of someone who's dying. I force myself to pull my focus away from the wound and onto his face. And there are those intense blue eyes, even more vibrant when contrasted with his raven-black hair.

It's not often that I want to know someone's secrets, but ever since I first met Foote, I've wanted to take hold of both his hands and let the skeletons in his closet dance with mine.

That's another reason I don't like him.

"So you *were* on the train," I say, quickly squashing down the flash of envy that comes with that revelation. Not that I would ever leave Gardnerville, but it's natural to be a little curious about what's on the other side. "Once you leave, you're not allowed to come back. Is that what happened here?" I flick a finger toward his oozing chest wound. "Did you have to fight your way back in?"

"Not exactly," Foote answers briefly, and then turns around and starts walking again. Even though he is several feet away, I can feel his secrets reaching out.

Well, not secrets exactly. People's thoughts tend to trail behind them, a stream of consciousness flowing like a river. Or a drippy faucet. It depends on the person. I hardly even notice anymore, but Foote's stream is more interesting than most. He isn't thinking about homework or buying more toilet paper. No, he knows something that I don't. Secrets of this sort are like the wild blueberries that come in the spring, growing everywhere the sunshine hits and begging to be picked. I take a deep breath, plucking one free.

And then there is a man with a beard, pointing a gun at the sickly girl I just saw. "Let me on this train, or she's dead," he says. An oxygen mask covers the bottom half of the girl's face, and the top of her head is lost to a thick fringe of bangs. Together the two create a frame for her wide eyes as they stare down the barrel of the gun and watch the man pull the trigger. Once, twice, three times. But none of the bullets hit her. Everyone turns to stare at someone who is groaning. As they gape, the groaning boy looks down to see the holes the bullets left in his white T-shirt. The man with the gun is taken away as others rush to help the bleeding boy who somehow absorbed bullets meant for someone else. Foote presses a hand to cover the wounds and waves them away. "I'll be fine."

"You can't keep a secret forever."

"What?" My voice is sharp, but nowhere near as sharp as Foote's eyes on mine. If I didn't know better, I could swear he knows what I've seen. But that's impossible. Even people who've grown up with me can't tell when I've taken one of their secrets. They suspect—oh, they constantly suspect—but the reason they suspect is because they never really know.

"This town," Foote says at last. "More and more people are finding out about it. Most shrug it off as an urban myth, but desperate people are desperate to believe and even more desperate to get their golden ticket. It's paradise to them, and they'll do anything to board the train."

"They're idiots. All of them. Gardnerville is more—" I stop myself. I'd been about to say it was more hell than heaven, but that felt disloyal. And wrong. "It's not what they think it is," I finish lamely.

Foote shrugs. "A place with no disease where everyone lives

past one hundred doesn't sound like paradise to you?"

I remember watching Piper run from the train. "That's only half the story. The rest is the reformatory and fourth years and kids turned into monsters."

I turn and point to the east, where the reformatory sits carved into the mountains, looming over Gardnerville. The windows glint in the sunlight. They are like the eyes in one of those paintings where the person seems alive and their gaze follows you wherever you go. No matter where I am, that great hulking beast of a building seems to watch me.

"Yeah, I've heard that story before." Mimicking my gesture, Foote points toward the station. "And right now all the people in there are hearing it too. If they don't like it, I'm guessing they'll leave."

"They won't," I reply sourly. "At least not right away, and by the time they do, it might be too late."

"So optimistic," Foote laughs, and then groans and presses his hand to his chest.

Instead of asking if he's okay, I take a step away and then another before spinning around and heading back to the station. He's fine. I've spent enough time with Foote to know that whatever happens, he's somehow always fine.

"You could get back on that train," I call over my right shoulder. "And this time not come back. It might be less hazardous to your health."

Foote doesn't answer, but it's not because he's thinking it over. A boy full of secrets who can take a few bullets and chalk it up as nothing more than a scratch is made for this town. He's doing just fine here, and I have no doubt that he'll stay.

I can't help but remember the day Foote arrived. I told him "good luck" the same way I said it to everyone—in a caustic tone that suggested they'd need it. A nervous smile was the usual response, but Foote gave me one of his crooked grins. It made me catch my breath, for reasons I didn't want to think about. "That's one thing I don't need," he'd said.

Now, as I pull the train-station door open and step inside, the mood is grim. This can only mean that Mom has finished giving the speech about the dark side of Gardnerville. Again, this is different than how Dad did things. He'd take the newcomers out, fill them with food and drink and stories that sounded like tall tales and skirted around the gruesome endings. He had a silver tongue attached to a sulfurous soul, and every single person around him eventually suffered for it. But not on their first night. And later, when they found out the truth, they couldn't hold it against him. It was too late—they'd already fallen in love with him the same way everyone always did. Once you loved Dad, you were halfway there to loving this town, because he was the same as Gardnerville—equal parts monstrous and miraculous.

You'd think Mom's way would be better, laying everything out clearly. Risks vs. benefits. But the newcomers never get it. Most of them barely hear the death-and-dismemberment part and instead whine about there being only one TV station, spotty cell phone reception that never goes beyond the mountains, and no internet at all.

"Any questions?" Mom asks with the same too-bright smile on her face.

Right on cue a man steps forward out of the crowd. "You're trying to scare us away."

It's the same man I'd pressed past earlier on my way out. The father of the sickly girl—the one the bearded man had shot at. His daughter is now on the floor playing with Wills. If I hadn't seen her with that oxygen mask and practically on the verge of death only a short time ago, I'd never have guessed she'd ever been anything but healthy. This is what Gardnerville does, and for a moment my throat tightens with something that feels like pride. The feeling passes quickly though. This girl's recovery is not without a cost. And Piper and at least fifty others held at the reformatory are paying it now.

"He's right." This time it's a woman, the little girl's mother. She clutches the man's arm as they both bear down on my mother, who stands stiffly with her back ramrod straight, not even trying to defend herself. "You just wanna keep this place to yourself," the woman accuses.

Now it's my turn to step forward. Piper would've loved this. All the tension and anger in the room, it's an explosion only needing a spark—and that was a role Piper was born to play. I don't have Piper's flair, so instead I take the part of the wet blanket.

"The train leaves in ten minutes," I say quietly. "Anyone who wants to return home should get back on. And if you decide to stay, don't say we didn't warn you, because everything my mother said is true."

"You're just a kid," the girl's mother sneers. "Why should we listen to you?"

I could tell them about the people I've seen die. I could tell them my own sister killed sixteen of her peers during the last fourth year. I could tell them I'd be surprised if this year isn't even worse. But none of that will touch them. The truth is they won't know the power of this town until they see it for themselves.

"You and your husband made your daughter sick. You didn't get her vaccinated, and then took her on an African safari specifically seeking out the countries where diseases like polio still exist. And you did this because even your most powerful and connected friends all told you the same thing: yes, the rumors about Gardnerville were true, but they only let in people with serious life-threatening illnesses."

There is silence for a long moment.

"How could you—" the father gasps.

"That's not—it's a lie," the mother screeches.

I am not paying attention to them. All I see is the little girl watching me with the same horrified look she had on her face when she stared down the barrel of a gun. Somehow that ended up okay for her. Maybe this will too. But I doubt it.

Then I meet the eyes of every person in that room. Or try to. Some refuse to look my way; the rest flinch after a few short seconds, afraid of what I might see.

Behind me, Mom announces it's time for them to head over to Gardner Manor, which means I've done my part and am free to leave. I don't hesitate to head for the door.

Ignoring the roads, I cut through the field behind the train station. It's filled with Gardnerville's version of wildflowers, which is essentially any seed that you put into the ground. In fields and between sidewalk cracks an amazing variety of flowers grow year round. An orchid someone planted years ago thinking it was pretty is now a tenacious weed that grows and spreads and never dies. Sometimes you'll even see their long delicate stems and colorful petals waving defiantly from a snow bank on a cold and sleety January day. Newcomers can't get enough of the orchids, but I prefer forget-me-nots. As I tromp along, I snatch a few and gather them together. As pretty as my forget-me-not bouquet is, the pills that the quints make from them are even lovelier. If I had some, I wouldn't hesitate to swallow one right here and now. Then I would lie down in this field, and for a short while forget the train exists—even as it roars right past me.

Ever since summer vacation began, I've been on the same schedule. I leave the house when the sun's barely risen, disappearing into the day before Mom and Wills even know it has begun.

Today, though, it looks like I'll be stuck in the solid and slightly sticky reality of a humid August afternoon. Then there is the evening thick with chirping crickets and croaking frogs, followed by the long stagnant night to get through.

But those endless seconds, minutes, and hours aren't even the worst of it. What I really dread are the memories that might bubble up to the surface. It's funny—I don't even remember what I am hiding from; all I know is that I don't want to know.

For a second I feel brave. Perhaps today is the day I'll quit being a coward and face those memories head-on. Or I can hurry home and plant myself in front of the TV, letting whatever old movie is on fill my skull and hopefully keep everything else out.

As I turn toward home, the reformatory catches my eye. I

stare at it, unable to tear my gaze away, wondering if Piper is inside. I can almost feel her looking out, wanting something from me.

But that's impossible, I remind myself, and then deliberately turn my back to the reformatory.

Piper is gone.

And tomorrow after I get more forget-me-nots, I'll be mostly missing too.

STAYIN' ALIVE

Eleven Years Ago

I PUSHED THE BINOCULARS THROUGH THE TALL grass, pressing them into your outstretched hand. You'd pawned Daddy's watch for them that afternoon. It was the new one he'd gotten for Christmas. Gold and shiny and big, even on Daddy's large wrist—he wore it only on special occasions, and I could see the way his chest puffed out when he put it on.

"Daddy'll be mad," I'd said, and you just smiled. You knew as well as me that Daddy would never say a word against you, no matter how many of his prized possessions you took and sold. Once, before I knew better, I thought it was because he loved you best. Later I saw that wasn't it at all. Daddy had it so everybody loved him, but he didn't really love anyone back. Not even you, Piper.

Me, on the other hand, he could never forgive. Probably because I didn't love him at all. Never did, as far back as I could remember. Or maybe it was because you loved me as much as you loved him. Maybe even more. That was the type of thing that would make him completely crazy.

"They're coming out," you whispered at the same time the buzzer startled a nearby flock of birds into the sky.

I squinted, staring past the grass and through the double-layered chain-link fence. I could see the dark, huddled forms exiting the reformatory one by one, like criminals on a chain gang. Some of them were nearly doubled over, yet somehow they found the strength to take another shuffling step forward.

You nudged me with the binoculars. I shook my head in response. I didn't want to look closer. I was afraid of the expressions I might see on their faces.

A moment later, I felt your shoulder shrug against my own, before you put the binoculars to your eyes once more.

"I see him," you said. "He looks miserable."

He was Benjamin Walker, the boyfriend of our favorite baby-sitter, Darla. She always made us ice-cream sundaes for dinner and let us eat them in front of the TV. Benjamin caught her kissing Johnny DelRoy in the middle of our living room while we were scooping the last bits of hot fudge from the bottom of our bowls.

Benjamin didn't say a word. He just stared at the two of them in this awful way. It was lucky it was only a first year and not a fourth year, everyone agreed—it could have been a real tragedy with those two little girls there. Since it was merely a first year, there was calamity but not full-on disaster. What that meant exactly was that Johnny's lips melted right into Darla's, and the two of them were stuck like that until someone got them to the hospital, where the doctors were able to surgically separate them. Benjamin was sent straight to the reformatory, and ever since then, Piper, you had been determined to see him in lockup. I thought you wanted to make sure he was paying for what he'd done to Darla, but sitting in the grass beside you, I suddenly wasn't so sure.

The line of teens disappeared as they circled around the other side of the reformatory. You put down the binoculars and then drew a finger through the dirt, forming a squiggly question mark. "Why do they do it?" You mumbled the words to yourself, wondering aloud.

"If they don't walk, they die." I answered your question without really thinking. Your head whipped toward me so quickly I would've jumped back if your penetrating gaze hadn't pinned me in place.

"How exactly does that work?" you asked softly. Gently. I was the little sister and you were supposed to be the one who knew everything and condescended to explain the workings of the world. It had never worked that way, though; the secrets revealed all the darkest corners of life to me, long before I was ready to see them. You were my night-light, Piper. You helped keep the darkness away.

"Sky?" You nudged me when I didn't answer immediately. Sometimes, I think, you craved the darkness. Looking back, I can see how impatient you were with me for always being so scared. I can see you thinking that if you were me, and knew what I did, then everything would be different.

Oh, Piper, you have no idea how much I wish that everything could be different. Come back from the reformatory and you can have all the secrets. I never meant to keep any of them from you; sometimes I just forgot that you didn't already know everything.

I told you then. I told you about how it was unnaturally cold inside the reformatory, and how you could see every exhale of breath.

You interrupted me, trying to guess, not wanting to be told. "They make them walk so they don't freeze to death."

I shook my head and explained how everyone bundles up in layers and they blast the heat so that it comes hissing and rattling from the cast-iron radiators. It doesn't help much; teeth chatter constantly. At first anyway. Eventually the cold settles inside them, and it gets so bad they hardly notice it except that every so often it feels like something is crawling up their spine. That's when they start itching and scratching at themselves. Sometimes it gets so bad they tear their own skin off. They're restrained then, and that's when they start screaming. The walks look like a punishment, but they're not. It's actually the best part of their day.

By the time I finished talking, I was shivering as if I were feeling the cold of the reformatory myself. You wiped my runny nose with the bottom of my shirt and then threw an arm around me. "Want me to French-braid your hair?"

"Uh-huh," I answered immediately, even though you always pulled my hair too tight. I loved when you paid attention to me and didn't want something in return. You had only just divided my hair into sections when the prisoners came tromping into view once more. I expected to be forgotten. Instead you glanced up for a moment and then went back to finger-combing my hair.

I was relieved. All you'd wanted was to see Benjamin, and now that you had, we would never go to the reformatory again.

I was wrong though. That was only the first of many visits, and every time you said the same thing you had that day as you'd French-braided my hair.

"We're gonna end up there someday, Sky. I can feel it."

"GG says that Gardners never go to the reformatory," I interrupted, hoping you would stop saying terrible things. "We always find a way out of it."

You kept talking as if you hadn't heard a word I said. "We're gonna do something terrible like Benjamin did, and they're gonna lock us up in there."

"No-oh," I half sobbed, because your words sounded like the worst kind of secret, the sort that I wished wasn't true. The thing is, secrets are awful in lots of ways, but they almost never lie.

"You can't fight a fourth year, Pollywog. People try, but it gets so deep inside them there's no digging it out." You were talking to me, Piper, but you were scanning the brick walls of the reformatory. "We're gonna end up in there, I just know it," you repeated. There was a strange gleam in your eyes as you reached out and grabbed hold of my shoulders. Your fingers dug into my skin. I could feel the cold in them through my thin T-shirt. It was almost as if you'd absorbed some of the reformatory's cold.

"Now, Pollywog," you said, "we just need to figure out how we'll escape once we're inside."

TWO

MOM IS BUSY THE REST OF THE DAY HELPING TO GET the newcomers settled, and I am left to my own devices. Normally, this is the way I like things. But I have this jingling, jangling feeling that keeps me pacing the front porch, while I wait for her and Wills to come strolling up the street hand in hand.

If they were to appear right now, I could grab Wills and start tickling him, which he loves. He'd fall to the floor, begging me to tickle him more, until suddenly it would be too much and he'd start to cry. Sometimes I don't notice at first. Screams of delight sound a lot like screams of discomfort. Mom and I would get in a fight. She'd say I'm too rough with him. I'd say she babies him. We'd scream at each other because sometimes it just feels good to scream, and Wills would watch us the whole time with eyes that are big and round and worried. Eventually, we'd forget what we were even fighting about—or I would anyway—and both stomp off to our respective corners, making sure to slam doors behind us. With any luck, I'd be exhausted and fall asleep quickly. It's an ugly but efficient way to use up the last scraps of an endless day.

But Mom and Wills do not appear, and I am stuck with the cassette recorder in my hand. I stare at the thing, wanting to hurl it at the big oak in the center of our front yard. Instead, I pull out the tape. I RAN (SO FAR AWAY) is written in round script on the sticker across the front of the tape. It's one of Mom's old mix tapes from before she came to Gardnerville. When we were kids, Piper and I used to record over them, filling them with tales of our daily adventures.

The last few months, though, I've been coming to after a forgotten day to find the recorder in my hand. The few times I've been brave enough to rewind and play it, I hear my own voice. Not my little kid voice. My current, teenage voice—gravelly and sleepy sounding from too many forget-me-nots.

I never listen for more than a few minutes because I am afraid of what I will say. What I will reveal. I keep putting the recorder back into Piper's room—beside the piles of tapes on her dresser that should be dusty from sitting there untouched for so many years. No matter how many times I put it back, it keeps turning up again. Today I found it between the couch cushions.

Popping the tape back into the recorder, I take a deep breath and press Play.

The tape hisses and there is a snippet of song, but that cuts out and is replaced by my own voice speaking slowly, yet sincerely.

"I can't forget you, Piper. But sometimes, I can't really remember you either."

The recorder falls from my hand and goes silent. My whole body is shaking and I'm not even sure why. I don't want to know.

I have a terrible suspicion that this is the fourth-year madness finding me. It strikes those between ten and nineteen years of age, but fourteen through eighteen is the sweet spot—we're the ones who seem to feel it the most.

It's an itch. An energy. Even the most obedient children can't stop from sneaking out of their locked-up houses, looking for trouble. Every hurt, every slight, every heartache, and every defeat is magnified by twenty during a first year. By the time you get to the fourth year, it's magnified by a million. Something that might have been shrugged off, instead festers. During a first year you might stop talking to your best friend; during a fourth year you might kill him or her. And for no real reason at all. In a fourth year people kill themselves and each other based on gut feelings, which the next day turn out to be nothing but a bad bowl of soup they'd had for dinner.

Of course, they always regret it. Almost immediately, even though it's too late by then. Killing your peers is frowned upon in Gardnerville, the same way it is everywhere else. And so crime is followed by punishment—or reform, as we like to call it. That sounds more altruistic, and hides the truth by letting us pretend that the reformatory is healing the people it holds. It's a lie every person in this town tells themselves. If the people of Gardnerville didn't believe this, then they'd have to admit they've made a deal with the devil. No sickness, no disease, none of the usual deterioration of the mind and body that usually comes with advanced age. These are the perks of living in Gardnerville, but they do not come for free.

When Dad was feeling big and effusive and proud he would tell us, "The good health we share all springs from the good earth of Gardnerville. The very dirt we walk upon fuels us." Dad was a one-half-of-the-story type of person, so he never mentioned why it was that no matter how many people drew strength from the land, it never ran dry. Like everyone else, he didn't talk about the troubled teens sent to the reformatory who came home hollowed-out husks, everything inside them leeched away. Their vigor. Their youth. Their joy. Their loss was everyone else's gain. But the earth absorbed their resentment, despair, and rage as well. Those heavier feelings sank deeper into the soil, creeping down from the reformatory and slowly penetrating every inch of Gardnerville, until it found a fresh victim to fill with sudden power and fury. Every year the dark power infesting teens grew stronger and stronger—until in a fourth year the explosions were catastrophic and inevitable.

"It's a totally messed-up system," Elton had said, years ago when Piper first explained the cycle to him. She was already half in love with him by then, but this sealed the deal. She thought they were on the same page, that he believed, as she did, that a broken system needed to be destroyed. It wasn't until much later—too late—that she realized how wrong she'd been. Elton had no interest in destruction, but rather in exploitation. The biggest problem with Gardnerville, as he saw it, was that we were "closing the barn door after the horse already bolted." He thought people needed to be locked away before they did something terrible, instead of after. Typical newcomer point of view. A simplistic solution to something bigger than they could even begin to comprehend.

I stomp a foot on the porch and push Elton out of my thoughts. It's bad enough that I have to deal with him in real life; there's no need for him to be taking up the increasingly limited space in my head as well.

Crouching down, I pick the recorder off the ground. The taped-on battery door came loose upon impact. I push the batteries back into place and then smooth the tape back down. It would be smarter to pull the batteries out and disable the damn thing. Or else suck it up and just listen to the damn tape. Minutes pass as I stand frozen, weighing my options. Who knows how long I might've stood there lost in uncertainty if Elton's Prius hadn't at that moment crested the hill and rolled into view.

It's not exactly a reprieve—more like trading one type of trouble for another. At least this is a type of trouble I'm familiar with. I shove the recorder into my front pocket and then, making it clear that I'm in no hurry, stroll to the end of the driveway, where Elton's car is waiting.

His window slides down. "Get in," he says.

I lean forward to peer inside. As I suspected, Foote is sitting shotgun. Straightening, I take a step back. "I'd rather not."

"Always so difficult," Elton says, directing his comment to Foote.

I'll give Foote this: he's not like Elton's other stooges. Instead of laughing or eagerly nodding in agreement, Foote just shrugs.

"Can't blame her," he replies, so softly I almost miss it.

The tips of Elton's ears go red. It's his tell. Has been since the day I met him. "Get in or I'm cutting you off." He growls the words at me.

I get in.

Elton laughs 'cause he's a dick and a sore winner. He knows those damn pills are the only thing holding me together. He hands me a bottle of water with a faintly pink tint. I don't want to drink it, but refusing to do so would only draw this whole thing out even longer. Twisting the cap off, I put the bottle to my mouth and tilt my head back. It has a faintly floral taste, reminiscent of the monstrous burps that plague me the day after a forget-me-not bender. My one small act of defiance is to fling the empty bottle at the back of Elton's head. I miss and it bounces off Foote's oversized skull instead.

Then there is nothing to do but stare out the window as the Prius slinks through town, searching for prey.

We begin by driving down the familiar streets that make up the nicest neighborhoods of Gardnerville. The house I grew up in is among these, and yet I almost have trouble recognizing the place. It's not that anything looks all that different. Maybe the yards are tended a bit better than usual. And windows that would normally be tightly closed are wide open, trying to catch a breeze. But those are small and barely noticeable things. Really it's the feeling of Gardnerville that is off. The fear, the tension—the constant strain of wondering who and where and when—is gone.

It's Elton's doing. He knows it too; his puffed-up pride fills the car as he surveys the changes.

Idiot. You'd think he would've learned his lesson about playing with fire after the way things turned out with Piper. But if anything, that only redoubled his ambition.

Still, even I have to admit that on the surface his two-part plan seems to cover all the bases.

Part one: drug everyone. He started slowly, about four years ago after he discovered the quints' genius for turning wildflowers into mind-altering substances. Scarlet runners, forget-me-nots, foxgloves. Each pill catered to a different part of the high school population. But that wasn't enough; too many teenagers were slipping through the cracks. So the sunflowers were invented. Instead of selling these like the rest, creating an artificial demand by only releasing one batch of pills a week, he started giving them away without anyone ever realizing it. For almost two years now he's been putting them in the water supply. With the heat wave we've been going through this summer, everyone is guzzling water, and now most people in town are so calm that they're nearly comatose.

But even all those drugs aren't enough to keep the bad stuff from bubbling up. Not during a fourth year anyway. That's part two and that's where I come in. Elton uses me to identify "troublemakers"—as he likes to call them—before they "act out."

My eyelids grow heavy from whatever the quints put in that bottle of water. Drawing in a ragged breath, I can feel my defenses crumbling. Secrets begin to trickle in, and then it's a flood crashing over me. They flow out of the houses around us, a steady stream of thoughts and desires. I drown in hidden sins and sorrows. Why aren't more secrets made up of joyful things like surprise parties and newborn babies? Those secrets run through me like cotton candy, sweet and airy and insubstantial. The others are sticky like spiderwebs—they cling no matter how you try to pull them away.

Closing my eyes, I begin the process of sorting through the secrets, separating them into individual threads. I swallow back a laugh and squint my eyes open to peer at the back of Elton's head while I hold one of his secrets. Such hubris, for him to believe that his secrets are safe from me. The quints told him that if he lined his "just one of the boys" baseball cap with aluminum foil, it would keep me out of his head. They must have known it was nonsense, which means they don't like Elton. That is a secret with potential future power and I try to shove it deep into my gray matter, so it doesn't dissipate the way the rest of the secrets will when this little car ride is over and Elton gives me a forget-me-not as payment.

My gaze shifts sideways, toward Foote. His expression in profile is severe, almost as if he is angry about something. I wonder what that might be and, without even thinking about it, reach out to take his secrets too.

Take them. A voice inside me whispers. *Take all their secrets. Strip them bare and leave them hollow.* It almost sounds like Piper. Except this voice is furious, calm, and conniving all at the same time. It's ugly in a way that Piper never could have been. Still I can't help but listen to it.

Take them, it says again. And this time, I consider it.

Foote's head swivels around and his eyes meet mine.

One one thousand. Two one thousand. Three one thousand.

I blink and look away, out the window, pretending to study the shops on Main Street but still seeing Foote's incredible blue eyes. I might once have compared them to blue pools of water, thinking of how I could plunge into them and dive straight to the bottom to find all sorts of sunken treasure. Now, though, they are more like ice, and all his hidden thoughts are frozen inside.

I hope my own thoughts are similarly locked away, because I'd hate for anyone to know about that whispery voice inside my head. I'd hate for them to suspect, as I now do, that it might be the fourth-year madness speaking to me, leading me toward disaster. If Elton had even an inkling of such a thing he'd have me guzzling gallons of sunflower water, or even worse—he'd send me straight to the reformatory.

Maybe I just imagined it. I comfort myself with the thought. Maybe it's this damn pink water making me crazy.

Honestly, I don't care what the voice was; I just want it to go away. I want everything to go away and I need a fucking pill to make it happen. But Elton's not gonna pay up until he gets something out of this little ride. So I turn my attention outward again, trying to hunt down some sort of secret that will satisfy him.

Luckily, a new secret comes to tickle my nose. I follow its trail to a boy heading up the steps of Milly's front porch. His name escapes me, but I recognize him from school. He might even be in my class. *Starving*. The secret screams.

Lord knows Milly makes the best pies on the planet, but this boy's reaction is extreme.

"Him." The drug makes my throat so dry that the word gets stuck. Giving up on speech, I reach forward to tap Elton's shoulder and to begin a chain of events that will end with that starving boy getting a one-way ticket to the reformatory and me taking a pill that will help me forget it ever happened. Better him than me, I tell myself the way I always do. Today, after hearing that whispery voice, it feels like more of a betrayal than ever.

But before I can alert Elton, I am thrown back against my seat and then jerked forward again, as the car screeches to a stop.

"Holy shit, you almost hit her," Foote says.

"She threw herself at the car," Elton spits back.

I look through the front windshield in time to see the object of their discussion climb onto the hood of the Prius. She deftly slides forward and begins to pound her fists against the glass.

"Cowards. Backstabbers. Traitors," she screams. I hardly hear her, though, because while the windshield keeps her taunts at a safe distance, her secret slides right through it with ease.

And it is unlike any secret I've heard before, because it sounds like something Piper would say as it loudly declares, *It's time, Pollywog. It's time.*

I gasp, but my dry throat interferes again, turning it into a choking sound.

As if it's a signal, the girl's eyes meet mine. And for an instant I could swear it is Piper staring at me. Then the girl is scrambling off the car and into an alleyway, where she disappears from view.

"What did you see?" Elton turns around in his seat and fixes me with what he thinks is a piercing gaze.

I clear my throat and then lie easily. "Nothing. She just got released from the reformatory, right? There's nothing left in there. Nothing that makes sense anyway."

Elton takes his time thinking this over, letting me sweat. Finally, he nods. "You know Jonathan, right?" he asks. He knows damn well that I do. Jonathan is another one of Elton's henchmen. He's in charge of selling the quints' pills, and I am one of his most regular customers. "That's his sister, LuAnn. She got out of the reformatory a few weeks ago."

LuAnn. Now I know why the face seemed vaguely familiar. Eight years ago she nearly killed Piper.

"Jonathan mentioned they've been having trouble with her. After that many years inside, you'd think she'd be bedridden, but she gets these manic bursts of energy. Disappears for hours. I should go after her, make sure she gets home okay." Elton scrubs a palm over his face, suddenly looking less evil and conniving and simply tired and human.

Sometimes I am so used to hating Elton, I forget that the rest of Gardnerville sees him as a hero. After he and Piper had their infamous last rendezvous on the trestle bridge, and he traded in his flesh-and-blood legs for metal ones, Elton started giving speeches about how Gardnerville needed to change. Then he went one step further and told people he knew how to make those changes happen. He promised the people of Gardnerville what they'd always dreamed of: health, long life, and freedom from fear. Four years later he's gone from being a high school teacher to practically running the whole damn town. People act like he's the answer to their prayers, and as long as he keeps delivering on his promises, nobody really cares how he does it.

Sometimes this makes me remember him the way that Piper used to see him, the way she used to love him.

But then Elton ruins it by chucking a plastic Baggie at me. It holds one tiny purple pill.

"Try to wait until you're home or somewhere safe before you take it."

Elton is right, I should wait, but between the fourth-year whisper and the run-in with LuAnn I am desperate for the forget-me-not's unique brand of oblivion. I open the bag, shake the pill into my mouth, and smile sweetly. "Haven't you heard, Elton? Thanks to you, Gardnerville is now one of the safest places in the world."

With that parting shot, I push the door open and climb out of the car. I don't make it very far before Foote shows up beside me.

"Let me walk you home."

"No thanks," I say. "Getting lost is kinda the whole point."

"Right," Foote replies, but he doesn't stop ambling along beside me.

I don't want him there. I don't want him to see me when I trip over my own feet and face-plant because I've forgotten how to walk.

"If you're looking to get laid by a girl who won't remember it the next day, try the park. That's where most of the notters hang out."

It's a terrible thing to say, but it does the trick. Foote is no longer beside me. I force myself to keep going, to not turn around and apologize. In a few more minutes I'll forget what I said, and who I said it to. And soon thereafter this whole day will be wiped away, like it never even happened.

EVERY ROSE HAS ITS THORN

Four Years Ago

I NEVER FELT LIKE THE ANNOYING LITTLE SISTER that you didn't want around until you started seeing Elton. He changed everything. He changed you. And since we have always been connected, he changed me too.

Changed for the worse. I want to be clear about that, although I don't know how there could be any doubt. He ruined us. He ruined everything.

Elton had arrived earlier that year, right around the time when Daddy was first beginning to show his age. It wasn't a dramatic change—no graying hair or stomach paunch. There wasn't one specific thing that you could point to, but rather several small cumulative shifts that made him seem older. Daddy no longer looked fresh and young and just barely twenty as he had for at least two decades. Now he looked, not middle-aged exactly, but on the brink of it.

He combated the change by doubling down. More women who weren't Mom. More languid strolls down Main Street, where people had no choice but to love him. More town meetings where Daddy sat at the front of the room like a king holding court, allowing the peasants a chance to kiss his ring.

In response Piper and I started spending less and less time at home. When Daddy was away, it was terrible to listen to Mom wail and moan, sick with missing him. Even worse, though, was when he wouldn't come home for several days. She would go quiet, her cheeks would burn bright pink, and her whole body would radiate heat. You could see the fever on the brink of breaking, but Daddy—using some sort of sixth sense—would return and she would succumb to the love sickness once more.

In warm weather, you and I roamed from one end of town to the other, measuring it with our bare feet. During the sharp winter days, we curled together under a pile of blankets in the shed out back. It also helped when Chance would curl up between us, and his furry body lent us a bit of extra heat. An extension cord gave us a single line of power that we used for a hotplate. We kept warm by filling our stomachs with cans of soup and hot cocoa. Sometimes you'd bring different books from the school library and read them aloud. You loved poetry then and would recite the same ones over and over until we'd both committed them to memory. Your favorite was "Mad Girl's Love Song" by Sylvia Plath. Do you remember it, Piper? I can't recall much of anything anymore, but that one line that repeated over and over throughout the poem sticks with me: "I think I made you up inside my head."

The way you said it—sometimes spitting the words out like they were burning your tongue and at other times exhaling them as if you were forming smoke rings that only you could see—still haunts me.

Perhaps it haunted Elton too. You recited that poem for him. You brought him into our little shed, saying there was room for one more, and when it turned out that it was in fact a little too crowded, I was the one who was told to go. It was only pride that kept me from sitting outside the door like Chance did, whining until I was let back in.

You had a crush on Elton before I even knew he existed. Later I learned he was a teacher at the high school and the number-one crush of every girl there. It was hard to believe you were just like the rest of the girls. Although, in the end you weren't. They wanted him, but you actually took him.

Later you told me that on his first day, he had asked you for directions when you were sitting on the front steps reading a book. "Follow me," you'd said, and he had, chatting with you all the while. He asked what you were reading and you both discussed the poems of Emily Dickinson. "She was so alone and sheltered, you'd think she wouldn't have much to say, but the exact opposite was true," Elton said, and in that exact instant—between one footstep and the next—you fell in love with him.

I don't know why. It doesn't seem like such a clever thing to say. I would've asked you, but I couldn't because you never told me this story. I took it. Please forgive me, Piper, but I couldn't accept being locked out from so much of your time with Elton. I needed a part of it, even if it wasn't mine to take.

"There it is," you'd said, pointing to the classroom that would be Elton's.

He didn't move toward it; instead he just smiled at you. "What's your name?"

"Piper."

"That's perfect. Like the Pied Piper. I'm sure I'm not the first person to say that I'd happily follow you anywhere."

You laughed and then, because you are fearless, you leaned forward and pressed your lips against his.

He stepped away quickly. "Piper, I'm a teacher."

"I know." You shrugged. "But who really cares about that?"

As it turned out, nobody did. They said it was only a five-year difference and what was that anyway? The thinking on the subject was so uniform it was almost like someone had gone around putting that exact thought into every single person's head.

And Elton eventually came around too.

Later, Piper, not so very long after, although so much had changed that it felt like forever, you and I had that big fight.

By then I was so full of jealousy. I had stolen so many secrets of your time with Elton that I had half fallen in love with him too.

An explosion was inevitable.

It came the day you returned home with grass in your hair. I didn't need that to know what you'd done. Before you even entered the house, I was reaching out and reading your secrets as easily as other little sisters crack the cheap locks on a sibling's diary. You could see on my face that I knew how you'd lain naked in the grass with Elton. How when it was over you held hands and stared up into the endlessly blue sky. How he had been gentle and—

You slapped me, knocking every secret out of my head for an instant.

"That's mine," you hissed, angrier than I'd ever seen you before. "I need something that's just mine and not ours to share."

I would rather you'd just slapped me again. Or punched me.

"He doesn't love you," I said. "He says he does, but he doesn't. *I know.*"

You turned white at that last bit. You believed me.

It was a lie, Piper. I admitted it later, but after that you were never quite sure, and then when he got Angie pregnant it seemed to confirm the lie. He had never loved you.

But Piper, Elton did love you and he still does. The thing is, he was afraid of you too. That was where the uncertainty came from—not a lack of love, just an inability to fully understand who he loved and why.

And despite being able to shake every last secret from Elton's brain, I can't say I've ever understood anything about what truly makes him tick—except that.

THREE

A BEEPING NOISE WAKES ME THE NEXT MORNING. IT takes me a while to realize it's coming from the little black square next to my bed, and several more long moments to remember it's my cell phone, and even longer than that to figure out how to make it stop. Mission accomplished, I flop back into bed and stare up at the ceiling, trying to remember yesterday. Bits and pieces come back to me. I recall something about the train station and a car. Foote. That name attaches itself to a face and a bloodied chest. And that's it; everything else is a blur, a beautiful swirl of images that never completely come together.

It would be scary, except the one thing I know is that I've been here before, and that I want to stay inside this bubble as long as I can. The last thing I clearly remember is diving into the forget-me-not's embrace. Why give myself a headache trying to clear the cobwebs when this is obviously exactly where I wanted to be?

The cell phone beeps at me again. This time when I flip it open, I notice the little message on the screen: *forget-me-nots, 9am.*

A bit of the fog dissipates and I remember. The quints spend their weekends making pills. Monday through Friday from 9:00 a.m. to 3:00 p.m. the pills are sold to whoever has the cash to pay for them. Usually they sell out by Wednesday, and then everyone who hesitated is stuck waiting for Monday to come around again.

I never hesitate, and take a sick sort of pride in always being the first in line ready to buy.

That's why I drag myself out of bed and pull some clothes on. By the time I'm dressed, my head is a little clearer. I even remember to walk softly and avoid the especially squeaky floorboards so as not to wake Mom and Wills.

At the end of the hall, I turn and step inside Piper's room. She hardly needs any sleep at all, so it's not often that I'm up before her. I grin just thinking of how she'll scream when I jump onto her bed and shake her awake the same way she's done to me.

Then I see the empty bed, neatly made, and my smile fades, forgotten.

Piper is gone.

I half remember writing those exact words on her door with a pink Sharpie pen. When I look, though, there is nothing except a patch of paint that seems a little brighter than the rest. Maybe it was a dream or maybe I had written those words and Mom painted over them, not seeing them as a simple reminder, but instead as some sort of condemnation of her parenting skills.

I linger in the room a moment longer, drifting toward the pile of cassette tapes on Piper's bedside table. Each one has a hand-written label. All song titles, I think. I reach for one, and then jerk my hand back. Something is telling me to leave them be. A few moments later, standing near the front door, I frown down at a small handheld tape recorder sitting on top of my flip-flops. Again, warning bells go off in some distant corner of my mind. Ignoring them, I pocket the recorder and slide my feet into the sandals.

The streets are quiet and I get to the school fairly quickly, only forgetting my way one time. As I cut across the parking lot toward the football field, I see the boys are already gathered for their morning practice.

They lumber around like overgrown babies, sucking water from their sports bottles and dragging their towels behind them like their favorite blankies. Gatorade mixed with a weekly dose of pansies has made them twice the size of your average high school kid.

The coach blows his whistle, and the whole herd of boys visibly startles. One or two run off. The rest manage to resist the flight instinct.

Barely.

Poor boys.

Poor Elton.

He'd wanted to build the football team into something you see in the movies, where the whole town comes out to cheer them on. That had never been our team though. And it wasn't our town either. Besides the obvious problem of finding opponents, there was the bigger issue that football tends to get the boys too excited. That's no good. The last time two boys got excited from a sporting event was a baseball game thirty-two years ago. A bad call led to a fight. Fists flew. One of the boys' fists turned into bricks. He killed three boys from the opposing team and two of his teammates before they could stop him. The victims' mothers could barely identify their dead sons' faces.

Arrogant Elton thought he could get around this type of thing with the help of the quints. Unfortunate side effects and unintended consequences later, he'd gathered enough boys for a team and pumped up their scrawny bodies while at the same time draining every last drop of aggression. He'd created a bunch of overgrown sissies.

If he had any sense, he'd admit it was a failed experiment and shut it down. But then Elton would have to admit to being a person capable of making mistakes, and that is never going to happen.

I turn away from them and begin my climb up the bleacher steps. What the pansies did to those boys should be the type of cautionary tale that would scare me away from putting another forget-me-not into my mouth. It doesn't. Sometimes you make bad choices to keep yourself from making other, even worse ones. Or at least that's what I tell myself.

It's not yet 10:00 a.m., but already the day is disgustingly hot. It's even worse inside the press box. All the windows are fixed closed and the only fresh air comes through the hatch in the roof. Everybody calls it the double-wide 'cause it looks like a trailer perched on top of the stadium stands.

"Whatcha know, pretty thing?" Jonathan Stimple grins so that all I can see are his yellow buckteeth. I'd think he was trying to distract me after I walked in and caught him using the edge of his polo shirt to mop up his sweaty armpits. But no, the guy thinks he's suave in his hand-me-down Lacoste. He doesn't know that Elton only gave him the job of managing the double-wide as a joke, keeping the white trash in a trailer.

Elton. Jonathan. I don't want to think about them. I might start remembering Jonathan puking so hard once in third grade that it came out of his nose. Or the morning I caught Elton leaving a bouquet of fresh-picked wildflowers on our porch. He'd winked at me before walking away. It's better not to think of those things. Not to remember who we'd been, or worse—who we've become.

"Quiet out there today," Jonathan says casually, like he's just making conversation. Except he isn't the chatty type, and he knows damn well I'm not either. His little rat eyes watch me, wanting some response that I don't care to guess at.

"It's early."

Jonathan makes a big show of turning to look at the clock on the wall behind him. "Ten to ten's not so early in most places."

This isn't most places. The words almost come out, but I stop them. If his goal is to get a rise out of me, I'm not biting. "Well, it's a hot day too." I try to say it pleasantly, but the early hour, the heat, and this conversation make it impossible.

"So you think our luck will hold? You think we can get through the year without a funeral?"

"We'll see," I say noncommittally, and then move the conversation back to business. "Pills, please."

"What kind?" Jonathan asks, even though he already knows what I want. He knew it before I walked through the door.

"The usual." I hold out my hand, a twenty at the center of my palm.

Jonathan takes my twenty but doesn't put any pretty purple pills in its place. "What if I told you prices went up? Just happened last night. Supply and demand, ya know? Ain't inflation a bitch."

I want to tell him that supply and demand has nothing to do with inflation, but my own grasp of economics is shaky, and besides, the last time I snarked back at Jonathan, he slipped a scarlet runner in with my usual pills. For three days my bones itched so bad the only way to shake them out was to run. I'd finally collapsed in a yard at the other end of town, and crawled under a rosebush. The next morning I woke to find the tread on my Converse sneakers had nearly been worn away.

"How much?" I ask, careful to keep my voice flat and expressionless, not wanting to antagonize him any further.

"Well . . ." Jonathan drawls the word out, as if he's thinking.

Look with your eyes, not with your hands. My mom would say that whenever I went near any of her little glass knickknacks. Jonathan must've been given the same lesson, 'cause he keeps his arms dangling at his side while his gaze travels my body. His eyes slide up my bare legs, to where the strings on my cut-off jeans tickle my thighs and the tips of the pockets stick out. Then up to the wifebeater. The other girls at school wear them bright white and tight. But mine is the dingy color of something that got washed with a load of black socks, and it hangs loose, dipping into a low U over my flat chest.

Wanting the imaginary groping to end, I reach into my pocket for the tape recorder.

"How much for this?" I ask, slapping it onto the table before I can change my mind. Sweat drips down my forehead and into my eyes, stinging, as Jonathan picks up the recorder and studies it for a moment.

"Old-school," he comments. Then he hits the Eject button, and pulls out the tape inside. "Heh," he says, looking at the handwritten label. He holds the tape out to me, sharing the joke. Generous of him.

"'Don't You (Forget About Me).'" He reads it aloud, just to make sure we're on the same page.

"It's the name of a song," I explain, not even sure why I bother.

"Ironic," Jonathan says, jerking his head from the tape to me and back again. Explaining the joke, 'cause I am still staring at him blankly.

It's not that I don't get it, but that I can feel something at the back of my mind, trying to tremble free. Something about that tape is wrong; I just have no idea what that might be.

Popping the tape back into the recorder, Jonathan presses Play. I hold my breath, suddenly afraid of what we'll hear. At first there is only the static hiss as the tape goes round and round and round. Then—

"Skylar, if you're listening to this—" It's Piper's voice.

I snatch the recorder back from Jonathan and eject the tape

once more. "You can have the recorder," I tell him, "but the tape is mine."

"Chill, Sky, you can keep 'em both. I was just messing with you anyway. We go back a long ways, you seriously think I would do you like that?"

"Whatever," I say, which seems nicer than laughing in his face.

Jonathan picks up the box that holds the pills, but instead of opening it and handing mine over, he nervously jiggles it so that the pills rattle inside. "Look, I want to make sure there're no hard feelings. Like I said, I was just kidding."

I don't know why Jonathan suddenly cares so much what I think of him. We are the type of strangers that only a town this small could produce—ones who know personal details of each other's lives going all the way back to kindergarten, but ones who will also not exchange friendly hellos when standing in the same checkout line at Al's Grocery.

"It's forgotten," I say, and then hold out my hand. "Or at least it will be soon."

Jonathan hesitates a moment longer, but in the end I am a risk that's easily calculated. The pills make me forget; chances are this conversation will be burned out of my gray matter before the day is even over.

Without another word he counts seven pills and places them in the hollow at the center of my palm. For a moment I stare down at them sadly, wondering why I'd wanted them so badly. Thinking I should throw them back in his face.

They take away sorrow, they take away pain, and they leave great gaping holes in my life. "You'll only remember the good times." That had been Elton's promise nearly four years ago when he'd pressed that first pill into my hand. Had it all been a lie? Did the pills take the good with the bad? Or is there just not that much good left to be remembered, after all the bad has been whittled away?

Even as my mind runs, my fingers curl inward, covering the pills.

Jonathan's feet shift nervously. I guess he wants me gone.

I linger a moment longer, just long enough to count my pills once more.

"Same time next week," I promise him.

I grab a candy bar as I walk out the door. One comes free with every purchase. Except it's actually the other way around. Supposedly my twenty paid for the candy, and the pills were the extra. The chocolate is soft and my fingers sink in, crushing the wrapper that reads THANK YOU FOR SUPPORTING GARDNERVILLE HIGH SCHOOL'S FBLA. I toss a pill into my mouth and quickly swallow. "Good stuff," I say. Half serious, half mocking myself.

"Wait!" Jonathan calls only seconds before the door clangs shut between us.

I stand outside, trying to decide whether to ignore him or not.

"Hey, Sky?" Jonathan calls out again.

Damn, he's persistent. Turning, I crack the door with my shoulder, just wide enough to poke my head back in. "Did you say something?"

Jonathan's beady eyes dart back and forth a few times before settling on me. "Yeah," he says. "Can you . . ." He waves his arm, gesturing for me to come closer.

Reluctantly, I take a step forward, back into the press box. I wish I had waited to take the pill. I have maybe ten minutes before I start feeling its effects and I don't want to be around Jonathan when that happens. "Well?" I prompt him now.

His gaze meets mine for a second before quickly sliding away again. "I know you do some work for Elton, but do you, like, really work for Elton?"

I stare at Jonathan, trying to figure out exactly what he's insinuating. "Well," I say at last, "I'm not planning on taking Angie's place as his baby mama, if that's what you mean."

"No, no, no, no." Jonathan holds both hands out, as if I might come charging at him. "That's not . . . what I meant was . . . do you support Elton? Like, philosophically?"

"What the hell are you talking about, Juh—" His name hovers somewhere between the tip of my tongue and my lips, and it takes me a long moment where my mouth quivers uselessly trying to find it, until at last my slowing memory spits out the necessary information. "Jonathan!"

"Hey, are you going away already?"

"It's just the heat." I wipe the sweat from my forehead. "But it'd be nice if you got to your point sometime this year."

"Okay." Jonathan nods, and then, as if he's made some sort of big decision, he blurts out, "I heard you ran into my sister yesterday. Or, well, she ran into you."

"Your sister," I repeat, trying to grab hold of the memory that Jonathan's words conjure up. It wavers before me as insubstantial as smoke.

"Yeah, my sister. LuAnn. She threw herself at Elton's car yesterday." He stares at me, as if he can force me to remember, but the memory recedes even further.

"Sorry." I shrug helplessly. "I don't recall any Lulu from yesterday."

"LuAnn!" Jonathan barks the name at me.

"Yeah sure," I agree genially, suddenly feeling happy and carefree for no reason at all.

Jonathan growls something else, but it's becoming difficult to concentrate. Through half-closed eyes, I watch as he removes a piece of paper from his pocket and begins to carefully fold it.

A moment later—or maybe longer than that—I feel something being pushed into the front pocket of my shorts. I shove the person away, or try to, but my arms move so slowly that my fingers only swish the air in front of me.

Cold water splashes in my face. I scrub it away with the back of my hand and glare at . . . Jonathan. "What the hell?"

"Listen, this is important. I put a note in your pocket. Don't let anybody else read it. Don't even touch it until after you're . . ." He twirls a finger near his temple.

I squint at him, forcing him to stay in focus. "What does it say? What do you want from me? And why wait until I took a pill to ask for it?"

"Damn, ain't it clear? I'm asking for your help, Sky. And I'm hoping that we'll both be able to forget I ever did."

There doesn't seem to be much I can say in response to that, and it's way past time for me to leave. I turn to the door and am halfway out when one last thing occurs to me. I look over my shoulder at Jonathan. "Give me my twenty back."

He shrugs in response, and then his mouth moves, but the words come out garbled—at least to my ears. All I hear is, "Sdfhwuiojlcj sjdfuoiwue hope gldljou stuck-up bitch slkjoiu owe you."

I nod like a bobblehead doll with blank eyes. My hand is held out, but I can't remember why. Maybe I was waving good-bye? It's possible. Wiggling my fingers at what's-his-face, I clumsily pivot and walk out the door. As it snaps closed behind me, I automatically reach for my pills, pop one into my mouth, and swallow it dry. "Good stuff," I mumble through numb lips.

Then at last I begin my slow descent down the bleacher steps. They clang as I clomp on dead feet. At the bottom I cross paths with one of the football players. I stare at him, trying to remember his name. But the pill is taking over completely. For the first hour or two, everything slips away. At its worst I can't even remember how to talk.

My cell beeps with a text. I pull it from my pocket. It's a barebones model or else I probably would've traded it for more pills. I have a message from someone named "O" that says: *News 4 u. Library Rm. 210.*

Somewhere at the back of my mind an ember of remembrance flares up. O is connected to Piper. I have a feeling it's not a good idea to meet him in this state, but my feet have already turned toward the school, and I am drifting through the front doors.

Clutching my phone as a constant reminder of my final destination, I stumble down the deserted halls and peer into empty classrooms. In the fall I will begin my fourth year here, and yet I cannot remember where the library is. I am having a difficult time even remembering to look for a place with lots of books.

I worry that it might be upstairs, but when I try to climb the steps, I'm turned away.

"Labs are closed," a girl tells me. "Go to the double-wide if you want pills."

Of course they're closed. I knew that. Because the things are up there doing that thing they do when it's that day that it is today.

I blunder on, the lockers blending one into another, when large block letters appear on the door in front of me. I hold my phone up, matching the word on the screen to the one on the door. LIBRARY. Pulling the heavy door open, I search again, this time through stacks of books. A long row ends at a wall, and I lean against it, feeling so incredibly tired. Still leaning, I make my feet move.

I don't remember who I am. Or where I am. Or why. I start to giggle, and look around for someone to share the joke with. But I am alone. The giggle turns into a sniffle. No tears come though. I've forgotten how to cry.

Something scrapes my cheek. I stop and push back from the wall just far enough to see. 205. A number on a door. It seems important. I try the knob, and the door opens to a tiny dark room. Closing the door, I turn to see more doors. A whole line of them going down the wall. 206. 207. 208. 209. I try every one, and find the same exact empty room every time. Like the lockers, and the books, these rooms could go on forever.

210.

I stop again. There is something heavy and beeping in my

hand. Shoving it into my pocket, I ignore it. This door doesn't open. I rattle the knob and then knock. Too loudly. The sound vibrates through me and the whole room. The door swings open. A boy is on the other side. Something wells up inside me when I see him. A feeling I don't have a name for.

And then he is kissing me. And I am letting him. Sort of. He doesn't seem to notice that my mouth is slack beneath his own.

Disappointment. That is the feeling. For some reason I'd thought it would be Piper here. Or hoped.

I jerk away, trying to remember how I know him. If I even know him at all.

He asks me what took so long. He holds my face between his hands, and I can feel his sweaty palms against my cheeks.

"You're all fucked up, aren't you?" It's mean the way he says it, and he laughs and his hands are under my shirt and I remember the word *no* and mumble it as I pull away from his grasping paws.

"C'mon, Sky," he says, his breath hot and whining. "Doncha want to hear about how I finally got a look inside the locked room? You know, the one I figured they've been keeping her in?" He tugs a chunk of hair, demanding my attention. "I finally got in, and guess who I saw in there?" He smirks. "I'm thinking that type of information might be worth a little extra something."

My heart pounds so hard it hurts. "Piper," I whisper. Her name brings everything into sharp focus. "Tell me."

"It was a lucky break. Simms dropped his keys in the john. I grabbed them before he even knew they were missing and high-tailed it to that room. It took me a few minutes to find the right key, but then I finally got in and . . ."

His mouth keeps moving, but there are too many words and I cannot process them. I close my eyes, thinking it will help me focus.

Someone is shaking me. I drag my eyes open.

"Whah-hut?"

The boy's face tightens, like this is a betrayal of him somehow. "Never mind." He pulls me closer, jerking my body against his. "Looks like fun first, talk later."

There is a loud banging. His eyes widen as he stares at the shaking door. I look at it too. Now the doorknob is rattling.

"Open up," a voice demands.

He turns to me, his mouth a wide O of surprise. The hands pressed against my back have gone slack and still.

Then he is grabbing hold of my shoulders, and steering me to the back of the tiny room. "Who did you tell?" He hisses the words at me.

My eyelids are heavy and I blink at him slowly.

His hand comes then, hard against my cheek. "You're not getting away that easily."

He's wrong. The pain brings him back into focus for the briefest of instants, but in the next he's blurred to almost nothing.

I hear a crash. He whirls away from me. The door opens, and then . . .

Nothing.

PEOPLE ARE STRANGE

Seven Years Ago

THE TEACHERS GATHERED IN THE HALLWAY, huddled tightly together. They closed the doors behind them so we couldn't hear them. We could only watch them through the glass and wonder what had happened. The whispers would begin soon. Usually someone had been in the principal's office or coming out of the bathroom just in time to have heard some tiny bit of information. Enough to give us something to think about as we sat there and wondered if this time it was someone we knew.

I looked away from the teachers and out the windows to the clear blue sky. February had finally melted into March, and even though the weather was still cold, I could smell spring trying to push its way up through the muddy fields that ran behind the school.

The classroom door opened with a jingle. I glanced over,

ready for Mrs. Wright's tight smile and encouragement to "stay calm."

Instead I saw you, confidently striding across the classroom. Immediately I stood, and you took my hand and led me out into the hallway.

"Skylar!" Mrs. Wright's voice was shrill as she moved in front of us, blocking the way. "Where do you think you're going?"

You didn't answer; you just gave Mrs. Wright and the rest of the teachers a look.

After a moment Mrs. Wright stepped aside, mumbling apologies, saying that she'd meant to let me leave early today. But she frowned, because her head was telling her one thing and her gut was saying something else.

Holding tight to each other's hands, we ran together, feeling invincible. We didn't stop until the school was out of view. Then finally we separated and slowed, needing to catch our breath.

The sun peeked out from the heavy blanket of clouds in the sky, and birds chirped. You whistled back, mimicking them perfectly. The day felt like an unexpected holiday, a gift, and we hugged it to ourselves for a moment.

I was the first to let it go, to remember real life and the whispering teachers and the something awful that must be occurring at this very moment.

"Are we going home? Is it something very bad then?"

"When did you get so serious, Pollywog?" You laughed and ruffled my hair. "It's only a first year, and everyone knows that'll hardly ever kill you."

I was more annoyed than reassured. You knew I hated it

when you called me Pollywog and treated me like a baby. "What is it then?"

You smiled. "That's for me to know, and you to find out."

"Piper!" I cried, but it was too late. You had taken off again and were running far ahead of me.

"C'mon, Pollywog, try to keep up this time."

I chased after you, sometimes losing sight as you took a turn, but never getting so far behind that I was tempted to give up. You finally let me catch you in the middle of Gardner Park. You leaned way over the railing of the big bridge, staring down at the trickle of water flowing below, and I came to a stop beside you.

"Look," you said in a soft voice.

I thought of stomping my feet and refusing. But I was too curious to pout, and so I peered down to see the little tadpoles wriggling in the shallow water. We watched them quietly for several long moments, while the wind whistled through nearby trees, chilling our fingers and toes.

"Cool, right?" you asked.

I nodded. "It's amazing."

You poked me with your elbow. "Not that amazing. Anybody anywhere in the world with a little stream or swamp or whatever can see something exactly like this. It's cool, but it's not that special."

You jumped back from the railing, pulling me with you. "Now do you want to see something truly amazing? That nobody else in the world will ever see?"

It was a rhetorical question and you didn't wait for an answer.

You'd already started walking across the bridge and over to the tiny forest of trees at the edge of the park. I, once again, was left to follow.

The sun had gone back behind the clouds and it was cold and quiet and dark between the trees. If you began running again, I wasn't certain that I'd follow this time for fear of losing you and being left there alone. But you walked slowly and deliberately until we reached the small clearing where a ramshackle fort had been built and rebuilt by constantly changing carpenters.

I tried to peer between the various cracks in the walls to see inside, certain that this was where the something extraordinary was, but an elbow in the ribs and a jerk of your head directed my attention to the opposite edge of the clearing. At first all I could see were the treetops swinging wildly. But then I realized only four of the trees were in motion. I moved closer, trying to get a better look. Without the fort blocking my view, I finally understood why you had brought me to this place.

Four trees that were unlike any trees I'd ever seen before moved—not according to the whims of the wind, but rather in response to the pirouettes and leaps of a dark-haired girl in a pink leotard and matching tutu. When she spun to the left, the uprooted trees shimmied sideways with her, following the movement. As she elevated onto her tiptoes, with her arms overhead creating a beautiful arch, the four trees did the same, their bare branches spare and elegant. The beautiful and bizarre dance performance made my throat ache.

"They're the girls from Miss Shelley's Ballet Academy," you whispered into my ear. "Word is little miss diva got the lead for their recital and it went to her head."

"And she turned the other girls into trees," I whispered back, as I detected impressions of their scared faces etched into the bark.

"Yes," you sighed. "Amazing dancing trees."

"Maybe not so amazing for them."

I felt your shoulder shrug against my own. "Angela Young was turned into a cheetah a few years before I was born. You can hardly tell now."

This was not exactly true. Angela was a cashier at Al's Grocery, so I had seen her plenty, and every time I had to remind myself not to stare. Even on the hottest days Angela favored turtlenecks, but they still couldn't hide the brown circles covering her hands and wrists and her entire face. When she bent her head to count out my change, the circles were visible through the part in her hair. Someone once told me that it had been worse. For the first two years after the initial incident, Angela had also had fur.

I sighed, while the trees creaked as they attempted to follow the girl in a low, toe-touching dip. "They'll close Miss Shelley's Ballet Academy," I whispered.

This was what happened after these types of things. The town board reacted by taking away whatever they thought caused the problem, whether that was putting down all the dogs in town after one kid turned his corgi into a ravenous killer, or shutting down dance classes that only a handful of girls attended anyway.

If I thought Piper would care, I should've known better.

My comment earned nothing more than another shrug. "Well, I doubt any of these girls will want to dance again after this."

That was probably true, but it didn't provide any comfort as we watched the strange ballet and waited for its inevitable ending.

FOUR

I STARE AT THE WATER SHOOTING OUT FROM THE
showerhead. My lips are open wide, drinking it in, trying to
moisten my cottony mouth. Bringing my hands up, I study my
fingertips. They are puckered and pruny. My soaked clothes
cling to my body.

I've been standing here for a while then.

I pat my wet pockets, looking for my phone. Needing it to
place myself in time.

Nothing.

Wildly, I search the tiled room. All ten showerheads are on
full blast. Steam billows out into the connected bathroom. Water
creeps out as well. I look down and see it beginning to lap over
the tops of my flip-flops. Taking a step back, I feel something
squish beneath my foot. It's a sodden ball of cloth, oozing red.

Gingerly I pick it up, exposing the covered drain. With a relieved gurgle the water rushes down. I give the shirt a hard shake and it opens up, revealing its secrets.

A Swiss army knife that echoes loudly when it hits the floor. I drop the T-shirt over it, and it falls with a familiar alligator symbol on top. Not a T-shirt then, but a polo. I pick the whole bundle up so that the knife is once more swaddled inside.

Flip-flops squishing, I step into the bathroom, not bothering to turn off the still-running water taps. There's a row of urinals to my left.

The boys' locker room.

The door to a bathroom stall yawns open in front of me. The tape recorder and my cell sit on the back of the toilet inside. I rush forward, reclaiming the phone first—my lost love. The screen lights up at my touch, delighted to see me too. The picture of the field full of forget-me-nots that I set as my wallpaper is unmistakably mine. But the time can't be right. Three a.m. I couldn't have lost an entire day. I've had some fuzzy moments, maybe even a few seconds that have slipped away completely, but never the white-outs that hardcore notters experience. I push the phone into my pocket, not caring if the wet kills it. It has betrayed me.

A drop of water from my soaking hair plops into the toilet bowl. I stare down at it, transfixed by the pretty violet-colored water. Then I see the five pills floating in the center. Their purple coloring has bled away, revealing a bland gray interior.

Fishing the pills out, I try to shove them into my other pocket, but a wad of wet paper gets in the way. Pulling the pocket inside out, I peel the paper from the cloth and shove the pills in its place. The paper is folded into a neat little origami square.

That's when I remember a hand pushing it into my pocket. Jonathan. And then a text from . . . Oswell Young. Ozzy to his friends. He works at the reformatory. We have an arrangement. He's been trying to find out for me whether or not Piper is inside the reformatory. He feeds me false hope and I give him—

I remember. His mouth and hands on me. Lately he's been pressing me for more, which makes me think it was no accident that he chose a Monday to meet up. If the door hadn't flown open . . .

My mind runs through the memories again, but it's all fuzzy and then goes completely black. After I get some sleep and sweat out the rest of the forget-me-nots, it'll come back to me. Probably. Maybe.

Somewhere nearby, a door bangs shut. Quickly, I shove the note back into my pocket. Slipping out of my shoes, I pick them up and then creep out of the bathroom and into the rows of lockers.

I scan the room, making sure no one else has stayed behind. It's empty.

My legs are stiff as I edge my way around the pool, not wanting to get too close. The sound of my ragged breaths echoes through the room by the time my fingers close around the door handle. It is a relief when the door shuts behind me, but I am not out of this yet. The hall is bright and empty. I hurry down it, feeling exposed. And then, finally, I'm at the south exit.

The early-morning air is as damp as my skin, and heat

lightning flashes against the far edges of the sky. I jog across the deserted parking lot, heading toward the housing development that borders this end of the high school. Jonathan's bloody shirt, along with the knife, has me shaken. Probably better to stay off the streets; I'll cut through backyards to get home.

Heart thumping, I reach the chain-link fence, a quiet green lawn stretching out on the other side of it. I lean against it, unable to believe it was so easy to get away. Wishing I knew exactly what I was running from. I look back, and that's when I notice the football field at the other end of the school is all lit up. They would never have practices this late; all the players are afraid of the dark.

I should go home. I should rinse the toilet water from my remaining pills, take another, and hope that this time it takes everything awful away. Instead, staying along the edge of the parking lot, I walk toward the field and its too-bright lights.

Broken and twisted, Oswell lies on the black asphalt that runs like a ribbon around the outer rim of the stadium. Directly above him the press box hovers menacingly. I look up toward it and then trace the line back down to Oswell. He started up there, that much is clear. The only question is what happened between up there and down here. I have a suspicion. Or maybe it's a hope. I take a step forward, with the idea that if I can get closer, if I can touch him, I might know for sure.

A hand grips my arm, stopping me. "No time for a close-up. You need to get out of here."

I turn and see Foote. A bandage is wrapped around his bicep. He is always bandaged up in one place or another. On his head he wears his fedora, tilted low so that it shadows his eyes.

"When I told you to run, I meant away." He increases the pressure on my arm, forcing me to take little steps farther and farther away from the light.

I stare at him. "When did you say that? What happened?"

"I thought the whole point of taking those pills was not remembering?"

"You don't want to tell me? Fine." I jerk my arm away from him. We are now deep in shadows and his face is nothing but a dark blob I'd like to drive my fist into.

"Wait." Foote's words stop me before I've gone two steps. "Elton said he needed your help getting the truth out of someone. We tracked you down in the library study room with that guy."

"Oswell," I say, and then, "Why are you even working for Elton?"

"Why wouldn't I? Once I heard you worked for him, I thought he was golden."

"He's not. And I don't work for him. We have a history, and I . . . It's really none of your business." I glare at his hidden face, wondering what I would see there. A part of me is tempted to reach out, but a competing instinct tells me to keep away. I listen to the latter one and take a step back. I should walk away, but Oswell is still there, silent and broken beneath the lights.

"Elton send you to clean that up?" I indicate Oswell with a jerk of my chin.

"That's not Elton's to clean up. Mine neither. We weren't even here when it happened." Foote pulls his hat off, and the moonlight hits his eyes, so I can see them glaring down at me. "But you were."

My stomach twists and I'm unable to hold Foote's gaze. I stare at my toes instead and then back at Oswell, again tracing the line from the top of the stadium straight down to the spot where he now lies.

"He jumped then."

"Didn't see it myself. Elton's girlfriend was here with you, though. Way she told it, he took off like he thought he could fly. What do you think put that thought in his head?"

Not what. Who. And there's only one person I know of who could do such a thing. Piper. The word is so loud in my own head, I wouldn't be surprised if Foote could hear it too. Then again, he doesn't need to; he's been in town long enough to have heard about her.

"How many of those pills did you take?" Foote asks, abruptly changing topics.

"Well, this has been fun," I say, deciding I've had enough of Foote. He's too damn comfortable for a newcomer. "But I should get going."

To prove it, I march back toward the fence line. Wishing I wasn't still wearing my too-short shorts, I push one foot into a diamond-shaped opening for a boost, and then grip the top of the fence, pushing myself up.

"You stopped breathing. And that was after you puked up a bunch of vile purple junk. Even then, there was still enough of that stuff inside you that you forgot how to breathe."

I feel right now like I've forgotten how to breathe. And how to move. And how to tell him he's a liar even when what he says sounds like the truth. So much like the truth that I can feel the way my chest would've grown tight, squeezing in on itself, begging for air. My heart frightened and galloping—that almost feels like a memory too, along with Foote's eyes staring into mine. "Breathe. Breathe." A chant, an order, a plea. Helpless, I heard the words, but couldn't remember what they meant any more than I could recall how to pull oxygen in and out of my lungs.

Somehow my toes find a grip on the other side and then I get my second leg over and hop down. Without looking back to see if Foote enjoyed the view, I start walking.

"Accidental overdose," I call to him. "Happens to notters sometimes." I shrug like it's no big deal, like I'm not totally shaken. Had I really been that bad? Could I really have come that close to dying?

I push the questions aside, unable to deal with them right now.

In the distance thunder rumbles, and I start to run, hoping to get home before the storm breaks.

EVERYBODY WANTS TO RULE THE WORLD

Five Years Ago

YOU STARED AT THE STATUE OF LACHMAN GARDNER like you were committing it to memory. And then you picked up the sledgehammer and swung. Lachman's right arm shattered into a pile of pebbles. You crouched down and began shoveling the pieces into a plastic bag.

"Help me," you ordered. "Hurry!" So I did. Using only the light from the crescent moon, we gathered every last bit of Lachman's crushed arm; you even had a small dustpan and broom to scoop up the bits too fine for our fingers.

That was how the destruction of Lachman Gardner, our illustrious ancestor and the founder of Gardnerville, began.

At first everyone was shocked. Who would hurt good old Lachy?

It was funny that people were so fond of him. Judging from the quotes etched at the base of the statue, he was a self-aggrandizing bastard. AS GO THE GARDNERS, SO GOES GARDNERVILLE. LONG LIVE THE GARDNERS. LONG LIVE GARDNERVILLE! Nobody seemed to hold it against him, though. Or if they did, perhaps they figured a little self-importance was to be expected from the man who'd built the reformatory and overseen the construction of the tunnel through the mountain that would bring the train and modernization to our sleepy town. If Lachman had never come upon this place, people would still be living the same primitive existence they'd been stuck with a hundred years ago.

But you, Piper, you hated Lachman Gardner.

I don't think I ever really knew why. Maybe you didn't quite know why either.

Maybe it was because Daddy was the spitting image of him and you couldn't hate him so you hated Lachman instead.

I think there was more to it, though.

I think it had something to do with the reformatory.

Over the next few weeks we returned to Lachman. With the sledgehammer or sometimes a little chisel and hammer, you broke him down piece by piece, and then together we swept him into plastic bags. Finally, only his clay shoes were left.

Daddy was furious. Every time another piece of the statue disappeared, he'd march down there to examine the damage. Then he would come home and ask me, "Who did it?"

At first when I told him I didn't know, he would shake his head and walk away, muttering that it must have been an accident. It was difficult for him to conceive of this type of betrayal—to his mind, an attack on Lachman was the same as someone planting a knife in his own back. But as Lachman continued to shrink, Daddy could no longer pretend that it was not deliberate.

He began pressing me harder.

"Tell me who did it.

"You know.

"I know you know.

"This isn't your secret to keep!"

I told him I didn't know. Every single time, that was my answer. He grew less and less satisfied until finally, when only Lachman's feet were left, he dragged me from our house all the way to the town square where the last bits of Lachman waited. I remember the look on your face, Piper, when he grabbed my arm and pulled me stumbling and tripping behind him.

"Tell me who did this," Daddy demanded once more.

"I don't know," I answered, my voice small and trembling.

He grabbed me by the shoulders and shook me so hard that my vision went spotty and little starbursts of color shimmered before my eyes. I blinked, clearing the spots away to focus on you instead. You stood frozen behind Daddy, looking even more frightened than me. Following my gaze, Daddy turned toward you.

"You know who did this?" he asked.

"How would she know?" I demanded, pushing myself between them.

Daddy gave me a careless shove. Still dizzy, I stumbled backward and fell.

Ignoring me, Daddy took a step toward Piper. "You love Lachman, don't you, Piper? Why don't you show Skylar the proper way to treat Lachman. 'Cause I think she's the one who's been doing this terrible thing. But she looks up to you. Doesn't she? C'mon now, Piper, set an example for Skylar and kiss that man's shoes."

You didn't even hesitate, Piper. You stepped forward and sank down to your knees so that you were kneeling before Lachman. Then you kissed the tip of each shoe.

Daddy laughed and turned to me. "Another piece of that man goes missing, and I'm taking it out of your hide."

Later that night, you let me take the first swing at Lachman. Then we alternated until he was nothing but crumbs to be scooped up and carried away.

Daddy kept his word. He beat me bloody while you watched and Chance barked himself hoarse.

A few weeks later, when I could walk again without wincing, we went up to the reformatory. Bit by bit, scraping the skin from our knuckles, we pushed our hands beneath the fence and left little fistfuls of Lachman scattered in piles on the grounds of the reformatory.

I still don't know what it was all about, but there was something satisfying in doing it just the same.

FIVE

I'VE ONLY GOTTEN THREE OR MAYBE FOUR HOURS
of sleep when the sound of my bedroom door banging open
shakes me awake. Reluctantly I force my sticky eyelids open.
Great-Grandma stands in the doorway, holding a stack of clean
and folded laundry. She invades our house a few times a week to
beat back the dust bunnies and the mountains of dirty clothes
that nobody else can quite bring themselves to care about. Grabbing a fistful of blankets, I roll away from her and squeeze my
eyes closed again.

"Where do you want these?"

I ignore her, but she doesn't seem to notice.

"This room is a mess. Not even a place for a clean pile of
clothes."

I could tell her my dresser drawers are mostly empty. But I

don't for the same reason I don't tell her to drop dead. Why does she constantly have to be cleaning anyway? Most of the centenarians in this town slow down a little and then a little bit more, until a decade or two into the triple-digit years, when they finally stop moving at all. Not GG though. She's determined to march straight through this century much like she did the previous one. "I'm gonna see two hundred. You just watch and see." That's what she says. I've asked Dennis, the town bookie, to give me the odds. He told me not to bet against GG, but if I were determined, odds were currently at twelve to one in GG's favor.

"All right then." I feel the laundry land on top of me. Still I don't move. The mattress squeals in protest as GG takes a seat beside me. "Are you trying to set some sort of record? Longest mope ever, perhaps?"

"Yeah, that's it," I agree. "Can you go away now, please?"

"You want me to go away and let you lie down on the tracks of life and wait for the next train to come along and roll right over you just like that stupid dog of yours did."

"Seriously?" GG knows exactly where to needle a person and dig it in deep. "Chance wasn't stupid. He was chasing the train. Dogs do stuff like that. And it didn't run him over. He only lost a leg."

"Oh, that's right. I guess I got things mixed up. Must be my old age catching up with me." I snort loudly. "Go ahead and remind me, Sky, where's that dog of yours now? Seems like it's been a while since I've seen him."

Flinging my covers back, I sit up and glare at GG, trying to see past the dark glasses she wears to hide her half-blind eyes. She's varying percentages of sightless, depending on the day. Sometimes I think she picks and chooses what she wants to see. "He's gone. Been gone nearly four years now, and you know it too."

I flop back onto the bed, and pull my blankets over my head. He disappeared the same terrible night that I lost Piper.

"Well, maybe he'll show up again one of these days," GG says, jerking the covers away from me. "You never know."

"You don't believe that."

"No, but you do," GG answers as she stands. "And for your sake, I hope that she does return."

I throw my pillow at GG, but despite being a blind old bat, she easily sidesteps it. "Chance is a he. We are talking about Chance, right?"

"I could give a damn about that dog. Let's cut the bullcrap and talk about Piper."

I shrug. "What do you want to talk about? She's gone."

GG waves her hand, brushing my words away. "But where has she gone, dear? That's the question, isn't it?"

"I think she's in the reformatory," I say, and as I do, I can hear Ozzy telling me—

Before I can remember, GG interrupts. "If she were there, they would tell us. The reformatory's pretty tight with information, but they do tell you when your loved ones have been locked away."

"What if they didn't?" I answer with the question that's been nibbling away at me for the past four years. "What if the people who worked there didn't even know for sure whether or not she was there?"

GG sighs and I can hear the pity ready to come pouring out of her. Poor delusional Sky, that's what she's thinking. But she surprises me. "I'm an old woman, Skylar, and I've tried to be patient these last few years, but lately I can feel my age catching up with me. My plan of giving you enough rope to hang yourself with has obviously backfired, since you've done nothing with it but play jump rope. So now I am going to tell you something, and perhaps this time it will actually stick to the inside of your skull for longer than a day. Piper does not belong inside the reformatory, and if that is indeed where she's been these past four years, then perhaps you should find a way to get her out."

"Is this one of those snobby Gardner things?" I ask. "We're too good to do time in the reformatory like everyone else?" It's something that GG has often told me with a certain pride.

GG's nose shoots up into the air. "You are speaking of me, I presume?"

"You, Dad, all the Gardners who found a way out of doing time."

"And you disapprove of this, I presume?"

I sit up, because it is hard to be snotty when lying down. "I'm just telling you what people say."

"What they say or what they think?" GG takes a thudding step forward. "Is there any person in this town whose secrets haven't been stripped from them?"

"I block them out."

Her lips curve in a mocking smile. "Oh, that's right. You're in control of what secrets you do and don't overhear."

"Yep," I answer, and even though I am wide awake, I retrieve my pillow and force myself to lie down again. "I'm tired so, if you wouldn't mind, shut the door on your way out."

"Always in control," GG snorts, as she pulls the door closed. "The girl who knows everyone's secrets—except her own."

"Get out," I yell, unable to keep my cool a second longer.

I snuggle deeper into my covers, trying to find sleep again. But it's not to be. I can hear the rain slapping against the windowpanes and Wills pounding away at the piano downstairs. My mouth has a terrible dry rotting taste from the forget-me-nots and from throwing them up. Worst of all, the rain has done nothing to drive the stifling heat wave away; if anything, the air feels stickier and heavier than ever.

None of this is what pulls me from my bed, though. In the end it is my consistently inconsistent memory whispering in my ear, reminding me of a piece of paper still wedged into the pocket of my shorts from earlier this morning. I roll out of bed, sluggish, the way I usually feel after a forgotten day. Except yesterday isn't just fuzzy; large chunks of it have been permanently lost.

I sink onto the floor, and it takes me several minutes to find the energy to move again. As I lie there in my piles of discarded clothing, I can't help but remember what Foote said about me almost dying.

On hands and knees I pull myself forward like a sick dog, nosing through my clothes. I find the shorts on the other side of my bed, tucked beneath my old friend Paddington. I've had him since I was a kid small enough to find comfort in squeezing a stuffed animal at night. Paddington's felt hat and coat and red rubber rain boots have long since been lost, his fur is more nubby than fuzzy, and gray stuffing oozes from an opening in his left armpit. Still, earlier this morning, when I'd stumbled into my room, soaking wet and shaking, I grabbed him as I crawled into bed. I fell asleep with my face buried in his soft belly.

Now I cannot help but clutch him once more as I dig the paper from my pocket, carefully peel it open, and read what is written inside.

> It sucks asking you for help. Not just because I don't like you—and I don't. Or because you don't like me—and you don't. It'd probably be better if I left this letter at the bottom of the Salt Spring, but I'm writing it anyway and giving it to you and asking for your help—not for me but for my sister, LuAnn.
>
> She got home two months ago after eight years in the reformatory. I couldn't believe it when she walked out of that place, she looked so sick and ugly, like she had been chewed up and spit out. She kept walking on these horrible wobbly legs, right past the bus and down the road and across town, until she stood in front of our house. Then she fell over. We thought she was dead. But she wasn't and I carried her inside to her bed where she didn't move again for so long she might as well have been dead. Then, outta nowhere, two weeks ago, she started talking. Or mumbling. We couldn't understand her at first, but then we realized what she was saying. "Piper." She was saying the name Piper.
>
> Three days ago, LuAnn disappeared in the middle of the night. We went from one side of town to the other at least a dozen times each, but couldn't find no sign of her.

Last night, Elton came over and started asking questions and talking about locking her up again. I tried to tell him that she was practically neutered after all those years living up there and besides which she's not even a teenager anymore. Nope. Too bad. That's what he said, but in his fancy Elton way. "It would be a last resort" and "We'll work together to keep her on track." Then when I started feeling a little better, he said I of all people should know his policy is always "better safe than sorry." And if that weren't bad enough, he asked if he ought to be worried about me too.

That shut me right up. I can't be sent up to the reformatory. I'd rather die and that son of a bitch Elton knows it too. I shouldn't write that down, I guess, but fuck it and fuck him too. If he gets hold of this paper I'll be going down for more than just name-calling. It's crazy of me to be writing this down at all, much less giving it to you, but I knew it wouldn't be of any use to tell you 'cause you'd just forget it two seconds later. And anyway, I don't think you'll give me up or LuAnn either, not when Elton's gunning for you too.

Yeah, that's right. You should know he keeps close tabs on you, always making sure you're coming to buy more forget-me-nots. Told me they keep you in line, but the minute you stop taking them he's got no problem sending you up the hill. Maybe you think that can't happen to you 'cause you're a Gardner, but you already hid behind that four years ago when you more or less got away with murder. To my way of thinking, you got it coming, and I wouldn't be sad to see you go. In fact, I'd be happy to escort you on up there and lock the gates behind you.

Damn. I'm rereading this and thinking that maybe I should be buttering you up, but that's not my way. I never liked the way everyone round here thinks they got to kiss some Gardner ass. And anyway, you'd see right through my lies anyhow.

Here's the thing I want you to understand: I need your help, but you need mine too—at least if you want to stay out of the reformatory. I can keep telling Elton you're taking pills, and I don't care if you do or you don't, but I need a little tit for tat.

You gotta keep Elton away from LuAnn. Don't ask me how, 'cause I don't know. What I do know is that half the people round here call you the Pied Piper behind your back, and I don't think it's a coincidence that LuAnn started using that name. I don't know if you put something into her head as revenge for eight years ago, or if the reformatory just made LuAnn crazy or maybe it's that everything seems to be going sideways lately. I don't care nothing about the whys, all I know is you're a part of this, and you need to fix it, or I'm gonna tell Elton that it's about time he locks you up too. So when you look at it that way, you can see this as helping me or you can see it as helping yourself.

I hope you're not so dumb that you can't see the smart thing to do here.

J.

A chill tingles down the backs of my bare legs, making my toes curl. Now I remember my run-in with LuAnn. Elton must not have been able to chase her down. I allow myself to enjoy the idea of her outsmarting him, sucking on it like a lemon drop. Then it occurs to me that I'm the one who needs to hunt LuAnn down. Damn. I'm not sure what was going through Jonathan's little pea brain when he was writing this letter, but I have no doubt that he'll rat me out to Elton in a second if something happens to his sister. I almost have to respect him for that.

Slowly I fold the paper back up into its neat little square. It doesn't go together quite the same way. I've noticed lots of things are like that once taken apart.

Tossing Paddington aside, I find a cleanish pair of cutoffs and another worn-out wifebeater. After pulling them on, I shove the paper square into my pocket. Seems like it belongs there now.

Dread should be pooling in my stomach. Jonathan's given me an almost impossible mission, and the price of failure is a steep hike up the hill to the reformatory. Instead, I feel almost giddy. LuAnn comes out of the reformatory after eight years and the first thing she says is "Piper." Jonathan's right, that's not a coincidence. Where he's wrong is connecting the dots to me and discounting Piper. Maybe he thinks she's dead. Or maybe he thinks anyone in the reformatory is as good as dead. He doesn't know Piper, though. Not like I do.

There are things I can't remember and others I can't forget, and in the midst of them is Piper. Maybe in trouble. Maybe causing it. Both sound like the Piper I know. It's indisputable that once you go into the reformatory you are never the same. Teenagers who enter vibrant and alive exit squeezed dry, afraid of shadows because they are shadows themselves. But even Piper's shadow would be a force to be reckoned with. A part of me is not surprised. A part of me has been waiting for this, and wonders why it took so long. A part of me knows exactly what to do.

I follow that part of me out of my room and toward whatever comes next. I won't turn back even if it takes me straight into hell.

And there's a good chance it might.

"Skylar was born during a fourth year." Mom's voice drifts up the stairs to meet me as I come down. I know before she comes into view that she'll be curled up on the sagging couch with Wills tucked into her side.

"I is a fourth year too," Wills says. Mom's gaze strays in my direction as I walk into the room, so Wills tugs at her long braid, demanding her full attention.

"Don't be an asshole," I say to him, pointing my finger.

"I'm not," Wills protests at the same time Mom warns me with a low "Skylar."

I roll my eyes at both of them and walk into the kitchen. A pot full of sticky gray oatmeal sits cold and unappetizing on the stovetop. It's the type of food GG loves to make for us: wholesome, nutritious, and tasteless. Sticking a spoon in, I shovel a few gluey bites into my mouth and quickly swallow them down one after another. As I eat, Mom and Wills continue story time in the other room.

"The year Sky was born was the year I decided I wasn't going to be scared and cower inside anymore. 'This baby needs to see the light,' I said. And so I took her for walks every day, rain or shine, without fail. Our next-door neighbor Mrs. Roberts was an outsider too, and she used to scold me. She said that we hadn't escaped one kind of danger to embrace another. She'd had a brain tumor and was given only a month to live when she moved here. Unlike me, though, she hadn't spent her whole life as a sickly invalid. Maybe that was the difference in our attitudes. I was diagnosed with cystic fibrosis when I was a baby and spent my whole life dreaming of how I'd live if I were healthy. When I finally got that chance I wasn't going to sit inside like some scared little mouse."

Mom sighs in that gusty way she has, hard enough to make the curtains twitch. "It was a shame really. We had so much in common, we should've been friends. I really needed a friend then, and I guess she eventually realized that she did too. She had a new baby just like me, and one beautiful June morning, instead of yelling out her window that I'd better be careful, she said, 'Wait for me.' A minute later she came running out with that baby on her shoulder. She didn't even own a carriage, she said, 'cause she hadn't thought she'd ever take him for a walk. Well, I pushed Skylar to the side of her carriage and we laid the two of them babies side by side, and they were just content as can be. So it became a routine, Mrs. Roberts and her baby boy John Paul coming along on our walk with us."

The oatmeal is gone, but I stand silently by the stove. I know this story. I have heard it so many times that it would be impossible to forget. It is my history. The beginning of being me. I know how it ends too, and I don't need to hear it again. Still I can't walk away until it is finished being told.

"The birds!" Wills interjects into Mom's pause.

"Yes," she says with an even heavier sigh. "The birds. It was July and Mrs. Roberts was having trouble with the humidity. She'd come from some place on the West Coast with cool ocean breezes. So I told her I would take John Paul on the walk, that the fresh air would be good for him and that she needed the rest. She didn't want to let him go. I didn't understand that then. I do now, but then I kept insisting she let me take the baby, until finally she settled him into the carriage. 'Good-bye, my sweet boy,' she said, and then she leaned down to kiss him, but I pulled the carriage away before she could. I told her she would make him hot and miserable, but really I was just impatient. When we reached the cemetery at the bottom of our street, I decided to pick some of the wildflowers that had sprung up there overnight. So we went in. I parked the carriage in the shade and tucked Skylar's blanket around both of those babies."

Mom pauses here. I can feel the transition, from her looking at Wills to almost reliving it.

"After that everything happened so fast. There was screaming and the town sirens went off. I rushed toward the babies, but the birds were already flying in. One sliced right across my cheek, and then a whole flock of them, so many they were just a black cloud, surrounded the carriage. I ran at them, yelling, praying, begging. The cloud lifted, and from the bottom of it, I could see Skylar's little baby blanket trailing along with them. My heart stopped. I was certain they'd carried her away. That's when I heard her high-pitched little scream. This brokenhearted howl. I reached the carriage and it was full of black feathers. I swept them away, and there was Skylar.

"I fell down and wept. I cried until I was sick with it, and then I cried some more. Mrs. Roberts found me. I don't know how, but it was like she already knew John Paul was gone. She stood beside me, staring at Skylar all alone in that carriage for so long, I was scared, not knowing what she would do. But then she just pushed the carriage back home. She must have told your father where I was, because he came to carry me home a little bit later. Later they sent out search crews, swept the Salt Spring and everything, but it was no use. No one ever saw a trace of that child again. Mrs. Roberts left town soon thereafter. Said a long healthy life had lost its appeal."

A shiver travels from the roots of my hair to the tips of my toes. That story, that loss, always goes straight through me. I was too young to remember. That's what everyone says. But then why do I flinch every time a bird flies by? Why can I still feel those feathers smothering me and blacking out the sky?

I rummage through cupboards, not really wanting anything but needing a moment to catch my breath. Grabbing a pack of Scooby-Doo fruit snacks, I stomp back through the front room.

"Stop telling him those stories," I growl, not even looking in their direction.

Sliding my feet into the flip-flops I left in the front hallway, I yank the door open. Humidity hits me like a wet blanket. Big lazy raindrops plop one by one from the sky, so slowly that someone swift could dash between them and get from one end of the town to the other and stay completely dry. I am not that person. The day has barely begun, and I am already tired. I'll be soaked before I reach the end of the driveway.

It would be so much easier to go back upstairs and take one of the pills I salvaged from the toilet. Getting it down without gagging might be difficult, but I'd soon forget where I'd last seen it swimming.

Something heavy lands on my shoulders. I turn and Mom is standing behind me. She places Piper's old yellow rain slicker—the one she found at the Goodwill and fell in love with—on me.

I have avoided Piper's old clothing. Wearing it would feel too much like she was dead and never returning. But also she was so much in everything she wore. Piper didn't simply wear clothes. She fell in love. Her red cowboy boots. This yellow rain slicker. Daddy's awful old brown sweater full of moth holes.

The slicker rubs against my skin just long enough for me to smell it and realize Piper has finally left that too. Her scent, a mixture of coconut shampoo and the red-hot candies she loved to chew, used to cling to everything she'd touched. Now the yellow rain slicker just smells like mildew.

This is why I am leaving the pills behind today. To find Piper. To bring her back home. I can't forget that, but I'm afraid that I will.

I shove my arms into the raincoat's sleeves. Mom leans in and pinches the snaps closed, starting down at my knees and not finishing until she reaches the one that closes it around my chin. Finally, she flips the hood up.

"It's just rain," I say, but the sharp-edged tone I usually use with her is gone.

She takes a step back. "You can never be too careful."

She doesn't add "in this town." She doesn't need to.

I nod, turn, and walk outside. Mom stands in the doorway, watching me.

"Where's Sky going?" I hear Wills ask.

"On an adventure," she says, and I guess that's the only thing you can say to a four-year-old. It beats "I don't know where she's going, and I don't know if she'll make it back."

SHE'S LIKE THE WIND

Four Years Ago

THE TRAIN CONTINUED TO ROAR PAST ME AS I watched you slowly swim toward shore, your arms chopping through the water as if it were your enemy. I made the same wish that I did every time—that you would finally be tired of playing this terrible game of chicken with the train.

You were twelve the first time you tried to walk the bridge's mile-long length. I stood at the far end and watched you shrink. Then the train whistle blew. You turned and started running back toward me, though there was no way you would ever make it. The whistle blew louder, or maybe that was the brakes screeching, and just when the train would've swallowed you, you threw yourself over the side of the bridge and into the water below. Ever since then you'd been trying to outrun that train. And I'd been watching it with my heart beating so hard I might as well be running alongside you.

You finally hauled yourself onto dry land and collapsed into the scrub grass. Chance barked at you the whole time, scolding. You flicked a wet hand at him, and with a yelp, he retreated to hide behind me.

"You're going to drown one of these days," I said.

For a long moment you didn't say anything, just stared out at the water that everyone else in Gardnerville feared. Almost no one in this town can swim. Fear of the water starts with the Salt Spring, but it doesn't end there. A few years back the Gardnerville town council put on the addition to the school with the pool, hoping it would encourage more people to learn to swim and lose their fear. An outsider was brought in to hold lessons, but he left after three months. He said it was because he only had three students, but everyone knew the town was more than he could take. It happened that way for a lot of newcomers.

"Last time you said one of these days I wasn't gonna jump fast enough and the train was gonna run me over," you finally replied with a laugh.

"That could happen too."

I didn't add that you wouldn't be the first to die that way. We both knew that people who wanted to leave Gardnerville but weren't brave enough to board the train threw themselves in front of it instead.

"Come on, Pollywog, you know the train wouldn't dare run me over. It would jump into the Salt Spring rather than take me down." You grinned at me in that wild sort of way you had, daring me to contradict you.

And of course I didn't. I couldn't.

Sitting up, you fixed your gaze on the train tracks. The grin faded but not the wildness. If anything, it flared. "Someday I'll outrun that train. You ever consider that outcome, Pollywog? One of these days, I'll run so fast and so hard that I'll become a stream of light. And then I'll burst into a million pieces. You'll try to collect them all, 'cause you and Mom and Dad will think I'll need to be buried and cried over. But you won't be able to. The pieces will be scattered everywhere; you won't even know where to begin looking. And when you do find one, it'll be so bright and hot and shiny that it'll burn through the toughest gloves and scorch the flesh beneath. So you'll have to leave me behind and you'll think it's sad, but it won't be, not really. 'Cause someday you'll be dead too and laid down under the dirt where no one can see you. You'll be forgotten. But people will find those pieces of me forever, and that's how they'll know I was part of something special."

I was speechless. You'd been weird like this a lot lately. You'd say the strangest things as if they were totally normal. I never knew how to respond. Usually, I tried to laugh it off. Pretend it was all a joke. Which was exactly what I did this time.

"Um, Piper, how much of that salt water did you swallow?"

You laughed. "Too much, Pollywog. Too much. Although not as much as the first time. I can still see the way you were staring at me when I finally came out of the water. You said to me, 'Gosh, Piper, I didn't know you could swim.' And I said, 'I didn't either 'til just now.'"

Standing, you grabbed the bottom of your T-shirt and

twisted it so that the water dribbled out. "This train was faster than usual, didn't you think?"

"It was the water train," I said, picking up one of the water jugs you'd dropped onto the ground and shaking it as a reminder. Not that you needed one. This was the errand you had invited me on.

"Oh, that's right." Gracefully, you swept three of the jugs into your arms with one swooping motion. "Our weekly allotment of natural springwater, which, unlike this natural salt water, will not increase your chances of going mad." You said this last bit in your deep theatrical voice, the one you used when you were try-ing to make me laugh. You knew exactly how much your train running upset me. This knowledge wasn't enough to make you stop. But you always tried to make it up to me afterward, going into extra-sweet-sister mode.

Usually, I gave in quickly, but that day I wasn't just upset about the train running. Your strange story was still bothering me too. So instead of laughing away the tension between us, I picked up my water jugs and started walking. You fell into step beside me, while Chance ran ahead.

"You know," you said, "they say the creeplings got the way they are 'cause their mother drank the Salt Spring water every day. Took baths in it too. Then after the five of them were born, she put the water in their bottles. She wanted them to be differ-ent. To be special. And I think everyone agrees that she got her wish." You paused for dramatic effect. "What do you think of that?"

I shrugged. I'd heard that story. I'd also heard the one where people said the creeplings' mother was in love with our father. According to the gossip, the woman was so much in love with Dad that she wanted him to leave Mom. Everybody knew he'd never do that, but she must've thought that maybe if she got pregnant he'd change his mind. Except he didn't. Then she thought that maybe if her kids came out incredible and different, it would change his mind. Having quints is pretty incredible. He still didn't care though. I didn't know if she tried anything else after that. I didn't know if any of that was true. But if it was, I felt sorry for her. It took her a long time, longer than most, to realize he wasn't capable of caring.

"You think they're related to us? Like, our half siblings?" I was certain this very question was the reason you'd brought it up.

But you brushed it off. "Oh, I don't know. Probably. Probably not. Take a peek inside their heads if you really want to know, I guess."

"No thanks," I said with a shudder.

"Oh, poor Pollywog. You've gathered enough scary stories to give your nightmares a nice variety."

"I haven't," I quickly protested. In some families you get known for being someone not able to keep a secret, but I was known for not being able to resist taking them. I hated it. And you knew it too.

You kicked a cloud of dust at me. "Don't get all scrunch-faced with me, Pollywog. I didn't mean it as a bad thing. Just think of all those people out there." You flapped your hand back in the direction we'd come, to the train tracks that disappeared into the mountain and the rest of the world that lived beyond it.

"Their nightmares must be so boring. If they were smart, they wouldn't take money for the natural springwater they send us. They'd insist on a trade instead. Our water for theirs. Then they could have a taste of the awful and awesome things we excel at."

Normally I'd agree. And then we'd spend the rest of our walk thinking up clever ways to insult the idiots that made up the rest of the world that wasn't Gardnerville. But I was still upset, so I said nothing and shrugged again instead.

You poked me in the side. "Don't shrug, Pollywog. It's nearly as bad as Mom's sighs."

Taking a deep breath, you did such an excellent imitation of one of those infamous sighs that although I fought it, I couldn't keep a snort of laughter in. You did it again and again, until I was laughing so hard I could barely walk. Then you finally stopped and laughed with me.

"You can't stay mad at me, can you?" you said later as we were walking home much slower, weighed down by the jugs now heavy with water.

I did my own imitation of Mom's sigh, with a little bit of a groan thrown in for added comic effect. You laughed. I did too.

But that sigh was genuine. I felt it down to my toes.

Since you've been gone, Piper, I've become as bad with the sighing as Mom. Sometimes it's the part of a sob that I just can't hold back. Sometimes the sigh's more like blowing out birthday candles to make a wish. And sometimes I do it hoping that it'll make you appear—even for just one instant—to laugh at me and tell me to stop.

SIX

NORMALLY, I CUT THROUGH SIDE STREETS AND across lawns to get around town. Today I take the main road. It runs from the north side of Gardnerville, where we live, through the center of town and then continues over the tracks to the school.

For the second day in a row, I'm going to visit Jonathan at the double-wide. He can't just hand me a note like that and not expect a few follow-up questions. My feet falter for a moment when a memory blooms inside my mushy brain of a sodden and bloodied polo shirt.

I decide not to think about that, which is easier said than done.

Trying to push the image from my brain, I begin to hum an old favorite of mine and Piper's—"Over the Rainbow." *The*

Wizard of Oz is one of the movies that plays as part of the constant rotation on our one and only TV station. We know all the songs and almost every single word of dialogue up until the part when Dorothy starts clicking her red heels near the end of the movie. That's when we turn it off. It's our tradition, going back to when I was four years old and began sobbing, crushed by Dorothy's choosing boring old Kansas over the Technicolor glory of Oz. "That's not the ending," you announced, desperate to comfort me. After that, whenever it came on TV, we turned it off before she could utter, "There's no place like home." Then, using props and funny voices, you'd perform the new ending so that Dorothy stayed over the rainbow.

I grin, remembering one of those imagined endings. You acted out Dorothy training the Wicked Witch's flying monkeys to be her pets. My chest suddenly aches, and I press a hand against my heart, trying to silence it. This is why it's better not to remember.

Unfortunately, once started, it's hard to stop.

Ten minutes later, I am still so lost in the memories of Dorothy's alternate futures, I don't even notice the car creeping up behind me as silent as a lion stalking prey—until it is almost on top of me.

It's Elton in his damn Prius again. Not many people have cars here. That's because a gas tanker only comes on the train every other month. During a fourth year, it might be longer than that. It's been this way ever since Marilyn Bingham turned the old gas station into a fireball thirty-six years ago.

The tinny horn beeps at me. I stare straight ahead, pretending obliviousness. Wishing he would go away.

He doesn't. Instead, I hear the soft whir of his window rolling down.

"Hey . . . ," he calls out, and it is the strange hitch and hesitation in his voice that finally make me turn. The moment my eyes meet his, I understand.

His widen and—within the space of a long, slow blink—dim. I remember then that Elton has not always been cool, calm, and calculating. Or perhaps he has always been all those things, but there was a time when he was also something else. Something more. It was there in his eyes, I saw it. It only disappeared when he realized that the girl in the yellow rain slicker was not Piper, could not possibly be Piper, and was, of course, only me.

He recovers quickly. "Skylar. I've been looking for you. Let me give you a ride." Leaning across the passenger seat, he pushes the door open, out toward me, inviting. Or, to be more accurate, commanding. An invitation can be declined.

I get into the car without saying a word. No Foote today, which is odd. Elton usually tries to avoid being alone with me.

"Where you headed?" Elton asks. One hand is on the steering wheel, the other on the gearshift, ready to move without hesitation at my say-so.

I wonder what he would say if I told him about the note burning a hole in my back pocket. What would he think about LuAnn using Piper's name as if it were her own? Would he feel desperate to get closer to LuAnn, just to feel some sort of connection to Piper no matter how tenuous it might be? Of course, the last time he connected with Piper, he lost both his legs. He's adjusted well to his prosthetics, moves on his silver limbs like he was meant to be made of steel. Still, it's obvious to anyone who knew him before that the train took more than just Elton's legs.

Elton's thumb taps impatiently.

"The school," I say, deciding to stick with the half-truth . . . and then embroider it around the edges. "Lost my stash of forget-me-nots yesterday; I'm hoping there'll be some left." I scrub at a bleach stain on my shorts, pretending obliviousness.

Elton says nothing as he drives us up the street, but I can feel his gaze on me. Heavy. Waiting. Urging me to say something. To blurt the truth out into the silence.

It doesn't work. I turn away from him to stare out the passenger window and watch my own reflection in the glass. I look tired. And sad. If I had a purple pill inside me right now, I'd be looking at that girl in the window, wondering who she was and feeling sorry for her.

At last, Elton coasts through the mostly empty school parking lot, heading toward the stadium. I reach for the door, wanting to get away already. Elton stops me with a hand on my knee. His bare hand. On my bare knee.

Elton never touches me. Won't even get close enough to lightly brush against me.

I remember then, visiting Elton in the hospital after he lost his legs, months before he was reborn with prosthetics. He radiated sorrow. And loss. He'd tried to save Piper. But no one had tried to save him. I admitted it in that moment: maybe I was a little bit in love with him.

I leaned forward to kiss his cheek. My hair fell forward, a coconut-scented curtain between Elton and me. He turned his head and our lips met. It was not the kiss I'd intended. Or maybe it was. I didn't pull away.

"Piper," he breathed against my mouth, and then grabbed hold of my arms, pulling me closer. That was when I finally shoved him into the mattress and pushed myself back with so much force my sneakers squealed against the linoleum.

I wanted to hurt him then. And I knew exactly how to do it. "I have all your secrets now," I told him, while making a show of scrubbing my lips with the back of my hand. "Touch me again and I'll know you better than you know yourself."

Elton has been very careful around me since then. Most people think I need touch to take their secrets. They don't realize that it is so much easier than that. Sometimes I can see secrets in the very air someone breathes. Sometimes I find them waiting in a chair long after its occupant has stood up and walked away. And sometimes, just sometimes, when I am sitting quietly with nothing much on my mind, even if there is no one around, secrets come searching for me, desperately wanting to spill themselves. Elton knows this, or he should since he's seen me work enough times in the back of his car, but he still keeps his distance.

I study him now, focusing on his true-blue lying eyes, straight nose, and lush lips. Oh, I can see why Piper fell for him. I could always see that. But I can also see the thousand damning secrets practically oozing from his pores.

I don't want Elton's secrets anymore. Not on purpose or accidentally.

I push his hand away. "What do you want?"

"I wanted to say I'm sorry," Elton says, leaning back just

enough so there is more space between us. "About last night."

"Last night?" I give nothing away, hoping he'll fill in the blanks.

Elton is equally cagey. "I'm not sure what you remember."

I take a stab in the dark. "I remember you knocking on the library door, scaring the hell out of Ozzy."

"Good. He had no business hanging around you like that."

Saying nothing, I stare at Elton. Hard.

He doesn't blush—I think he's become too cold-blooded for that—but he does at least have the decency to look away.

Good. One small victory for me.

It is short-lived, though, as Elton quickly recovers and tosses this little grenade my way as reprisal: "He's dead, by the way."

"I know," I reply, trying to match his blasé attitude but failing utterly when the words come out a watery whisper. As horrible as Ozzy and his wandering hands might have been, he was my connection to Piper . . . even if the information he'd given me about her over the last four years was barely enough to fill a thimble. "I'm getting close to finding something out," he'd say. "It's been tough. The guys don't wanna risk their necks to help me. When I mention Piper, they pretend to not even know who I'm talking about. Then they tell me there's nothing in that locked room, and to stop talking crazy. But if it's empty, why lock it, right?"

"I never see her on the walks. How would that even be possible?" I'd press.

He'd shrug. "It's Piper, you know?" It wasn't an answer, but I'd still nod and agree.

Then he'd tell me it was okay and not to worry. *Okay, don't worry* was an Ozzy phrase that covered all situations. Piper was okay, don't worry. The reformatory was okay, don't worry. "It's okay, don't worry," he'd assure me as his hands slid under my shirt.

"You shouldn't feel guilty." Elton's words pull me back into the present, and I realize that in his own cold way he's trying to comfort me. "You know, it's not uncommon for reformatory workers to kill themselves."

It wasn't suicide. No way. No how. I almost laugh at the idea. Sure, reformatory workers kill themselves sometimes. And they're not the only ones. Suicide is common in Gardnerville. Distraught parents. Kids who can't stand the pressure of waiting to see whether they or one of their friends will implode during a fourth year. Old-timers who decide to create their own expiration date.

"Yeah," I say to Elton, since he seems to be waiting for some sort of answer.

"I can see you're upset," Elton replies. "Why don't you take some time off? Or should I say, time out? I thought these might help. A gift from the lab boys." Elton produces a plastic Baggie full of little purple pills. He must have had the quints up all night producing them.

"Shit," I say, my hand reaching out before I remember that I can't have one today. Maybe tomorrow though. Or later, after I talk with Jonathan. A reward of sorts. My fingers close around the bag.

"I promised Piper I would look after you and I mean to keep that promise."

"Uh-huh," I say, only half listening, trying to count the pills.

"And I want you to know I never would have gotten you involved in that Jonathan situation if I'd known he would react that way."

My fingers go slack and the bag of pills drops to the floor between my feet. I have this terrible feeling that I'm falling too, but I can still feel the cold leather seat slick beneath my bare legs.

The bloody shirt. The knife. I see it again, and this time something else. We are in the pool room at school. Jonathan rushes at Elton with an army knife. But suddenly Foote's between them, getting stuck with the knife instead. It doesn't even scratch Elton, who is now punching Jonathan until blood pours from his nose. Jonathan pulls his shirt off and throws it at Elton, all the while shouting about how this is all going to blow up in Elton's face, that he's playing with fire. He repeats *playing with fire*. Once. Twice. The third time, flames shoot from the tips of Jonathan's fingers. Elton rushes him then, with enough force to send them both into the pool. Foote jumps in after them. The water begins to foam and then giant bubbles appear. It's almost as if the pool water is building to a full boil. I try to count, wondering how long they've been under, but keep losing track of the numbers after I get past fifty. The whole room is hot and steamy by the time Elton comes up gasping for air. Around him the bubbles pop, disappearing as quickly as they appeared. Foote surfaces several long moments later. At first I don't even recognize him; every bit of visible skin is red and blistered. Elton pulls Foote into the locker room, and I am left to wait for Jonathan to pop up next. But, of course, he never does.

"He's dead," I say, still not quite able to believe it.

"Yes, it's unfortunate," Elton replies, but I think the word he wanted was *inconvenient*, because he continues, "I have some other people minding the press box for now. You won't have to worry about that, though. Those pills should keep you for a while, and the next time you run out, I want you to come straight to me. I know we've had our differences, but I think we both know how important it is for you to stay out of trouble during a fourth year. We wouldn't want to repeat the mistakes of the past."

"Why?"

Elton chuckles, and the sound is about as musical as our garbage disposal chewing up eggshells. "I think that should be obvious."

"No, why did you—" I was going to say "kill Jonathan," but Elton's eyes stare at me hard and cold. I wouldn't say that I've ever felt safe with Elton, or that I trust him. Elton was bad news from the moment I met him. But he loved Piper. I always thought that was enough to protect me from the worst of him. Now I can't help but wonder if the opposite is true. "You had me read Jonathan, didn't you? What did you find out? What did I tell you?"

"It was a betrayal," Elton says. "One I envy your ability to forget."

I am ready with my follow-up question, but the hell with that. Enough dicking around. I take a deep breath and in the same instant swipe the answer straight out of Elton's skull.

And I find out something that Jonathan apparently didn't feel was necessary to divulge in his letter. When LuAnn regained her voice she didn't just say "Piper." She also told Jonathan, "The reformatory is the center. Don't be afraid. We'll go together. You and me and everyone to the top of the hill. We'll call it the uprising. It's the way Gardnerville was always meant to be, everyone gathered together in the reformatory."

There's not a lot there to freak out over. Mostly just a crazy girl's ramblings. But that word *uprising* is surrounded by flashing neon lights in Elton's head. In his mind that was enough for him to lock her up again.

"Well, Sky, since you've already gotten what you came here for, why don't I drive you home?"

"No thanks," I say, pushing my door open. "I'd rather walk."

Elton's hand closes around my wrist, while the other reaches for the bag of pills I left on the floor. "Take the pills, Skylar."

I stare at the pills, nearly trembling with wanting them wanting them wanting them and—Piper. I use her name like a magic word to break a spell. I can't find her if I'm all fucked up.

Elton gives the bag a little shake, the same way I used to with Chance's treats when I wanted him to beg, sit, heel. "I'd like to see you stay out of trouble," he says. "Lots of people are wondering why you aren't being sent to the reformatory with the rest of the precautionaries."

"And what do you say to them?" I ask, remembering Jonathan writing in his letter that Elton used the pills to keep me tame. It's not like I didn't already know that on some level, but to see it laid out so clearly makes me feel like a chump.

"I tell them that I have it all under control," he answers softly. "Now take a pill like a good girl, and I'll drive you home."

I squeeze the bag so that pills erupt and then I lean back and hold it over my head, letting them rain down on me. My mouth fills with pills. My teeth clench into a hard smile. Elton's hand squeezes my wrist.

"Skylar," he warns.

I spit the wad of pills onto his cream-colored leather car seats. They will leave a wet, sloppy purple stain. I know this. I once fell asleep with my cheek on a pile of pills and had a purple mark on my face for a month. One pill remains on my tongue; I stick it out at Elton and then close my mouth and swallow it.

With a smile that doesn't come close to reaching his eyes, Elton releases my wrist. "Have a good day, Sky."

"You bet I will." I slam the door behind me and start running with no clear destination in mind, except away.

PARADISE CITY

Eight Years Ago

EVERYONE WENT TO THE FUNERALS RESULTING from a fourth-year event. It was a way to pay respect and to count your blessings that it wasn't you or yours being put into a pine box.

LuAnn Stimple left twelve victims between the ages of nine and seventeen to be buried. For four days in a row, we went from one funeral service to another, mouthing the same meaningless words, throwing down handfuls of dirt to cover one dead body before moving on to the next.

Daddy loved these funeral-filled weeks. Any large gathering of people put a spring in his step, never mind the reason they'd come together. He'd work the crowds with one arm around Mom's waist and the other free to shake hands, slap backs, and every so often reach over to pat your head or mine while he turned his eyes heavenward and intoned in a solemn voice, "The silver lining here is that we're reminded to cherish our loved ones and hold them closer."

I hated it, but got through it with you at my side.

Except that week you refused to go.

I thought Daddy would be furious and drag you down to join us, but if he noticed there was one less head to pat, he never said a word about it.

The nine-year-old's funeral was last. There were always more tears at the final funeral, as if people had been saving them and now needed to use them up before it was all over.

I skipped the feast they always had after the final burial. Daddy would be mad, I knew. He always made a big speech, talking obliquely about the sacrifices these brave young people had made for the greater good of Gardnerville. As if their deaths were noble. Or a choice. I didn't know how anyone could listen to it and not hate him, but more than once I'd been told that his words were a great comfort.

I trudged home, my whole body heavy with four days of grief. As I walked, I began to feel angry with you for making me go through this alone. Yes, you had almost been one of LuAnn's victims yourself, but that seemed a better reason than any to attend the funerals of those with less luck. By the time I burst into the house and stampeded up the steps toward your room, I was steaming.

I threw your door open, and froze.

Every square inch of your room was covered in crumpled and torn paper. And you . . . you sat in the middle of the madness, muttering to yourself and stripping pages from a book one sheet at a time, and then tossing them this way and that, adding them to the various piles. You were so absorbed in your task, you didn't hear me come in.

"Piper?" I called softly, my throat already aching with unshed tears.

Startled, you looked up. "Oh good, you're here. Come help me." You held a book out to me. *Alice's Adventures in Wonderland* read the gold lettering along the spine. Taking it, I flipped through the book. It looked like you had already stripped half the pages from it.

"Hurry," you said, flapping a hand at me. "We need to take them apart before we can put them back together."

I sank down to the floor, papers crinkling beneath me. "Piper, are you okay?"

I wanted you to laugh and say it was all a joke.

You didn't. Instead you snatched *Alice's Adventures in Wonderland* back from me. "These are my books, my stories. I can change them if I want to."

"Okay," I answered, gently taking the book back. I opened it and tore a page out. "I'll help."

We ripped the pages, not just from *Alice*, but also *Peter Pan* and the entire Chronicles of Narnia. As we began to put the books back together, heavily edited and with entirely new endings, the pattern became clear. Characters in these books made the same terrible mistake that Dorothy did in *The Wizard of Oz*. They left a magical and sometimes dangerous place for the relative safety and comfort of home.

You called the characters idiots and cowards. You pounded the book covers and said these books equated ordinary with good and extraordinary with evil.

I nodded and agreed, but all the time I couldn't help finding the new stories unsatisfactory in a slightly different way. In our Gardnerville story, we were born into the magical and dangerous place, and that left us with a new problem and no easy solution that I could see.

Maybe it was all those funerals, but our predicament seemed much worse than anything that Alice faced. How could we ever have a happy ending, Piper, when the mysterious and deadly land is where we've grown up, and there is never any hope of finding a safe place to call home?

SEVEN

THE WORLD COMES INTO FOCUS, THEN GOES OUT again. Blurry. Sharp. Blurry. Sharp.

The first time I took one of those purple pills, I tried to stand up and walk. It didn't go well. I had fallen flat on my face and lay on the floor, straining my eyes, fighting to bring the world back into focus. Until I realized my vision wasn't the only part of me impaired. Every bit of me was blocked up. All five senses and my sixth sense too. Without them, it was quiet, wonderfully so. There were no secrets to be guarded against. Everything was easier.

But that was a long time ago. It's not easier now. The sharp moments are cutting into me, reminding me. Piper is gone. Or maybe she isn't. Maybe I gave her up for lost, when all this while she's been waiting for me to break her out. From the fog a memory swings toward me like a lighthouse lamp, blinding me with its sudden glare. With painfully intense clarity, I can see Piper. Her hands grip my shoulders and her nose is less than an inch away from my own. She is telling me something I must do. Something I must do after. But after what? The light begins to dim, and before it blinks out, I recall my response. "Impossible." That's what I told her. I attempt to remember something more, but the darkness is worse than ever, and when I try to penetrate it I am rewarded with a terrible pressure pushing against my temples.

Too late, I stick my finger down my throat. I gasp and gag, but nothing comes up. The pill is long dissolved. I could have done that before. I had enough time before the pill worked its ugly magic. Hell, I could've hidden it in my cheek and spit it out when Elton drove away. But I didn't want to. That's the truth. I am a coward. That's even more true. Always looking for the easy way out. Always have been. It was never a problem when I could hide in Piper's shadow, when she made the decisions and I marched behind her.

Now I stare up at the sky. Except there is no sky, only a sagging ceiling with a dark-brown water stain. I wriggle my fingers and touch dirt. In fact, I can now feel dirt covering me, crumbling around my shoulders and sprinkled over my bare legs. It seems that while I was out of it, someone tried to bury me alive.

Everything blurs again, but this time it's because of the tears in my eyes. I try to wipe them away, but my arms are still limp and useless.

The tears stream. The dirt itches. The dark-brown water stain begins to take the shape of a monster with fangs. Having no other choice, I wait. Time passes. My mind churns. It is impossible to avoid the memory of Foote asking whether I am suicidal. I told myself that it was just an accident. A mistake. A one-time thing that would never happen again. Now, though, it's as difficult to shrug off the question as it is the dirt making my skin itch.

At last, motor function returns. My legs flex and, pushing against the floor, I inch myself into a seated position. The room wobbles and wavers, then finally comes into focus. I recognize it immediately as the headquarters for the Gardnerville Historical Society, aka one of GG's spare bedrooms. I'm sitting on the wood floor in a pile of dirt. Across the room, with her back to me, GG is seated at her ancient wooden desk, which is so warped that none of the drawers fully close anymore. I watch as she bends over some piece of paper with a magnifying glass.

"What the fuck?" I say. Or not. My tongue gets twisted. All that comes out is, "Wah?"

GG swivels to face me. "Oh good, you've returned from your little trip to nowheresville. How was the weather there? Do anything interesting?"

I glare. Well, I stare and try not to drool on myself.

GG shakes her head at me sadly. "You're making me feel very old, Skylar. I watch you and see the choices you're making, and then I come here and look at all these stories I've written out by hand over the years. My handwriting was always so neat. So small. I can't read a damn word of it now. Not that it matters. It's the same damn story every damn time. The Gardners who reap what they sow. So this afternoon when I found you collapsed on my doorstep, I thought I would try something different. I said to myself, 'Let's plant this Gardner and see what grows.' And that's exactly what I did."

This is the part where I would be saying something sarcastic and then walking away, but with both my legs and tongue out of commission, I am actually listening instead of thinking about my escape route. That's why I notice that something is wrong with GG. She seems different. She seems . . . old.

The change is so dramatic; I can't believe I didn't notice it earlier. Her famous snowy white hair that she wears long and flowing over her shoulders is striped through with wiry gray. The barely noticeable laugh lines around her eyes have spread like ever-widening chasms. Most troubling, though, is the unmistakable curve to her usually ramrod-straight back.

"Whatever you're thinking—stop it," GG says.

I scrub a hand across my face and then—with effort—push an answer through my stiff lips. "Not . . . think . . . any . . . thing."

"Can't argue with that," GG answers as she stands up in her usual brisk way. For a minute I think that I imagined it all, but then she wobbles, wavers, and slowly sinks back into her chair.

"Shi-it," I stutter, struggling to get up from my place on the floor and having no more success than GG.

GG waves a hand at me. "Settle down, Skylar. I'm honored that you took a moment to think of someone else's troubles for a change, but you needn't bother. I've been feeling it more and more these last four years, what with that newcomer's tampering. Although who knows, perhaps in the end it will all be for the best."

"Best?" I ask.

GG ignores me. "And I am especially feeling my age at this moment, after dragging all that dirt in here." With a jerk of her chin, she indicates the soil covering me. I'd actually forgotten about it, once I realized I wasn't buried in it.

Since she obviously doesn't want to discuss the aging thing, I focus on the dirt instead. I let a handful of it run through my fingers. "Practical joke?" I am relieved when the two words come out of my mouth fairly smoothly.

This earns me one of GG's imperious sniffs. "Hardly. I was simply returning something that I believe belonged to you."

"Whaddaya mean?" I ask at the same time GG says, "Do you know what I'm looking at here?"

My hand clenches around a handful of dirt. Anger trips up my still-recovering tongue and I blurt out, "Bullshit."

"Good guess, but no," GG answers. "These are papers that might do you some good, Skylar. I know you think the way forward is to forget the past, but I guarantee that will only cause more trouble in the end."

"Seriously?" I roll my eyes, but honestly I'm scared. GG's right, I am comfortable with forgetting. "Two lectures a day is a bit much even for you."

In response, GG clears her throat. "In 1856 Lachman Gardner discovered this valley. It was love at first sight."

"Lachman?" I can't help but feel relieved that we're discussing my great-great-grandfather. I can deal with history when it's of the ancient variety.

"Yes, Lachman," GG snaps back at me.

I hold my hands out in a "hey, chill out" gesture, but the effect is ruined by their trembling and I quickly drop them back into my lap. "I know 'bout him."

And I did. Not just because we had studied him in school. Although we had. We also celebrated Lachman Gardner month every March. I seem to recall a statue of Lachman once standing at the center of town, posed with one clay fist clenched over his heart, but maybe I'm remembering that wrong, because all that's in that spot now are some words etched into cement.

"You know, but you don't really know anything," GG says in response to my protest. "Now listen. Lachman loved this valley and he ruined it too."

"Ha," I say, forcing myself to my feet. The room swims. I stumble forward like a newborn calf and have to clutch GG's desk to keep from falling. GG smirks at me while I catch my breath. The old lady gets under my skin. She always has. Just once I'd like to win an argument with her, and maybe this is my chance. "Lachman ruined it? How about—he built it."

"You're wrong, Skylar." GG stands as well. "He only built it after he broke it. And this is exactly what I am talking about. You don't know why you do anything, because you don't know what has already been done. I am trying to make you understand."

"By covering me with dirt?" Releasing the desk, I take a lurching step back to where I'd been lying on the floor. "Enough." Leaning down, I scoop a handful of dirt from the floor. "Explain this."

GG stumbles away, but there is nowhere to go. Her chair hits the back of her legs and she sinks into it, looking . . . defeated.

It's what I wanted. Or what I thought I wanted. It's not the first time that the two haven't matched up the way they should.

I look down at the soil in the palm of my hand. Beating GG with a handful of dirt shouldn't be possible, which means that this isn't just any old dirt.

A memory rises, of Piper handing me a plastic shovel and telling me to dig. She points to the ground on the other side of the fence that surrounds the reformatory. "You can feel it, can't you?" she asks. "The reformatory poisons everything it touches, even the very ground it sits upon."

"It's from the reformatory, isn't it?" I ask now.

After a long moment GG nods. "Couldn't you feel it? Even with gloves on, I was sick from touching it. The reformatory has that effect on most of us. Except lately some people are immune—including you."

GG's right—I should have felt it. I did a little bit. That itching along my skin. Wool sweaters give me the same scratchy feeling. But it should've been much worse. This is what powers the reformatory, something in the dirt. The very land it is built upon makes people sick. We've all seen it. The fourth-year villains go into the reformatory able to bring down buildings with a snap of their fingers, but with every step taken during four years or more of lockup, a little bit of that power seeps away, until by the time they're let out, they can't even snap their fingers. This is how the reformatory works, how it has always worked. No one is immune.

Except, I apparently am. The dirt has no effect on me. This information doesn't feel surprising or new. I knew it but momentarily forgot. The surprise is that someone else found out. "How did you know?"

"I didn't know. A long time ago, I guessed, but it wasn't until recently that it seemed important enough to know for sure." GG lifts a shaky hand to smooth back a bit of hair. "So, you see, you're not the only person in this family who sometimes prefers to hide from the truth."

"Yeah? And do you feel better now that you know?"

"No." GG laughs in this hollow sort of way. "I don't feel better. But I do feel more prepared."

"Prepared for what?" My voice is too loud, because I am annoyed with myself for asking another question, and even more annoyed with GG for not spitting it out already.

"'Things fall apart; the centre cannot hold,'" GG answers. "That's a poem. Maybe you've heard it before?"

Opening my hand, I let the dirt trickle from my fingertips. It takes everything inside me not to fling it in GG's face. Quoting poetry at me. Maybe I'd heard it before. Yeah, I'd heard it all right and I knew who GG heard it from too. "The Second Coming" by William Butler Yeats was one of Piper's favorites. She made me memorize it along with her. I thought I'd forgotten it along with everything else, but with that one line it all comes back.

Here's another thing I remember: I don't need to be here anymore now that my legs are working again.

"Skylar, someone needs to be the one," GG calls after me, as I walk out the door.

The one to what? I would ask if I wanted an answer. I don't, so I give her both middle fingers in response instead.

"'The best lack all conviction, while the worst / Are full of passionate intensity.'" GG's voice follows me down the hall spewing another line from that damn poem.

Who the hell knows what she means by it all. It's vague. Like everything else GG is tiptoeing around. Making words but not saying anything at all. Some people would find it tantalizing. Some people would still be standing there like idiots, asking questions, trying to get a straight answer. Not me. GG can go digging through the dirt and history too. She's certain to find some skeletons. If she keeps digging long enough, eventually one of the skeletons will probably be mine.

Me, though, I'm more interested in searching out the living. Piper is up there at the reformatory, waiting for me. I'm beginning to feel more certain of that. Ozzy found a way into the locked room and he must've seen Piper in there. I don't know what he said to her, or what he did. Something terrible, I'd guess. She'd have to be furious to make him jump like he did. And she's somehow gotten to LuAnn too. The other day when she jumped onto Elton's car, I felt like she was trying to communicate something to me. Maybe Piper sent her to me with a message.

Maybe. Perhaps. Possibly.

I want certainties, not endless indefinites.

It'll be okay, though. Once I figure out how to get to Piper, I won't have to worry about what questions to ask. She'll have them all and the answers too.

At least I hope so.

KARMA CHAMELEON

Six Years Ago

I STOOD AT THE FRONT GATES OF THE REFORMATORY.
Waiting. It felt strange to be there out in the open, instead of hiding in the tall grass around the back side. I pressed the button to announce myself and, in a trembling voice, spoke into the black box. "Skylar Gardner here for Piper Gardner."

"Relation?" The disembodied voice crackled through the speaker.

"Sister," I said, although they already know. It wasn't a question asked to gain information; it was a reminder of who was in charge.

"Discharge papers?"

I looked down at my empty hands, as if the papers might have magically appeared. "Sorry, I didn't get anything," I finally answered.

I waited, but there was no response. My mouth was dry, my

tongue stuck to the roof of my mouth. What if they didn't let you out? What would I do then?

For the millionth time, I wished that you hadn't fought with Ms. Van Nuys. She was just a dumb newcomer, so who really cared if she gave daily lectures on how every kid in town should be tagged and monitored? Yes, I got that you were pissed, but you could've just stopped after calling her an idiot. That would have been enough for most people. But not you. You had to take it even further and tell her to do herself a favor and either leave Gardnerville or jump out a window.

As if that wasn't bad enough, a day later you actually made her jump out a window. She was on the first floor, so she wasn't hurt, but Daddy still had to ooze a whole lot of charm to keep you out of the reformatory. And then after all that, you walked up to the reformatory, pressed this very same intercom button, and said, "My name is Piper Gardner and I'd like to commit myself for two weeks." I stood at your side, dumbfounded and hoping they'd send you home with a sharp warning about messing with things you didn't understand. But, of course, they didn't. Instead the gates opened up. I tugged at your hand, begging you not to do it. You pulled away. "See you in two weeks," you said to me with a brave smile, and then you disappeared inside the reformatory for the first time.

I pressed the button once more. "Hello?"

A long moment passed. I reached toward the button, ready to push it again.

"WAIT." The command blasted out. I snatched my hand back.

I didn't have a watch, but it was a long time before anything else happened, and when it did, it happened all at once. A buzzer shrieked, the front door swung open, and then, at last, you stepped out into the sunlight. I tried to see past you, to the interior of the reformatory and your home for the last two weeks, but it was pitch-black inside.

Everything about you sagged. Your shoulders and neck bent forward, giving way to the weight of your head, which hung at such a low angle you seemed to be studying your own belly button. Instead of walking, you shuffled along, not lifting your feet but sliding them through the dusty yard.

"Piper," I called out. "Piper!"

You didn't look up. Maybe you didn't hear me. Maybe you were angry. Or lost in your own thoughts. I couldn't bear for it to be anything else. I couldn't stand to think they broke you in only fourteen days.

At last, you reached the gate, and after several long moments of making you wait in front of it—never looking up, not even seeming to notice me only inches away on the other side—someone inside deigned to buzz it open.

A few more shuffling steps brought you to my side, while behind you, the gate slammed shut once more.

I stared at you, waiting, wanting to follow your lead. You drooped like the bouquets of roses Dad sometimes bought for Mom, which she held on to for so long that they began to rot.

"C'mon," I said, slipping my hand into yours. It took only a gentle tug to get you moving alongside me down the hill. "Chance is waiting at the bottom. He wouldn't come any closer, that chicken dog." You knew this already, but I needed to fill the silence. "Ms. Van Nuys is okay. If you were worried."

I didn't add that Ms. Van Nuys had also left town, but not before she visited us. She stood in the doorway of our house screaming at Mom and Dad, while I hid in the stairwell, hugging Chance close to keep him from barking and giving me away. "Your daughter is a menace. She should be locked up permanently."

I waited for our parents to say something. To defend you and your strange powers. But they were silent. I wanted to step forward then, but I was afraid she might recognize me. That would only bring more trouble. The day before Ms. Van Nuys jumped, you and I had seen her in Al's Grocery, pushing her little cart through the store with her nose in the air, probably annoyed that it wasn't like the big grocery stores she was used to. "Touch her and tell her something awful about herself," you'd said. I didn't have to ask why. You'd already told me about your ongoing feud with Ms. Van Nuys. The worst of it wasn't the stuff about tagging and monitoring. No, what you could never forgive was Ms. Van Nuys saying that she'd seen dozens of girls like you during her teaching career and, despite your notions to the contrary, you were nothing special. Even now, thinking about it, I felt the same outrage I did the first time you told me. Holding on to that outrage, I marched toward Ms. Van Nuys and wrapped my fingers around her arm, forcing her to stop.

"You came here because your baby died and your husband couldn't stand to look at you anymore," I told her.

I felt her skin prickle and go cold beneath my fingers. And

then I ran. I had hoped never to see her again, but there she was at our house, demanding in her screechy voice, "Well? Don't you have anything to say?"

I knew the exact moment Dad unleashed his smile on her. There was this strange high-pitched titter from Ms. Van Nuys. Then in his Mr. Smooth voice I heard Dad say, "It's a good thing you were only on the first floor."

Instead of slapping him, Ms. Van Nuys tittered again.

"I heard you're leaving town. I'm real sorry about that. How about I walk you over to the train station? I'm sure you could use an extra hand to help carry your things."

"Oh. Why . . . thank you," Ms. Van Nuys answered in a breathy voice. Mom said nothing. She never did, not even when Dad walked out the door arm in arm with Ms. Van Nuys. Neither of us was surprised when he didn't come home that night, or when we heard that Ms. Van Nuys had waited to take the train out the following week.

Now, as we walked home, I made myself be patient and wait for you to talk to me, instead of reaching into your head to find out for myself. About halfway down the hill, where it curves and the reformatory becomes hidden from view, you skidded to a stop.

"Sky," you said, grabbing my other hand. At last, your eyes met mine. They were shining. Radiant. Burning with a victorious light. "I was right, Sky. It's a terrible place. Worse than we ever imagined."

"Are you okay?" I couldn't help but ask.

"Silly." You gave me a little shake. "That doesn't matter.

What matters is that I figured out what I'm meant to do. What we're meant to do. The reformatory began with the Gardners and it will end with us too."

I said nothing. For years you had said the reformatory was our destiny, and I'd believed you. I'd thought you meant doing time. Getting drained. But this . . . this was a different plan entirely.

"Sky, you're with me, right?"

I hesitated. Taking down the reformatory was about as impossible as shooting the sun from the sky, but that wasn't the problem. If you had wanted it, I believed you could have shot down the sun, the moon, and a couple of stars too—you'd collect the whole set. The problem was imagining Gardnerville without the reformatory. How would our town even work?

"Sky?" You interrupted my thoughts, wanting an answer. I must have looked as panicked as I felt. A part of me was afraid that I'd agree and you would pull a pack of dynamite from your pocket, and then rush back up the hill, ready to blow the whole thing to kingdom come.

"I need this, Sky. It's what I was meant to do." You shook your head, correcting yourself. "No, it's what *we* were meant to do."

Piper, you never really needed powers to make others do your will. Not with me, at least.

And that was why there was never any choice to make.

"Yes, of course I'm with you," I said. "Always."

EIGHT

STILL SHAKY AFTER ESCAPING FROM GG'S AND uncertain about where to go or what to do next, I end up back at school. In the girls' room, I use the cheap brown paper towels to scrub the residual dirt from my skin. They're like sandpaper, which is usually a bad thing, but right now I welcome their ability to remove several layers of skin with a single swipe. After tossing the last wad of towels into the trash, I turn to the mirror for the first time. I could blame the green tile and fluorescent lights for my sickly gray color, but who am I kidding? I'm a wreck.

Enough. Nothing good ever came of staring into a mirror and wondering who was the fairest of them all. Still, while great beauty has never been something I've been terribly interested in, I do try to avoid looking like a corpse. With this thought in mind I give my cheeks a few hard pinches until two patches of dull pink color bloom. It'll have to do.

I march toward the door but hesitate before opening it. I roll my shoulders back. Wiggle my hips. Tilt my head back and forth, then left and right. Residual fog lingers somewhere behind my eyes, making me feel dull and heavy. Otherwise, though, everything is back to normal. Relatively speaking.

On my way down the hall, I check the time, wanting to make sure I haven't lost a whole day like yesterday. It takes me a few minutes to remember how to read the clock. Sometimes even hours after a pill, when I think everything's back to normal, little things like this trip me up. Right now, it's the meaning of the big hand that has momentarily stumped me. Then it comes back, suddenly. 2:45. If I hurry, Jonathan will still be at the double-wide. There was something I'd wanted to ask him about. . . . My hand reaches toward my back pocket, and paper crinkles beneath my fingertips. All at once I remember. Jonathan is dead. LuAnn is missing. She and Piper are somehow connected.

And I've lost hours.

The forget-me-nots have been a crutch allowing me to hobble through my days. Now, though, I need to move faster. It's time to go cold turkey. Not forever, but until I find Piper and know for sure if she's dead or alive or something else in between.

The thought is enough to hurry me down the hallways. I burst through the front doors and into the merciless afternoon sun that has replaced the earlier rain. I have time to feel only the shortest moment of relief at my escape before I catch sight of Angie. She is tapping on her phone with bright-pink fingernails, while her foot jiggles a bedazzled baby stroller holding a wailing child. Angie spends her life clinging to Elton, or—after he's managed to shake her loose—trying to hunt him down again. I should hate her for being the girl Elton cheated on Piper with, but I've never been able to do it.

Hoping that if I ignore her, she'll return the favor, I stare straight ahead as I stride past.

It doesn't work.

I can feel her gaze on me as I draw even, and then a moment later she calls out, "You seen Elton?"

The question stops me in my tracks. I have seen Elton. He gave me pills. Made me take one. And he told me Jonathan was dead.

I hear the clatter of her wooden heels clomping against the sidewalk, and then the stroller pulls up next to me, the kid screaming louder than ever. I stare at the red-faced monster, wondering why it's still in a stroller at almost four years old.

I throw a dark look Angie's way. "Make it stop."

She returns my look with interest. "Right. 'Cause it's that easy."

"It's crying 'cause it wants something. Whatever it is, give it what it wants."

"*It* is a she," Angie snaps. "She wants her daddy. You might know him. Handsome guy. Metal legs."

"Sounds familiar. Is he also cold and incapable of feeling?"

Angie turns her fingers into shotguns and aims them both at me. "Bang. Bang."

I shake my head. "Don't shoot the messenger 'cause the truth hurts."

Her guns turn back into hands and she places them on the stroller to push as we start up the hill toward Main. "Actually, I was saying you were dead-on. But yeah, the truth hurts. Hurts every damn day."

"Yeah" is the only comeback I have. We continue to trudge up the hill. The little girl doesn't stop crying for a second, not even to take a breath.

"Hey," I snap when we reach the top of the hill. The kid's wide eyes snap toward mine, curious. Not curious enough to stop howling, but enough to look. Leaning down, I press my index finger against the tip of her nose. "Knock it off."

She gasps, shudders, and breathes in like she's gonna start all over again, but then pops her thumb into her mouth instead.

"Well shit," Angie says. Our eyes meet and she shakes her head. "She usually goes for hours. I'd never have guessed you were good with kids."

If that's being good with kids, you're an even worse mother than I already thought. The words are on the tip of my tongue, but I don't say them. Angie looks tired in a way that goes beyond the sag in her shoulders and bags beneath her eyes. She looks to have the type of exhaustion that goes bone deep. I remember before she took Elton from Piper, when she was just a girl in Piper's class with a sassy, hip-swinging walk that ensured everyone would notice her. I liked her then. Admired her in the same way I did Piper or anyone else who lived life bright and loud, unafraid to be seen, not concerned that the next words to come tumbling from their mouth might make everyone hate them.

"I saw Elton a few hours ago. He dropped me off at school."

Angie nods. "He was supposed to meet me an hour ago. I told him to pick us up, but he said we should walk, that it would be good for us. Good for us. In this godforsaken heat. And during a fourth year. It's like he wants his daughter to be taken by whatever terrible thing happens. That's what I said to him, and then he said that we needed to set an example for everyone else. To show them how not to be afraid. To show them fear didn't have to win. So then I said, 'And what about when your daughter's dead? What's that gonna show everybody?' You'd think that woulda shut him up, but it didn't. 'She won't be dead,' he says. 'She'll be fine 'cause there aren't gonna be any more fourth years.' And I said, 'Bullshit.' And he told me to drink more water." Angie throws her head back and laughs with a complete lack of mirth. "You believe that?"

I shrug and look away.

"I don't even like water," Angie mutters beside me, still replaying her argument with Elton. "He knows I prefer my beverages carbonated."

I stare at her, unable to believe that she doesn't know. That Elton wouldn't tell her. Then I turn away once more, reminding myself it's none of my business.

Angie doesn't say anything else as we hang a right onto Main Street. You'd think I'd be happy for the silence, but instead I hear myself asking, "Why don't you just leave?" I gesture to the kid, who is now happily singing "Twinkle, Twinkle, Little Star" to herself. "Go somewhere you'll be safe, somewhere without fourth years."

Angie looks at me in this measured sort of way. "And

where would that be?"

I shrug. "Anywhere the train stops that isn't here."

"Uh-huh." Angie nods slowly. "Don't you ever read the newspapers the newcomers bring in? Out there, in all the other places the train stops, are school shootings and starvation and drownings and cancer and five thousand other horrible ways to die. Bad stuff happens everywhere. There is no safe place."

"Yeah," I say, unconvinced, but not wanting to hear the rest. I've heard this argument before. Hell, I've used this argument before. The joys of small-town life, fresh air unpolluted by the smog that plagues the big cities on the other side, and the biggest bonus of all—if you survive puberty—the chance to live well into your second century.

"Is this about Jonathan?" Angie asks as she reaches over and gently pats my arm. "I'm sorry about what happened. Elton was really upset about it too. He did everything he could to save him, but he blames himself, I think."

I slip my tongue between my front teeth and bite down to stop myself from telling Angie that Elton was the reason Jonathan needed saving.

Oblivious, Angie keeps prattling along. "Anyway, with you and Jonathan being close, I bet you're pretty upset about it. Just remember, it's okay to cry."

I stare at Angie, certain she's joking, but when she gives me another sympathetic pat, I realize she isn't. "Jonathan and I weren't friends. Where did you get that idea?"

"Oh." Angie wrinkles her brow in confusion. "I forgot, you probably don't remember—you were pretty out of it last night.

You weren't feeling too good, so I sat with you for a while. I mentioned that Elton wanted you to talk with Jonathan, and you got kind of upset. Then you pulled out this piece of paper from your pocket, said it was a note from Jonathan. You tried to read it, but . . ." Angie trails off, looking embarrassed for me.

I save her with a shrug. "I couldn't remember how to read. It happens."

"Right," Angie says. "Well anyway, I offered to read it to you, but you kept it folded up all neat and careful and told me it was private. The way you acted, I figured it was, like, I don't know, a love note or something."

I want to make barfing noises like a third-grader at the idea of exchanging love letters with Jonathan. Instead, I widen my eyes, hoping it comes across as innocent instead of scared shitless, and ask in my sweetest voice, "Don't tell anyone, okay?"

"You poor kid," Angie says. "Of course, I wouldn't tell anyone. You've been so unlucky in love. First with Elton and now—"

"Elton?" I interrupt. "No."

Oh, the pity on Angie's face as she looks at me, like I am the saddest, most delusional person on the planet. Somebody needs to get this girl a mirror. "Sky, we've never talked about it, but I know you and Elton had a thing. For a long time I thought you hated me because of it. But maybe you've realized that you were just a kid then, and Elton was much too old for you. . . ." Angie reaches out to give my shoulder a comforting squeeze. "Anyway, for a long time, I've wanted to apologize. So here it is. I'm sorry."

I step away so that Angie can't touch me again. And so that I don't punch her in the face. "I'm not the person you need to apologize to," I tell her, trying to keep my voice even.

"You're right," Angie quickly agrees. "A lot of people got hurt because of my thoughtless actions, and I probably owe a lot more apologies. But I'm not the only person responsible for that, Skylar, and I really don't appreciate the guilt trip."

She's right, of course. What Piper did . . . All those young lives just over. No matter how many forget-me-nots I take, I can still hear their screams—and the deadly silence after so many of them drowned.

"I gotta get out of this heat," Angie says, interrupting my dark thoughts. I realize we are standing in front of Milly's. The old-timers stare down at us from the wide front porch. They don't say hello or smile. They just stare. Piper used to charm them. She'd go into Milly's, steal the coffee pot, and insist on refilling everyone's cup. Then we'd sit at their feet and beg them to tell us their stories. And they would. They would tell us about every fourth year they could remember. The more interesting first-, second-, and third-year anecdotes too. We soaked them up and made them our own.

Somehow I get wrangled into dragging the stroller up the stairs and inside, while Angie pops the kid onto her hip and sashays past. I consider telling Angie I need to use the bathroom, and then escaping out the back door, but the AC blasting from the vents is so icy cold and refreshing, I can't help but enjoy the way it almost immediately raises goose bumps up and down my arms. An hour later I am still there, drinking coffee to keep the chill away and finishing off my second slice of Milly's famous peach pie. The last bit of murkiness from the nots has cleared and the combo of Angie and her kid—one mushing her own piece of pie into her hair, the other futilely yet repeatedly asking her to stop—has become more annoying than cute.

Outside the skies have once again darkened, and a storm is threatening, but that isn't what's keeping me inside. What holds me here are the posters plastered across every inch of Milly's walls. They've been there since before I can remember, always faded and curling at the edges. A brilliant blue sky is a central motif in most of them. Grinning people in bathing suits or ski gear are another. And they all have the name of a place in big, bold letters. Sometimes it is preceded by "Come See" or "Visit," but mostly just the name, as if they know that you'll say it out loud and the feel of the word in your mouth—Vail, Cairo, Waikiki, Cornwall, Havana, Grand Canyon, Portugal, Mont Blanc—will be enough to make you want to go there.

Piper loved them. I think they spoke to her, the same way the secrets whispered to me. They said, *Look at all there is to still be discovered.*

I never disagreed with Piper. Not out loud anyhow. We were strange sisters that way. Those posters were the closest we ever came to having a disagreement. When I looked at them, I couldn't help but think about how large and frightening the rest of the world seemed. But Piper saw a treat constantly dangled in front of her, always out of reach. She loved the posters, and hated them too.

The day before that terrible May Day, Piper added her own poster to the wall. Imitating the drawing style of the other posters with their clean lines and bold colors, she drew the trestle bridge cutting through the center of the page. She captured the way a full moon looked hung high in the sky and reflected in the water below. At the top in thick, bold letters she wrote GARDNERVILLE so that it stretched across the whole page. She made Milly hang it up on the wall then, but as we had our customary second piece of pie, she kept staring at it all squinty-eyed. That unsatisfied look remained no matter how many times I assured her it was brilliant. "It needs something else," Piper insisted, pulling it back down. She curled her arm around the drawing, huddling over it as her pencil scratched against the paper, hiding it from my view. It wasn't until she placed it back on the wall that I saw her addition. And she was right. It did complete the poster. In smaller, right-slanting letters, she'd printed in the bottom corner, *Where magic happens.*

"Now," she said, "I can finally say I've been to one of the places on Milly's wall."

The memory makes me ache for Piper. More than once, I've dreamed of her escaping from the reformatory. And I've wondered where she would go. If she stayed in town, she would come to me. I know she would. But what if she couldn't stay? What if the only way to remain safe was to leave? Maybe right now she was in one of those other places from the posters, and maybe right now she was writing a letter to say she was safe and that I should join her there.

It's a fantasy. Piper would never leave without me. But for a minute I let myself believe it. I let myself imagine boarding that train to join her. I imagine the darkness as the train chugs through the long tunnel cut into the mountains and then the light bright and blinding on the other side.

I must make some sort of noise—a murmur or a moan of someone caught inside a nightmare—because Angie glances up at me with a startled expression.

I look away from her. Scan the nearly empty restaurant. Through the wide front windows I see that the rockers on the front porch are empty. The old-timers must have gone home. Inside the café, there is only one other person besides us, a scrawny boy I vaguely recognize from school. I feel a shiver of some memory warning me to pay attention as I watch him down an endless pile of cheeseburgers and french fries. I've seen at least five burgers delivered to his table since we've been here. He eats almost desperately, shoving the food in, his panic palpable. His secrets flash like neon signs—bright enough for anyone to read them.

That's when I remember that I saw him yesterday, right before LuAnn jumped onto Elton's car. He'd been heading into Milly's then. I wouldn't be surprised if he practically lived here. It's the best place for a boy who knows that no matter how much he eats, it won't be enough to fill him up. He's trying to fight it, but this is a losing battle. Right now it's taking everything inside him not to eat the plate along with the food. And then the table, the chair, the pie display case, and Milly herself. He's battling the urge. Who knows how long he'll succeed. He's drinking glass after glass of Elton's drugged water too. I watch him take a sip, and for a moment the hunger recedes, but then it roars back stronger than ever.

It's like this when a fourth year drags on into August. Kids who thought they were normal, who thought they were safe, suddenly find out otherwise. Sometimes they are able to keep it at bay long enough for someone else to implode and drain all the excess energy away. For them, that's all it takes for their newfound powers to disappear.

Every teenager is a potential fuse during a fourth year. Usually there are a few tiny flare-ups that quickly fizzle out, like Jonathan shooting fire from his fingertips. It was a cool party trick, but it wasn't much good for saving his sorry life. You never know, though; in another month he might've had enough power to level the school. Now that would've been a fourth year. One person all lit up, consumed by the power and taking as many other people as possible down with them. Later they come to in the reformatory, like they are waking from a bad dream into an even worse one.

That's why the plan to place the potential troublemakers preemptively in the reformatory is silly. Anyone can implode at any time. There is no prevention. No damage control. There's only counting losses and cleaning up.

I push my chair back with a loud screech. "I'm going," I announce. Angie nods but doesn't look up from her phone. It must be Elton on the receiving end of all that furious typing. I wonder what she's writing. If she's mentioned that I'm with her. I decide that I don't care and turn toward the door. The rain has started; it pounds against the roof, demanding to be noticed. I reach behind me for the rain slicker, and only then do I realize that it's gone. That I haven't seen it since I ran from Elton's car, the forget-me-not melting away inside me.

Piper will be pissed, I think. Then I remember.

Always remembering. Damn these memories that will not die. And every time is as painful as the first time. Every time, everything inside me rebels against the idea.

I dig into my pocket to throw some cash onto the table. My eyes are still directed at the window, but I'm not really seeing it anymore; instead my gaze is directed inward, lost once again in the fantasy of Piper escaping from the reformatory.

That's why I don't see her at first, and by the time I do, she is almost out of sight. She travels along the sidewalk, right past Milly's front porch. Her hands are tucked into the pockets of the yellow rain slicker, and the hood completely covers her bowed head. She moves quickly, without hesitation, as if she knows where she's going and is in a hurry to get there.

I run toward the exit, tripping over my own feet. Piper's name is on my lips, but I choke it back, not wanting to jinx it. My hand is on the door when I remember Angie. I glance back at her and then at the boy, who is plowing through another cheeseburger.

"Hey, Angie," I say. Her fingers pause, and she looks up, clearly annoyed. I jerk my head in the direction of the boy. "Unless you want to rename your kid Pork Chop, you might want to get out of here too."

I don't wait to see if she understands my warning or follows my advice. I don't hear the heavy door clang shut behind me or feel the rain or the way my whole body is shaking.

I scan the street from right to left, but there is no sign of the yellow rain slicker anymore. I run down the empty road, looking up and through the little alleys between shops. Finally, I spot her three blocks ahead of me. I pick up speed, trip on my flip-flops, kick them off in opposite directions, and take a skidding turn onto Jefferson.

I've lost her.

I keep running. Keep looking. It is everything I can do to keep from screaming her name, to let her know that I am searching for her.

I slow when I reach South Street Park, feeling lost but unwilling to give up. A lot of the notters hang out here. They take turns drifting away, leaving one sober person to act as their anchor. I joined them a few times, but when it was my turn to stay behind in the harsh glare of reality, I flaked and decided to take a pill anyway. It was just bad luck that one of the girls stumbled into a hornets' nest. She was fine. All's well that ends well, I thought. The group disagreed. They made it clear I was not welcome to join them anymore.

Now I see a group of them lying on the picnic tables in one of the pavilions. They are so still they might be dead bodies, except for one who is on her feet and twirling this way and that. Her eyes are closed and her arms are up as if she's dancing with an invisible partner.

"Don't mind her," someone calls out to me, and that's when I notice another girl, sitting cross-legged atop the middle picnic table. "She's in the sweet spot."

"Right." I nod, even though I have no idea what she's talking about. Crazy notters—they forget that not everyone understands their made-up lingo. "You see someone in a yellow rain slicker around here a few minutes ago?"

She tilts her head and considers the question. "Yeah," she says at last in the slow way that heavy notters have. "Maybe not so long ago. That way." Her finger stretches out, pointing north toward the duck pond.

"Thanks," I say, dashing back out into the rain. It is coming down slower now, no longer blurring everything in front of me. I see her then. At the opposite end of the duck pond. She's heading into the trees. Piper used to call it the forest and scare me with stories of grizzly bears that waited in dark tangles of underbrush for small children to walk by and become their afternoon snack. I must have been almost ten before I realized that only harmless bunnies and squirrels hid in the scant half acre of trees and underbrush. The real woods were farther out, winding through the mountains, a true wilderness that stretched for miles.

I thump across the rickety wooden bridge, scaring the ducks, which launch into the air around me. The bit of bright yellow grows smaller, sinking into the tangle of trees. I plunge through the underbrush, tripping over fallen branches, but never take my eyes off that hint of color, determined not to lose her again.

Of course, I do.

A spiderweb coats my face, and in the second it takes to scrub it away, she's gone. I continue pushing through the trees, scanning them, until I burst out into the open and the back of Al's Grocery. No sign of Piper. Spinning, I head back into the trees. Now slower and more methodical. Again, I see a hint of color. I run toward it, and instead of moving away, it comes closer until it is on top of me and we nearly slam against each other.

Foote stares at me, the rain slicker clutched in his gigantic fist. "I was calling your name," he says. "Didn't you hear me?"

I grab the slicker away from him, pressing it against my nose, wanting some evidence that Piper has been inside it. "Where did you get this?"

"It was snagged on a tree back there." He gestures behind him to his left, and although I know it is futile, I jog in that direction, still looking. Still hoping.

Foote is on my heels the whole time. I abruptly stop and spin to face him. "Where was it? Show me the exact spot."

He looks at me for a long moment, like I am someone to be pitied. I suppose I am. "This way," he says at last. We take only a few steps before we reach a small tree with low, gnarled branches. "It was hanging here," he says, but I can already tell the spot because there are several strands of long blond hair caught in the V of the branch.

Forgetting Foote is beside me, I reach for them and bring them close. Piper was not blond. Although as sisters we don't look much alike, we do share one physical trait: our golden-brown hair that glints with bits of red on sunny days. LuAnn, though, does have blond hair. And lots of other girls do too, of course. I could've been chasing anyone. Disappointment floods through me. Then a beam of sun breaks through the tree branches overhead, and one of the strands separates from the rest. In the sunlight the reddish hue is unmistakable. I can't say how it ended up among the other, white-blond wisps of hair, but right now it is just enough that it's here.

"Let me walk you home." Foote puts a hand on my shoulder.

I shake it off. "Why were you following me?"

"I saw you by the pond. You looked lost. I was worried. Elton said that when he saw you this morning, you were—"

I cut him off. "Fading fast. I know. Did you see anybody else by the pond? Someone in this rain slicker?"

"I didn't see anyone but you," he answers immediately, without hesitation.

"Okay," I say, and then because he is still looking at me and because he's been nice, I add, "Thanks."

He shrugs it off and holds out his hand. "Now let me walk you home."

Instead of refusing, I reach out and take his hand. I probably shouldn't trust Foote. I shouldn't trust anyone. But I am so tired of doing this alone.

"Do you believe there are bears in these woods?" I ask him.

His lips turn up slightly, but he doesn't laugh. "Bears," he says, considering it. "Probably once, but not recently."

It's a fair answer. I press on. "Do you think it's possible for someone to escape from the reformatory?"

"Someone?" Foote questions.

"My sister, Piper. Four years ago she led a bunch of kids to the trestle bridge at the same time a train was scheduled to come along. A bunch of them drowned." He's probably already heard the story, but I remind him since he is new to the town and has never met Piper, and the tragedy would just seem like another crazy, unbelievable story.

"I'd heard something like that." He nods. "But most people say that it was . . . I mean, they say you were there too. Right? That's why people call you the Pied Piper?"

"No." I shake my head, impatient with his newcomer confusion. "They call Piper that. Her name was Piper, so obviously."

"Okay," he agrees, still sounding uncertain. "You would know better than me."

"I do," I assure him. "But what I don't know is what happened to Piper after that night. She was on the trestle bridge and then . . . I don't know. It was chaos. I didn't see her again. But I think she was sent to the reformatory."

"Wouldn't they tell you?" Foote asks.

"Usually yeah, but Piper's a Gardner."

"And?"

"Gardners always find a way out of getting locked up. I think this time, someone decided they didn't want one of us to get away."

"Yeah," Foote says, after a long moment of hesitation. "I guess that makes sense."

"Which brings us back to the original question. Do you think it's possible to escape from the reformatory?"

"Well . . ." Foote pauses again, this time for even longer. For a moment I think he's going to duck the question and I feel an unexpected sting of disappointment, as if I expect more from him. But then he answers, and he does so perfectly.

"You probably know best about the possibility of your sister escaping from the reformatory too. But for what it's worth . . ." He takes his hat off, runs his free hand through his hair, and puts the hat back on. "I think it's possible," he says at last. "She could escape. Someone with the will to do it could escape."

My heart leaps. Foote is new, I remind myself once more.

He's never done time in the reformatory, or had a family member in there either. He has no idea what it's like. What it does to a person. Only a stupid newcomer would believe that someone could escape—especially after four years. This should be proof that I can't trust him. It should be a warning to stay away.

Instead, I squeeze his hand, warm and solid inside my two cold ones.

And because I am stupid too, I tell him to walk me home.

Once we start walking, Foote is different. Distant. Fidgety. He reaches his hand into his pocket and then pulls it back out empty, with an angry sigh on his lips.

It reminds me that I don't really know him, and it makes me nervous. "Forget something?" I ask to fill the silence. The moment the words are out of my mouth, I wince. It's like Helen Keller asking someone if they've gone blind.

But Foote doesn't seem to notice. "No," he says shortly, and then a moment later, "Yes." He kicks at a rock and sends it flying down the street. "I used to smoke. Bad habit, I know, but I figured I'd give it till twenty and then quit. Didn't count on moving here though."

I nod. "Yeah, they stopped bringing cigarettes into town after—"

"I know," Foote interrupts. "I mean, I mostly know, but not the exact story. I don't have the name of who did it or the year or how many were harmed, but I've lived here long enough to get the gist of it. It was a fourth year—"

"A third year actually."

"Okay, well, then that probably means there were no casualties."

"Right," I agree. "Just second-degree burns."

"He blew the cigarettes up in their faces."

"She," I quietly correct.

"She," Foote amends. "She blew the cigarettes up in their faces during a third year, resulting in second-degree burns for her victims. I'm guessing that kind of damage would have earned her . . ."

"Three years in the reformatory," I answer. "One year for a first year, two for a second year—you get the idea. Unless, of course, there are casualties. Then it doubles. Most fourth years end up doing eight years."

"Oh," Foote says.

He doesn't say anything more, just buries his hands in his pockets and points his eyes up toward the gray sky that seems to be biding its time, waiting for the perfect moment to come raining down on us once more.

The silence stretches out longer; between it and the sticky humidity pressing against my skin, I can barely find enough air to kick-start our conversation again. But I want it to start. I want to ask him about what happened last night. And maybe I also want to know if Foote has officially switched from enemy to ally.

Perhaps the silence bothers Foote as well, because he begins to whistle. It isn't the cheerful whistle of Snow White's dwarfs or a bird building its nest while preparing for spring. No, this whistle has the slow, mournful quality of a funeral dirge. It suits me; this wet, dark day; and this give-and-take town perfectly.

As I listen, my eyes drift half closed. My feet keep moving me forward but I am not thinking about them any more than I am about Piper's rain slicker hanging heavy over my arm, the strand of reddish hair wrapped so tightly round my ring finger that the tip is turning blue, or Jonathan's letter in my pocket. It's so habitual I hardly even notice the way I am always trying to keep secrets away. But now, with my feet splashing through puddles and Foote's whistle pecking away at little bits of my soul, I let that control slip just a bit. Like a boat loosed from its mooring, I slowly drift out toward sea. . . .

But the sea is more than just waves and sand; there are so many shipwrecks buried there, and I can see them all through my glass-bottomed boat.

From far away, I feel my shoulder brush against Foote's and then—

A dark, flapping cloud rushes toward me, picks me up, and carries me away. I think that I will become a part of the cloud—that it has swallowed me whole—but it spits me out, dropping me so that I fall through tree branches that scratch and grab at me, until finally I land with a splash. Water rushes over me, filling my mouth, my lungs. I drown a million times while my blood leaks into the water, turning it red. I close my eyes, wanting escape, when strong hands find me, cradle me, lift me—

The whistle ends. The vision ends. I am dragged back to dry land by two hands wrapped around my throat.

I stare into Foote's eyes, only inches away from mine and furiously angry. His hands loosen slightly, allowing air in, but he keeps them on my throat, ready to cut off my oxygen supply again.

"What did you just do?" he demands, his voice an angry, low growl. I stare at him. There is no sign of the Foote who took a knife for Elton and barely seemed to notice. The laid-back Foote I'd known before is also nowhere to be seen. And the gentle Foote who coaxed me into letting him walk me home seems like a figment of my imagination. "What did you see?"

"See?" I ask, trying to buy time while I sort out what just happened. I'd let down my guard for just a few moments, but that was more than enough time for Foote's secrets to whisper in my ear. And somehow he knew what was happening. Foote had felt it; he knew I had taken something and he didn't like it. Maybe he even wanted it back, maybe that was why he kept his hands on my neck.

"Talk," Foote demands.

I try to gulp, but it gets hung up on his fingertips. "I didn't mean to. I wasn't thinking and then . . ."

"And then what? What did you see?"

"This big, dark cloud. It picked you up and you were kind of flying in it. Then you fell into water. You were bleeding and drowning. Then someone grabbed you." I give him a CliffsNotes-style summary. The main facts are there, but all the feelings—from shock to terror to despair—have been stripped away.

"Is that it?"

I nod and my chin brushes against his fingers. "That's it."

He takes a step away and I am free. With a deep breath, I

stumble backward, needing more distance. My hands go to my neck, massage the skin.

"I'm sorry," Foote says, his voice shaking as if he is the one who was just assaulted.

This is what comes from trusting someone and relaxing for a few minutes. I want to lie down in the street and cry. With any luck, Elton's Prius will come by, run me over, and finish me off. I don't have that kind of luck though. I would end up waiting hours for his car to pass. The thought almost makes me laugh. I don't, though, because it would end up being just as hysterical as the crying. Instead, as the rain begins sprinkling down once more, I shove my arms into Piper's rain slicker and flip the hood over my head. I try to feel the way that Piper felt in it. The way Piper felt in everything. Strong and certain. Able to bend anyone to her will.

I glare up at Foote from beneath the hood. "What happened last night?"

"What do you remember?" Foote says, and it feels like the conversation I had with Elton earlier today. Except this one isn't going to end with me running away.

"No. What do *you* remember?"

Foote nods, understanding. Giving in. "Elton and I were looking for you. He called your cell, but you didn't answer. Then someone said they saw you heading into the library. We found you in the study room with that Ozzy guy. You were totally out of it. Elton told me to pick you up, take you into the bathroom, and that he would call Angie over to help make you throw up. In the meantime he was going to deal with Ozzy. I got you to the locker room, laid you down, and was waiting maybe fifteen, twenty minutes when your breathing got really shallow. I couldn't wait for Angie any longer, so I carried you into the bathroom and stuck my finger down your throat until you gagged. Then you puked. It was all this purple-colored crap, and I thought you would be okay, but then you stopped breathing altogether. Angie showed up around then and went running for the defibrillator. Between the two of us, we got you breathing again. Then you seemed okay. Out of it, but okay. You were trying to talk, and you opened your eyes and recognized Angie. Since you still couldn't walk, I carried you out to Elton. He was in the parking lot with Ozzy, who was refusing to leave until he saw you. Then after he did see you, he still insisted on staying, 'cause he said we were all out to get you."

"I don't remember Angie being there," I say, not that it really matters or concerns me overly much. I just feel like I need to say something and right now I can't deal with my near-death experience or Ozzy's odd show of concern.

"She left after . . . well, I'll get there. I carried you, and everyone else walked up to the press box. It was an ambush, but Jonathan must've had an idea that Elton was coming for him, because he saw us and ran. Elton and I took off after him, while you, Angie, and Ozzy stayed up in the press box. We finally cornered Jonathan in the pool room, and Elton had me hold him there while he went to get you."

"And Ozzy?" I ask. I don't really want to know, but I have to ask.

"He jumped sometime when you were out there with him and

Angie. I guess she freaked out. So I took Angie home while you and Elton talked to Jonathan. Although, I'm guessing it wasn't talking and more like Elton asking you to, I don't know . . . read Jonathan, I guess? Anyway, from what Angie told me, Ozzy's jump seemed like it happened out of the blue. She said you and him were talking softly, when suddenly Ozzy climbed to the top of the press box and without hesitation did a swan dive off. She said he must have seen the ground coming right at the end, because he tried to scream."

I hold a hand out. "That's enough."

"I dropped Angie at home and then headed back to the pool," Foote continues as if he didn't hear me.

"I said that's enough."

"You wanted to know what I remembered." He takes a step toward me, and somehow I manage to hold my feet still and keep myself from taking an answering one back.

"I can figure out the rest. I remember the . . ." The words catch in my throat, sticky like taffy. "The knife. The pool. The bubbles. I remember."

Foote nods. "You passed out once more after Jonathan . . ."

"Drowned," I say, although I wonder if boiled would be more accurate.

"Yeah." Foote nods again. "Anyway, Elton told me to wake you up, and then to keep you busy so that he could talk with you again. I thought you'd had enough for one night, so I took you to the showers, and once you started coming to, I told you to take off. I went to run interference with Elton, try to buy you some time."

Hazily, I can remember it now. Foote's hands tight on my

upper arms, propelling me toward the shower.

"Cold," I said. He released me then to spin the knobs; the water became warm and pleasant. I turned my face into the spray, letting it wash over me. Distantly I heard someone telling me to hurry, but I closed my eyes, letting the shower wash that away too.

Now I stare straight at Foote, wondering if I owe him a thank-you. He helped me, that's obvious. But the hands-on-the-neck routine also proves that he doesn't trust me. Which seems like a good enough reason for me not to trust him either.

"I'm going home," I tell Foote. "Don't follow me."

He looks like he is going to argue, but then changes his mind. He tugs his hat down, and a stream of water drizzles from the front brim. "Okay."

I take a few steps and then several more, and the whole time I can feel him watching. He doesn't follow, though. A block away, I can't stop myself from turning. He is standing in the exact same place, the exact same position. At this distance, it's impossible to see his expression, but I imagine it's troubled. I can also now imagine him with a cigarette, like a detective in an old movie, trying to decide if he should help or run from the messed-up dame.

Run.

That's what I should say. Return the favor. But I don't.

"Foote," I call out. "Like a rabbit's foot, right?"

His chin lifts and then falls again in a quick nod. "Right."

I can remember now, him holding me, cradled in his lap, as I slowly learned how to breathe again. He talked to me quietly, and

I couldn't understand the words then, just the tone and the calm. It soothed me. But it's coming back to me now, in bits and pieces. "My uncle found me, and called me Foote, like a rabbit's foot, 'cause he thought I was lucky. And for years I believed that was true. When I got older, though, I found a quote from some guy that summed up the lucky thing pretty perfectly for me. It went like this: 'Depend on the rabbit's foot if you will, but remember it didn't work for the rabbit.'"

I don't totally understand what he was trying to tell me, but the memory is enough for me to make a decision.

"I'm going to the reformatory tomorrow. I need to see it. I need to . . ." I almost say that I need to figure out a way to break in, to find out whether Piper is in there or not, but it is too ridiculous. "I haven't been there in years. It's a horrible place, and you should avoid it whenever possible." I take a deep breath, and then add in a rush, "Wanna come with?"

Foote doesn't hesitate. "I'll meet you here at ten sharp." He points to the blacktop at his feet. I wonder if he intends to continue standing there until tomorrow morning. It occurs to me then that maybe he is the messed-up one, and that I should be the one running away. Of course, I don't.

"Tomorrow. Ten," I confirm, and then I pivot and slowly walk away, already certain that we'll both be here again even if we shouldn't be.

WE GO TOGETHER

Seven Years Ago

I WATCHED OUT THE FRONT WINDOW AS YOUR BIKE glided down the driveway and into the street, plastic buckets dangling from each of your handlebars. You did not look back.

Almost immediately, regret choked my throat. You had left me behind. It shouldn't have been a surprise, but it was—I was constantly forgetting that just because I couldn't be without you, you didn't necessarily feel the same way about me.

I raced out the front door, not bothering to grab my coat even though there was a wicked bite in the air. Chance came running out behind me, as attached to me as I was to you.

I'd been an idiot to think I could talk you out of this. When I told you it was crazy, I hadn't meant it as a compliment. But you took it that way.

It was not a fourth year, but I was afraid regardless that this would be the year you broke. You talked about the reformatory more than ever lately. Sometimes at night I'd find you staring out your window at it. You told me you could hear it calling your name.

Eventually you'd let me pull you away from the window. Then I would remind you that a Gardner had never done time at the reformatory. Not Daddy. No, of course not Daddy. They'd wanted to send him away, but every time they'd come for him, he'd given them that smile and they'd ended up shaking his hand instead, telling him he was going to be a hell of a man. That was why his was the longest fourth-year event on record. It had gone on for three weeks, and by the time it was over, thirteen of his peers had died for him. He'd had the whole high school competing to be his favorite person. It had started small. Baking cookies. Serenading him at night. Doing his homework for him. But then it built. A girl shaved her head. A boy one-upped her with a tattoo across his entire chest. And then a third girl went one better and chopped off her little finger. That was when things got bloody. Kids would lay on train tracks, jump off buildings, and drink poison—all to prove their love. It had ended when a boy set himself on fire and then ran toward Daddy, wanting to give him one last hug.

All of this raced through my head as I hopped onto my bike and took off down the street in pursuit.

I couldn't help wondering how far I'd go to prove my love to you. Leaning over my handlebars, I spun the pedals as fast as they'd go, determined to catch you. Chance yipped with excitement as he kept pace beside me. My bike pitched sideways as I took the corner too fast, and I had to drag my foot along the asphalt to keep from falling. Moving again, I pumped harder . . . only to hear laughter behind me. I slammed on the brakes and my whole body lurched, wanting to continue hurtling forward. Getting my feet on the ground, I twisted to see your bike parked against a tree and you lounging in the grass beside it, a half-eaten bright-red apple in your hand.

"What's the hurry?" you said.

Slowly, I pedaled my bike back toward you. A hot lump of tears waited in my throat, and I swallowed past it, determined not to cry, uncertain why I even wanted to. I should have been happy. You didn't leave me behind.

"Why'd you stop? Tired already?" I jutted out my chin, trying to strike the same casually confident tone that always came so easily to you. Instead I sounded petulant and whiny. As if channeling my mood, Chance whined too.

You cocked your head, considering me for a moment. Then, chucking your apple aside, you took several slow, measured steps until you were standing directly in front of me. Gently you reached out and smoothed my wild hair down and tucked it behind my ears. "What's wrong, Pollywog?"

Your pet name, paired with the tender tone of voice, was too much for me. The tears spilled down my cheeks as I wailed, "You knew I'd come!"

"Hey, stop that." Your words were harsh, but you said them softly while your fingers ran along the tracks of my tears, wiping them away. With a gulp and a shuddering sigh, I managed to keep the next sob at bay.

"That's better." Taking my hands, you pulled me from my bike and led me to the shady spot of grass where you'd been sitting. We sat cross-legged across from each other.

"Pollywog, I knew you'd come because you and I are like that. You go where I go. I go where you go. The two of us, we're more than just sisters. More than just friends. The two of us . . ." You held out your right hand, with your fingers spread and the palm facing me. I pressed my own palm against yours so that our fingers lined up. "See that? We're one and the same."

"One and the same." I repeated the words whisper soft, then peered past our connected hands to watch you between the space of our fingers. You stared right back at me, unblinking, completely open. Except I knew there were secrets there. I would never listen to them, any more than you would put a thought into my head. Still, sometimes it was tempting, to know there was something I wasn't being told; it made me wonder whether everything was just a lie. "Would you have followed me?"

"If you had asked me to go to the reformatory and dig under the fence and fill our buckets with the dirt to bring home and sprinkle into our food? Honestly, if it hadn't been my idea, I would have said no at first too. But I would've gone. If you got on the train and rode out of town, I'd follow you there too. All the way to Waikiki or the Grand Canyon if I had to."

"Oh," I said, feeling less than comforted. I didn't understand why you had to bring the rest of the world into it. Instead of letting it go, I added, "But I would never leave Gardnerville. Not ever."

"Never say never," you answered with a mysterious smile.

Then with one of those quicksilver changes of mood, you yelled, "Race you to the hill."

Moments later we were on our bikes, with the wind whipping through our hair as we sped down the streets. Chance raced between us, getting as close to our wheels as he could without getting caught beneath them.

You thought that was the end of that conversation, Piper. But later that night and many other times—I thought about it. Never say never. That's what you said. It was almost like you didn't understand that here in this town, we are the Gardner sisters, we have strange powers, and we are one and the same. But anywhere else we'd just be two girls, no different from any others, with nothing to connect us but blood.

NINE

BY THE TIME I REACH MY FRONT PORCH, THE SUN IS
setting, I am exhausted, and Piper is not any less gone than she
has been these past four years. In the glass of the front door, I
catch a glimpse of a girl in a yellow rain slicker, and for a split
second my heart leaps, thinking Piper has found her way home.
The illusion pops like a soap bubble, but still I walk toward the
door slowly, keeping my eyes on the reflection, trying to hold on
to the idea of it being this easy to find Piper once more.

Reaching out, I press my fingers to the glass, meeting the
cold mirror image. "One and the same," I whisper. The girl-
in-the-glass's lips move with mine, and I wish like hell I had a
forget-me-not right now, so that I could pretend it really was
Piper and have a tiny bit of comfort to take to bed with me. But
since my conversation with Foote, it's become increasingly clear

that my memory problems are making things more complicated than they need to be. How can I ever get closer to finding Piper when I have to keep stopping to have someone explain what happened to me yesterday? And then there are all the days much further in the past that are big, gaping black holes that will eventually need to be filled in too.

Not tonight, though.

I peel the rain slicker off and leave it hanging on the porch railing, hoping it might lure Piper home.

The stairs up to my room feel steeper than usual. I flop onto my bed and stare at the ceiling until exhaustion pulls my eyelids closed. Even then, though, I don't really sleep. Too many unanswered questions chase through my head and keep sleep away. Sometime later I hear footsteps padding down the hallway and then pausing outside my door. I sit up, my heart pounding.

"Piper?" I whisper into the darkness.

"Sky?" a tiny voice answers.

I fall back onto my bed. "Go away, Wills."

My door creaks open. The hall light behind him casts his shadow into my room. "I had a bad dream."

"It happens." Even as I say this, I slide to the far side of my bed, pulling the covers down. Wills runs across my room and jumps in beside me. He wiggles around like a puppy until his warm little body is pressed against mine.

"Tell me a story, Sky."

"Go to sleep."

"Tell me a fourth-year story."

I snort. "I thought you were having nightmares."

This stumps him for a moment. A very short moment. "Not about that. Please, Sky." His tiny fingertips trace the scar that runs along my left arm. "Tell me 'bout the lightning year."

I push Wills so hard that he rolls right out of bed, landing in a pile of blankets with a thump. For several minutes the only sound in the room is my too-heavy breathing, as I try to control the shaking. "We don't tell that story," I finally say.

Wills says nothing, and I half-expect him to return to his own bed. The kid's more determined than I give him credit for, though. He scrambles back into my bed, this time making sure to put a little more distance between us. "Tell me 'bout the year Piper lost her baby toes."

I close my eyes, but sleep feels far away. An apology is on the tip of my tongue and my arms itch to pull Wills closer so that he is once again snuggled against my side. Instead, I start to talk. "Piper was eight that year, and I was four."

"Like me!"

"Yeah, like you." Except I didn't have Mom constantly at my side, waiting to wipe my nose for me. I don't say this out loud though. It feels too disloyal. Not to Mom, but to Piper. She was the one who was there when Mom wasn't.

"It was hot that year," Wills says, prodding me.

"You want to tell it?"

Wills shifts next to me, and I can feel him considering it. He's heard it enough from Mom; I'm sure that he could. "No," he finally says. "You."

"Okay then. It was hot that year, just like it's been this year, except it was only March."

"Global warming," Wills breaks in.

I poke him with my elbow. "You don't even know what that means."

"Do too. It's a house in Ozone that's making everything hotter."

"No, that's not . . ." I stop, realizing I don't have any idea of how to explain global warming. "Well, it wasn't global warming that year. Everyone thought it was just freak weather, but later we realized it had been Franklin and Violet Foster the whole time. But that was at the end. At first, all we knew was that it was hot."

"How hot was it?" Wills asks with a big smile on his face.

I sigh. "It was so hot Milly started serving all of her coffee frozen on a stick, and if you didn't finish it within five minutes it'd be running down your arm and dripping from your elbow. It was so hot that the power went out every twenty minutes. It was so hot Piper and I filled the bottom of the baby pool with ice and took turns sleeping in it at night. It was so hot that after two weeks, most people didn't even move anymore. Even sitting up made you hot. All the ice was gone and the power was permanently out. The water came burning hot out of the tap, but you drank it anyway because your tongue felt like it was covered in cement. The air was so heavy you felt it covering you like a winter coat. People died and their bodies began to rot and reek, and the whole town smelled like death, but no one moved them—it was too exhausting to even try. That's how hot it was."

The smile has faded from Wills's face. This is not the way Mom tells the story. She has a way of making the danger and terror seem like something that happens to other people.

"I fell asleep. That seems like a good thing, but it was too hot to sleep. Piper knew that. She could see I wasn't truly sleeping, I was dying. She shook me awake and dragged me out of bed. It hurt to walk; it felt like we were moving through fire. Chance usually followed me everywhere I went, but that day he stayed where he was, lying on the floor by the front door. He didn't even wag his tail as I went by. Outside, the grass crumbled to dust beneath our feet. Dead birds littered the ground, and more fell from the trees. We didn't get very far before I fell too. Piper tried to pull me up, but she had used every last bit of energy by then and collapsed next to me. I don't know how long we lay there. It felt like a very long time. I could see the sun, burning hot between the tree branches above us. It seemed so angry, that sun. I kept trying to close my eyes against it, but every time I did, Piper slapped me until I opened them again."

"And then," Wills interrupts, "you felt the breeze."

"No," I snap back at him. "Not yet. It wasn't just that we were hot and then there was a breeze and everything was instantly better. We were dying. Every single one of us was slowly being cooked in that heat. It was killing us, but that wasn't even the worst part. The worst of it is that we were waiting to die, the same way you wait in line at the grocery store, impatiently waiting for it to be your turn. I wasn't old enough to understand, but I felt it. All I wanted to do was close my eyes and go somewhere cool. I would've gone that way too, long before the breeze ever came along, except that Piper kept me here. Every time her palm stung against my cheek, I could feel her telling me to stay alive. She willed me to live, and I think she may have even willed the weather to change."

"You mean with powers?" Wills whispers the question, probably afraid I will snap at him again. Or maybe he already knows that speaking aloud of these things is not something that's done.

I suppose this would be a good opening for us to have Gardnerville's version of the birds-and-bees talk. I remember Piper explaining it all to me when I was even younger than Wills. I hadn't understood everything she said at the time. She told me that being a Gardner made you different, and as we got older that difference grew too, getting stronger. We weren't like the normal kids—but the normal kids didn't always stay normal either. With puberty came the possibility of inexplicable changes for everyone. But we Gardners were superpowered from the get-go. "That doesn't mean fourth years don't affect us. It's hormones, and we have those just like everyone else," Piper had said. "They make everyone crazy. Sometimes you can fight it . . . and sometimes you can't."

I don't say any of this to Wills though. Maybe because I can't tell it the same way that Piper did. I can't say that he might be able to fight it and not let it control him. And I can't promise that I will do the same. Everything I've seen tells me that the reformatory is my destiny just as it was Piper's. And I don't know of any reason that it won't eventually be Wills's as well.

"We should go to sleep," I say, suddenly feeling incredibly tired once more.

"Noo-ooohh," Wills whines.

"I'm tired."

"But the story. The end. Please, Sky."

"Fine." I take a deep breath. "Then the breeze came. It tickled my toes, climbed up my spine, and breathed an icy-cool breath down my neck before coming to lick my nose. Piper felt it too. It gave us the strength to sit up and then it came again, stronger, and we stood and followed it. As we got to Salt Spring, the breeze grew stronger and stronger, until by the time we reached the water, there were gigantic waves crashing against the shore. Half the town had followed that wonderfully cool wind to the same place, and we could feel the mist from the water, cold and refreshing on our baked skin. People who would go a mile out of their way to avoid even seeing the spring waded in without a second thought. No one could swim, but we all went as deep as we dared, and then bent to scoop the water up to reach the rest of our too-hot bodies.

"The water felt so good, goose bumps were a welcome novelty. We didn't notice when the waves slowed or when the water began to crackle. The chill came so quickly that the water froze right around us, trapping us inside ice as solid as cement blocks. Then the snow began to fall. Piper and I were lucky. We weren't in that deep. And she had a necklace GG had given her when she wasn't much older than me. It was a lion claw dipped in gold. GG said the oldest child always wore it. Piper never took it off. Ever. Except there, trapped in the ice, she did. There was a red mark all along her neck and at the place on her breastbone where the necklace had rested. It must've gotten so hot that its image was branded on her skin. Piper took that claw and she used it to chip away at the ice until I was freed. I wanted to help get her out then, but she told me to run to all the houses and get blankets and boiling water. So I did."

"You left Piper in the ice?" Wills asks, even though he already knows the answer.

"She told me to."

"But didn't you want to stay and help her?"

"What do you think, Wills? Of course I did. But because I went to get help, lots of people survived who might've died. Lots of people who might've lost their feet lost only a few toes. And Piper got herself out. I knew that she would. If you knew Piper, you would've known that too. Piper is unstoppable."

"But—"

"Go to sleep." Cutting Wills off, I make my voice as hard as the ice that held me and Piper and so many others captive. I know what he was going to say. That either the train or the reformatory had stopped Piper. And that when she got out, she wouldn't be the same. He's seen enough of the reformed to know. I hope, though, that he will be able to meet his oldest sister sooner than planned. The more my mind clears, the more I get the feeling that a plan already exists to get Piper out—I just need to remember exactly what that plan is. Then he will see how Piper is different. Then he will finally have a story of his own to tell.

"Sleep." This time I say it softer and gently tuck the blankets around Wills.

He curls onto his side, and the curve of his back brings the delicate bones of his spine pressing through his thin T-shirt. "Night, Sky."

"Good night, Wills."

He falls asleep almost immediately. I usually end up spending forget-me-not-free nights staring into the darkness. When Wills is nearby, though, I get this calm sort of peaceful feeling. It's been that way ever since he was a baby. I also cry whenever he gets hurt. Sometimes even louder than him. My guess is that he can manipulate emotions, like the way Dad did. I don't tell him this, though. If it were up to me, he'd never find out what he can do, because I can't imagine anything worse than for him to turn out like his father.

Now I gently sling an arm around Wills so his small body settles onto the mattress once more. With him anchored solidly beside me, I, too, at last fall asleep.

PAPA DON'T PREACH

Twelve Years Ago

I WATCHED AS DAD WALKED INTO THE INFIRMARY. He scanned the room, searching for us. You were lying on one of the cots set up for anyone who had frostbite or heat stroke. Both of your feet were wrapped in bandages. I had been sitting on a cold metal chair, swinging my legs because they didn't reach the floor. I froze when he walked in.

I'd seen other kids my age run to their fathers, screaming, "Daddy!" It puzzled me; my instinct had always been to run to him and then kick him in the shins. He was made of secrets and lies, many more than I could count at four years old, but that wasn't what made me hate him. He mostly ignored me, but sometimes—as if he was testing me—he'd stare at me and I would feel my heart squeeze like he was trying to pull it from my chest. The whole time he'd have that oily smile on his face, but behind it his teeth were clenched.

Now he walked straight past me, and took the chair on the other side of the cot.

"It's going to be okay," he said, taking your hand in his own.

His saying it made it feel true—to you at least. "Okay," you agreed weakly.

I felt invisible whenever Dad was around. I didn't care about not getting his attention. What I really hated was being so easily forgotten by you.

The doctor, seeing Dad, immediately came over to talk with him. I wanted to sit beside you again, and retell the day's story. I didn't have the tape recorder on me, but sometimes we liked to tell a story one or two times without recording, just so we could get everything right before we put it on tape.

I only half listened as the doctor explained about your injuries. He talked about third-degree frostbite and how a few lost toes shouldn't slow you down. Then the doctor called you a hero and Dad agreed and they shook hands, congratulating each other on something they had nothing to do with. You stared past them, your eyes meeting mine, a wry smile pulling at the corners of your lips.

At last we were allowed to leave. Dad cradled you in his arms like a baby. I followed several feet in your wake. When we reached the house, he carried you all the way up to your bedroom. I watched as he gently lowered you onto your bed and then turned to shut the door behind him—right in my face. There was no lock, but even so, I didn't dare come in. Instead, I stood in the hallway, listening to the rumble of Dad's voice and your softer humming responses. I couldn't help but wonder what you were both saying.

I waited for what felt like a very long time, shifting my weight from one foot to the other. Finally, I heard the floorboards on the other side of the door creak, and a moment later the door opened. Dad brushed past me without acknowledging my presence. I watched his back as he descended the stairs and for a moment thought of rushing at him, pushing him down. With any luck, he'd break his neck.

The thought shocked me. It wasn't the first time I'd had a hateful thought about Dad, but it was the first time I'd wished him dead. It was the first time I'd imagined it and felt a flash of satisfaction. I could've killed him a thousand times, Piper, but I didn't because of you. I knew that hurting him would hurt you too.

"Sky?" you called from inside your room.

"Right here." I walked in and flopped onto the bed beside you. The spot was warm, as if someone else had recently been lying there.

"What did Dad say?" I asked.

You shook your head.

"Piper," I whined out of habit, but a part of me was relieved. I could sense just enough of the secret to know that it was several shades darker than any I'd encountered thus far.

"No." You turned from where you'd been staring up at the ceiling to meet my eyes, then said, "Forget it." Just like that, the secret that had been slinking closer and closer drifted away. "That isn't part of the story." You handed me the tape recorder.

I took it. "What story?" I asked, trying to remember what I'd missed.

"Start with two weeks ago," you said, ignoring my question. "On the day when you woke up and said it was so hot it felt like your bones were turning into noodles."

"Cooked noodles," I corrected.

Then I cleared my throat, pressed Record, and began to tell our story. I thought it was the true and complete story of our lives that we put onto those tapes; it's only now, looking back, that I realize how much you might have left out.

TEN

THE NEXT MORNING I STAND IN THE MIDDLE OF A quiet street, waiting and second-guessing myself. I don't know exactly what I'll accomplish by going to the reformatory with Foote. The only way you get past the front gates is if you're doing time. But even if we can't get in, I can lie in the field where Piper and I spent so many afternoons together. I can watch the inmates do their daily walk.

The low bleat of a horn brings me back to my surroundings, and I see an ambulance slowly coming down the street toward me. The siren is silent, but the lights on top whirl as the vehicle rumbles past, almost luridly bright against the overcast sky. I turn to watch the ambulance roll through the stop sign at the end of the street and take the left that leads toward the Salt Spring.

It's not an active decision, but suddenly my feet are moving, following the ambulance's path. While I walk, my brain works, wondering what could be happening. If it was a fourth-year event, the siren would be screaming. Not to move people out of the way but as an early-warning system. *Get in your houses. Lock the doors.* If it isn't fourth-year-related, then somebody is drowning. Probably someone released from the reformatory after a long stint. They're often drawn to the water. Nobody really knows for certain what the link is between the two. Some say the spring formed when they were clearing the land to build the reformatory. Others say it's the tears of the inmates. All that's known for certain is that when former inmates are found there, they often seem to be searching the waters, diving in again and again, as if looking for something they've lost and will never be complete again without.

Shit.

Suddenly, remembering LuAnn, a girl who seems to have lost more than most, I start to run.

The land rolls in a steep downward slope toward the Salt Spring and I let gravity push at my back, propelling me faster and faster until the water spreads before me with the ambulance parked at its edge. The back doors are flung open, and a cot waits with an empty black body bag draped carelessly over the top of it.

Not a rescue operation then. I wonder why they even bothered with the lights.

My steps slow and I let my feet drag through the scrub grass and shale that make up the beach. I hear the sound of vomiting as I get closer, and I wonder if maybe the body bag was just a mistake and someone has been saved.

Up. Down. Up. Down. My heart is like a yo-yo attached to the thinnest of strings that sends it flying up and down with the slightest of tugs. I round the ambulance and the string is cut.

The ambulance driver, bent in half with his elbows braced against his thighs, heaves into the water. Beside him, just inches from the water—as if the spring chewed him up and spit him out—lies Jonathan. It's his blond hair I notice first. Maybe because it is so similar to his sister's. Or perhaps because it is the only part of him that looks the same, that has not bloated and deteriorated.

I am grateful I skipped breakfast. My stomach churns, but finds nothing to spit out onto the sand. I turn my gaze up toward the hills just in time to see Elton's Prius gliding down. There is no time to run from him, and even if there was, I find that I don't wish to. I want to look in his face when he sees Jonathan's body and I want to hear what Elton's secrets whisper. I want to know why he would have done such a thing.

But when the car stops, it is Foote at the steering wheel and Foote who opens the passenger doors to let two adults out. Jonathan's parents. They both worked up at the reformatory once but were let go after LuAnn went in. Standard policy. It's seen as a conflict of interest.

They hold hands tightly as they walk toward the ambulance. I think about stopping them. Warning them. But they have worked at the reformatory. They've seen worse. Caused worse. I let them go, and a terrible part of me is glad to hear their cries of anguish and sobs filled with sickness. It feels like justice, although, of course, it isn't. The reformatory is the main employer in this town, and most people end up working there due to a lack of other options. It changes the people who put on the uniform. Changes them for the worse. I watched it happen up close and personal with Ozzy. He was a sweet boy once, who wouldn't reach for a girl's hand without asking her permission first. After he'd been at the reformatory a few months, I could see the kindness decreasing, like a slow leak. Years later, if there was good left in him, it was buried too deep to be easily seen.

"You should stay in the car," I hear Foote say.

I turn to see LuAnn sliding from the backseat of the Prius. In the brisk wind from the Salt Spring her long hair flies behind her, undulating gently as if imitating the waves. She ignores Foote's advice and walks toward her parents. As she passes by me, I notice that her clothes are wet and that she is singing softly, her lips barely moving with the words, "Don't, don't don't don't, don't you forget about me."

LuAnn is not Piper, I know that, and yet . . . she is singing that song from the tape.

"Piper?" I whisper, the word escaping.

At the same instant, Jonathan's dad growls, "LuAnn, get back in the car. Now!"

It's like neither of us spoke as she stares out at the water and then slowly, as if it is calling to her, continues toward it with springy little steps.

"LuAnn!" her mother calls.

"Let her go. Let her drown." Her father spits out the words. "Who is she anymore anyway? Not our daughter. Just someone who ruined our lives."

"No," her mother replies, but not convincingly.

Once she's waist deep in the water, LuAnn turns back to where her parents kneel beside their son's dead and bloated body.

"C'mon, little brother," she calls, sounding young and girlish. "Enough pouting, you sore loser. You always were terrible at hide-and-seek. Your blubbering gave you away every time. Maybe you thought I wouldn't hear it if you were underwater. At first I didn't, but then you got so scared down there alone in the dark. You were always good at finding dark places but always had trouble getting out of them. Lucky for you the water's not as deep as it used to be." She leans forward to splash at the water with her hands, sending a spray toward her silent and stricken parents. Then she turns to me. "I'm going to hide again. Want to come with me? When Jonathan wakes up, he'll come and find us."

Her hands meet over her head, and she looks poised to dive and disappear into the water when Foote grabs her from behind. She flails her limbs and shrieks loud enough to drown out every other sound, but Foote has her in a tight bear hug and doesn't release her until they are back on dry land. As soon as he frees her, she sinks to the ground.

After a moment of hesitation, Foote reaches for her again, this time handling her more gingerly. A hand on her elbow to pull her up and then just the tips of his fingertips against the small of her back, pressing her into the car. Finally, he scoops up her feet, still dragging in the sand, and places them inside so that he can ease the door shut behind her with a soft click.

I have been staring at Foote this whole time, and when he finishes this task, his eyes meet mine. Our gazes hold for however long it takes for me to breathe a hundred shallow breaths. I can feel my heart racing, scared and hopeful and ready to be torn to pieces.

The sound of a zipper grabs my attention. I close my eyes, needing to extract myself from the laser beam of Foote's focus. It doesn't work. I can still see Foote on the backside of my eyelashes, the same way Piper pinned a picture of Elton to the back of her pull-down shade.

I turn my head and open my eyes just in time to see the body bag now filled and on the ground, being zipped up to the top. What's left of Jonathan is placed on the gurney and in the ambulance. The driver gets in and turns off the swirling lights before steering the ambulance across the sand and out of sight. Jonathan's parents watch until the vehicle disappears. Then they trudge back toward the Prius and get in without another word or sob.

I guess after the initial shock and denial wore off, they accepted it fairly quickly. Everyone knows that the chances of surviving adolescence are about fifty-fifty during a fourth year. Even if Jonathan's death wasn't exactly fourth-year-related, the end result is the same. A plot in the cemetery, with a headstone that labels him as "Taken Too Soon."

Foote closes the car door behind them, then turns back toward me. I expect nothing from Foote. He doesn't owe me explanations or anything else. But as he has from the moment I first saw him, Foote defies my expectations. He crosses the space between us with his long-legged stride, takes hold of my elbow, and then leads me several more steps until we are at the edge of the water right beside the indention left behind by Jonathan.

It's hardly a romantic spot, but nobody told my central nervous system this, and the tingles in my arm where Foote is touching me spread like a wonderful disease through the rest of my body.

I wonder if Foote is feeling it too, and with his hand on me it would be all too easy to find out. So I take a step away and disconnect from his touch, evading secrets that aren't mine to take. I am left like any other girl starting to crush on a guy—staring at him and wondering what he's thinking.

His gaze is focused on the water and the train tracks beyond it that disappear into the mountain. I try to look at it through his eyes, but even with the forget-me-nots, I have too many memories of this place. I blink as one of those memories nearly overtakes me.

"Piper used to sing 'Over the Rainbow' when we came here," I tell him, not even sure why I'm sharing it with him. "We watched *The Wizard of Oz* so many times we memorized the whole thing." I feel the need to explain this to Foote, even though chances are if he has a TV, he's already seen it. The same movies play on a constant loop.

"Yeah, I've seen it a couple times now," Foote says. "Although personally, I prefer *The Maltese Falcon*."

Of course, I've seen that one a million times too. It starts with a girl asking a detective to help find her missing sister. But it turns out there is no sister and she's just another bad guy.

"Piper and I always liked musicals," I say, moving us back toward Oz. "And there was this one line in 'Over the Rainbow' about troubles melting like lemon drops. That's what Piper always said the Salt Spring smells like."

Even as I tell Foote this story, I can almost see Piper, farther down the shoreline, singing a different part of the song. The end part where Dorothy wonders why the bluebirds can fly over the rainbow, where she is unable to follow. "Why, oh why, can't I?" Sometimes Piper belted out that last line and at other times she sang it so softly the waves drowned her out.

In my memory the waves were bigger. The whole Salt Spring was bigger, in fact. I look at it again, remembering what LuAnn said about the water being deeper before. Could the Salt Spring be shrinking somehow?

"What is it about this place?" Foote asks, distracting me from my meaningless speculations.

"This place specifically, or the whole town?"

Foote pulls his hat off, and slaps it against his leg a few times. "I don't even know."

"You can leave," I remind him gently, not with the sneer I use for most newcomers.

He doesn't respond, just puts his hat back on and spends a full minute adjusting it so that it sits right. When he's done, he glances back toward the car where the remnants of Jonathan's family wait. "I was on my way to meet you when Elton called. He said that he received a call about a girl swimming in the Salt Spring and asked if I would come down here to pick her up. When I arrived, she wasn't swimming, she was on the shore next to Jonathan."

I want to ask how Jonathan went from the bottom of the

school pool to the bottom of Salt Spring. Did Foote help load him into Elton's car? Did they work together to fill Jonathan's pockets with rocks to make sure he'd stay sunken? The one thing that's certain is no one counted on LuAnn dredging her brother back up.

"I called the ambulance and then decided to take LuAnn home. She didn't seem . . . I just thought it would be best if she was with her family. But when I got there and explained what had happened, Jonathan's parents insisted on seeing him and I agreed to drive, and I believe you've been here for everything else."

For a second I think I might tell Foote about the note from Jonathan, but then LuAnn bursts from the car and makes another run at the water. Her parents don't even try to stop her; they just stare out the car window with cold eyes and dead faces. Foote runs at her, but LuAnn is watching for it this time and quickly veers around him. He stumbles in the loose dirt, and then it is up to me. I throw myself at LuAnn, tackling her and bringing her down so that we are a tangle of limbs. She looks stunned for a moment, but then her eyes meet mine.

"Pollywog!" she exclaims, and her face lights up, like she's a toy that's just been given fresh batteries. Her arms wrap around me in a squeezing hug, her cheek presses against mine, and then she whispers in my ear, "The plan is the plan. She told me to tell you. It's the uprising. It's time."

Before I can respond, she is jerked away by Foote. Apparently spent, she sags in his arms and her eyes drift closed.

Before reaching the car, he calls over his shoulder, "If you'll wait, I'll meet you in an hour. Same place."

I nod, or try to, but am feeling pretty worn out myself. Foote, on the other hand, looks calm. That scene was enough to send most other newcomers screaming. It almost sent me in a similar direction. But Jonathan's note in my pocket acts like an anchor, holding me to this spot and making me wonder how much of what he'd told me was true. Making me wonder more than just that.

Collapsing onto the sand, I pull out Jonathan's note. He wanted me to find his sister. But she found him instead. And me too.

The plan is the plan. That was the one thing I sort of understood. Because I'd heard it before. Four years ago, the plan was the plan, but then Piper went away and I forgot about it the same way I did everything else. It would be helpful if I could remember that plan, but all I remember is the sick feeling I got in my stomach every time Piper said the plan was the plan. That sick feeling is back now.

Crumpling the paper into a ball, I throw it out to sea and watch the waves curl around it and carry it away.

LET'S HEAR IT FOR THE BOY

Four Years Ago

WE WAITED ON THE FRONT STEPS OF MILLY'S. FROM there we could see the bus and everyone who got on or off. School was ending in a few months, and you said this was the best time to find the new people who'd be working at the reformatory—this was when they started recruiting. Every year at least half of the high school graduates would take the bus up the hill to apply for positions. "We'll be able to pick the new workers out right away," you assured me. "They'll be the ones carrying uniforms instead of wearing them."

As usual, you were right. About ten people got off the bus at 4:00 p.m., and among them were two girls and four boys, each carrying a stack of clothing. You eyed the new workers as they walked past us in a silent clump. There was no excitement or happy chatter about their jobs like I'd expected. Instead they were morose and silent, as if they'd just been sentenced to serve time at the reformatory instead of work there.

"I feel bad for them," I whispered to you after they were a few feet away.

"Hush. The plan is the plan." You tugged on my hand, pulling me to my feet. We followed them for a few moments, and then you pointed to one of the boys. "Him."

I studied the one you'd marked, trying to see what made him so special. His shoulders slouched and his greasy dark hair was short in the front, but long enough in the back to touch the collar of his wrinkled button-down shirt. He took shuffling little steps like his feet were shackled, and his too-long dress pants were already frayed. Maybe this was what you liked about him, that he looked a little sloppier and more beaten down than the rest of them. Maybe you had some thought of wanting to help him out, give him a new purpose in life. Or maybe you just saw an easy target.

As if feeling the pressure of our eyes on his back, the boy stopped and turned. You smiled at him. It was like having a flashbulb go off in his face; he was left half blind with spots of light dancing in the space between your smiling face and his own. He looked around, stunned, trying to figure out who that smile was for, unable to believe it might've been for him. You began to walk toward him with your hips swinging and that smile still there but turned down a few notches from *stun* to *confuse*.

The others kept going, not even noticing they'd lost one of their own.

As he watched you coming, his eyes got bigger and bigger while his Adam's apple bobbed with each gulp of air so that it looked like he was choking on something. When you finally reached him, you placed your arms around his neck like you were hanging a medal on him, and then you pressed your lips to his cheek. As you pulled away, I finally understood why you'd bought that tube of red lipstick instead of your usual shimmery pink lip gloss. Stamped on his cheek, in candy-apple red, was the perfect bow shape of your mouth.

"I'm Piper," you said, your voice pitched so low that I had to lean in to hear.

"Oh." He finally smiled back at you, a big, goofy grin. "I think I know you from school maybe?"

I almost laughed at the question. Was this his idea of trying to be cool? Even in a school three times bigger than ours, everyone would know who you were. You weren't someone who would ever go unnoticed.

"I'm Oswald," he added. "But my friends call me Ozzy."

"Well, maybe we should get a little friendlier, so that I can call you Ozzy too." You laid it on thick, like you were imitating Marilyn Monroe or one of the other glamorous actresses from the old movies we constantly watched. Then you led him away, down one of the dark lanes that broke off from Main Street.

For a second I thought of following, but if you'd wanted me to come along, you would've made it clear you were including me. Later that night, though, you climbed into bed beside me and shared all the details. You told me his kisses were sloppy and that he kept asking, "This okay?" No matter how many times you assured him it was just fine. I asked if you thought you'd fall in love with him, and you laughed.

"No, Pollywog," you said. "This isn't about love. This is strategy."

ELEVEN

I DRAG MYSELF HOME FROM THE SALT SPRING thinking I will crawl back into bed and ditch Foote. But I want a fuller escape than sleep can give me. I want to let a forget-me-not slide down the back of my throat and make the world slowly dissolve. For the first time in longer than I can accurately say, I am 100 percent forget-me-not-free. I wouldn't say I'm suffering from withdrawal, but I am finding reality to be a little too real for my taste. It's like somebody has cranked all the control buttons so that everything is too bright and too loud and too pushy, wanting me to notice every fucking little thing.

It's making me more than a bit cranky, and it doesn't help that the early-morning overcast skies have burned away so that the sun is now beaming down at me, brighter than I remember it ever being before on any other day of my life. And, of course, I can't remember where my sunglasses are, or even where I last saw them or what they look like.

Without the forget-me-nots dulling my memory, I'm starting to remember other things, too. And those other things take my feet away from the front door and around the side of the house to the garden shed. The building that was once Piper's and my sanctuary now leans forward like a hunchback. Or maybe the roof is getting ready to slide off. Either way, I have to lean all my weight against the door to open it, and when it finally gives, I half fall inside. A streak of sunlight illuminates the dust and spiderwebs that have claimed the small space as their own. I am content to let them have it as long as the place holds together; I just need to retrieve something I left behind and half-forgot. My old bike. They say nobody forgets how to ride a bike, but those people have probably never tried any of the quints' pills. After falling off one too many times, I put mine into permanent storage.

I wheel the bike from the shed, and then go in one last time to rescue the air pump as well. After brushing the worst of the cobwebs away and inflating the tires, I grab hold of the handle-bars and start walking.

Foote is already waiting for me. Although, maybe *waiting* isn't the best word. He sits on the curb, elbows balanced on his knees and a book in his hands. Whatever he is reading must be good because he doesn't even notice me until I am almost on top of him.

"Hey," he says, hopping to his feet and tucking the book away in his jacket pocket before I can catch what it is.

"Hey," I reply. "I brought my bike, thought it'd be faster to get up there that way."

Foote looks at the bike and then back at me. "I don't know if I'll be able to keep up with you."

I shake my head. "One of us pedals and the other sits on the handlebars or rides the back bar." I point to the long bar poking out of the center of the back wheel. "After Piper and I outgrew our kid bikes, we couldn't get another until the next shipment came in, and who knew when that would be. So we frankensteined our two bikes together to make one that we could share."

Foote gives a low whistle. "That is some crazy-good mad-scientist work right there."

I grin at him, unable to stop myself. "Thanks."

Foote grins back. "Okay, so since I outweigh you by at least fifty pounds, I think I'm obligated to volunteer for pedaling duty. Which leaves you to choose the stern or bow."

When I rode with Piper, I almost always used the bar on the back wheel. Putting my hands on her shoulders, I'd sometimes lean forward so far that Mom said we looked like a two-headed girl riding down the street.

"Handlebars," I tell Foote.

It takes us a few minutes to get situated. First Foote has to raise the seat, then there is a series of shifts after I take my place on the handlebars so that Foote's hands aren't touching my butt. Then, at last, we are moving. The wind grabs hold of my hair, sending it into Foote's face. I hold it back with one hand and keep the other on the bike, to do my part in helping us balance. The red, white, and blue streamers at the ends of the handlebars, which Piper insisted on keeping even though I thought they were too babyish, create a crinkly, crackly sound that makes it feel like we are going much faster than we actually are. At the first corner we almost wipe out, but Foote gets a foot onto the ground and we are quickly righted and moving along once more.

A couple guys I recognize from school, who are clearly full of scarlet runners, come up behind us, their feet pounding the pavement in unison. Foote pedals harder, and they pick up the pace too, the pills inside them urging their bodies to go faster.

"This is awesome," Foote shouts into my ear, and I nod in agreement, but what I really want to say is that I had forgotten how much I love this. I've never been a fan of cars. They are too climate-controlled and cushy. Riding in one is as much fun as taking a living room couch out for a ride. Walking is not especially thrilling, and I've never seen the point of running unless you're in a hurry to get away from or to something. But a bike is a brilliant form of transportation. On hot, sticky days like this, it creates the perfect amount of wind to keep you cool. If you're feeling lazy, you can turn the gears down so low that you're practically pedaling in place. And on days when you just need to escape and know that there is none available, you can at least have the pleasure of pushing the pedals as hard as they will go until you reach the farthest edge of town.

When we begin climbing the last big hill leading up to the reformatory, Foote stands up to pedal.

"Want me to jump off?" I yell back at him.

"No," he answers immediately.

I throw a glance at him over my shoulder. He looks so intense and focused and—

I face forward again, staring straight ahead.

"Everyone falls eventually," Piper told me. "You think it'll hurt. But it's falling with no bottom. You just keep going and going forever, just falling deeper and deeper. And once you stop being scared, it's kind of fun." It was after she'd met Elton and I'd asked her what the angle was. I'd been certain that he was just another part of the plan. I'd never thought Piper would be distracted by something as stupid as a cute boy.

The pleasure of this moment drains away. The sun is in my eyes, and the breeze is no longer cool but scratchy against my skin. Staring at my knees, I hunch forward and try to make myself as small as possible, so that we can get to the top of this hill and I can get off this bicycle and stop feeling Foote's hot breath against the back of my neck. I don't want to fall. It's a distraction I can't afford right now. And also, I'm afraid.

Just before the front gates come into view, I point to the dirt path that runs through the overgrown grass and weeds that edge the road on the right side. "That way," I shout back to Foote.

He immediately turns the bike, and we begin to bump along the narrow trail. I grab hold of the handlebars with both hands to keep myself from sliding off and am about to shout that maybe it is time to walk when we hit a rut and the bike slips out from underneath us.

The ground comes up at me, hard and fast. My arms go out to absorb the blow and then quickly give way so that my face— with my nose leading—smacks into the dirt.

I lie stunned for a moment and then sit up, spitting out dirt and expecting to see a few of my teeth too. I wait for the pain . . .

that never arrives. No blood and broken bones either. Somehow, I've come through the crash totally unscathed.

Foote groans behind me. Apparently, he has not been as lucky. He and the bike lie together in a tangled pile.

"Foote?"

He looks up at me when I call his name. Blood streams from his nose and drips down his chin. The arm underneath him sits at an unnatural, twisted angle. Instinctively, I reach down toward him but then stop, uncertain if there is any place I can touch him that wouldn't cause him additional pain.

"Foote, what can I do? Should I get help?"

"No. Just . . ." Foote pauses to use the back of his good arm to wipe the blood from his mouth. "Give me a minute, okay?"

"But—" I start to protest feebly.

"Go!" Foote barks the word at me, and it is more than enough to convince me to take a few steps away and then a few more, until I turn and start running. I play chicken with the trees, darting at them, and then at the last second, when I am about to collide, I feint left or right. I get so close the bark skins my arms. The trees never flinch.

I am veering around a gigantic oak when suddenly a chain-link fence, and beyond it the brick walls of the reformatory, looms before me. For a second I am tempted to run at the fence, but unlike with the trees, this time I won't give way. I know the layout of the reformatory. I could get inside and find Piper. And then I would . . .

As the fantasy gives way to reality, I feel that old fear the reformatory always awakens in me. My palms sweat, my throat closes, and my heart starts doing jumping jacks in my chest. When you're a kid, the reformatory is the boogeyman and the haunted house on the hill all rolled into one. It's a scary story you whisper at night under the covers. But as you get older, it becomes something else. It is the worst day you can ever imagine and it is coming straight at you, as unavoidable as destiny.

"So this is it, huh?" A low voice speaks into my ear.

I scream a high-pitched shriek that you'd expect from a toddler, and then whirl to find Foote.

"Damn it," I say, punching his arm. "Don't do that." Then, realizing I've hit his bad arm, I wince. "Sorry. I just . . . You scared me. Are you okay?"

"Right as rain." Foote grins at me.

"You've got blood on your teeth," I tell him.

The smile fades. "I'm fine. Just got the wind knocked out of me."

"And blood."

"I get nosebleeds from stress. Sucks, but I've learned to always carry tissues." Foote holds up a hand clenched around a fistful of bright-red tissues.

I squint at him, unable to believe he's fine after looking so beaten up only moments ago. "You're sure?"

"Look." He stretches his arms over his head, then brings them in an arc back to his sides. "Like I said, right as rain."

"Okay, good," I grumble, not even sure why I care. "You're right as rain, whatever the hell that means. Now c'mon and follow me. There's a spot around the back where we can get a good view of the yard."

"Would you prefer 'fit as a fiddle'?" Foote sounds amused, which only annoys me further.

"I'd prefer you to be quiet," I hiss at him. "If anyone sees us poking around back here, they'll send the guards out to chase us away."

Foote says nothing in response, and for a moment I am disappointed. I realize then that I sound like GG during the lectures she used to give Piper and me. One minute she'd be telling us to keep our mouths shut if we knew what was good for us, and the next she'd bellow, "Answer me!" There was no winning with her.

I stop and turn to tell Foote I'm sorry, but his head is down and he keeps plowing forward, crashing straight into me. I nearly hit the ground for the second time, but Foote grabs hold of me, pulling me back and bringing my body against his. I twist my head so that my nose isn't pressed into his chest, breathing him in, but then my ear is right over his rib cage, which cradles his heart and broadcasts its frantic beating. I jerk away, feeling like I've taken a secret.

"Sorry," I say, taking a few shuffling steps backward, needing a little more space. "If we want to get closer, we should probably crawl. That's what Piper and I used to do."

Foote nods. "Okay. I'll follow your lead."

Feeling silly, I get down on my hands and knees and begin to crawl through the weeds. Dust rises and I can feel it sticking to my sweaty face and arms. I glance back to see Foote behind me, in a bloodied and ripped white tee, looking similar to the other day when I caught him at the train station. I never did get a straight answer from him about why he was on that train, which should remind me to be more careful around him. To stop trusting him. To stop wishing that when I was pressed against his chest I had leaned my head back and waited for his lips to touch mine. I can see it so clearly that for a minute it almost feels like it actually happened. Then my hand hits something cold and hard and metallic.

It's an old Zippo lighter that Piper found at the secondhand store. For a while she used to say she was going to use it to burn the reformatory to the ground. The lighter was cheap because it was broken, so Piper never even bothered to put lighter fluid in it, but just the same, every time she flicked it open, I expected a flame to come shooting out. This lighter. Piper. They are real. And Foote; Foote is just a newcomer. Even if he lives here for the rest of his life, I'll never see him as anything but temporary.

I collapse onto my belly and motion for Foote to come lie beside me.

"Now what?" he whispers, his gaze caught on the bricks and steel bars that make up the reformatory. At this moment it looks like a deserted building. The sun bounces off the iron-barred windows, making it impossible to see if anyone is peering out. The grounds are empty. But not for long. I pull out my cell to check the time. It's 1:15. The walk is usually right around now. After everyone has finished lunch.

"Just wait," I tell Foote.

He sighs and then is still. But not quiet. "I don't like this place." He whispers the words so close that they tickle my hair.

Hiding the movement behind an arm stretch, I shift a few inches away from him. "Nobody does."

"It's funny," he says, leaning in closer to me. "I've been to some terrible places, but this, the feeling here . . . It's like nothing I've felt before."

"Terrible places like where?" I can't stop myself from asking.

Foote shrugs. "It's not that interesting. Just your run-of-the-mill people-doing-terrible-things-to-other-people stuff. Tell me about Piper instead."

"You could just say you don't want to talk about it."

"Okay, I don't want to talk about it. Not right now anyway. And I really do want to hear about Piper."

"You've been living here for three months. You've probably heard all the Piper stories by now."

"Maybe I want to hear them from you."

"Well, maybe I'd rather not talk about it."

My tone is more sharp than playful, but Foote laughs anyway, a low rumble that gives me goose bumps. "Okay, then."

But now, of course, I can't stop thinking about Piper. I wonder what he's been told and who's been telling him. Was it Elton's version of Piper? The old-timers at Milly's? Or maybe it was someone else.

"Do they all hate her?" I hear myself ask in a small voice. The question never reaches Foote's ears, because at the same instant the alarm wails.

"What's happening?" Foote says, and I can hear the tension in his voice.

"The daily walk."

"Like a get-fresh-air kind of thing?"

"No." I shake my head for emphasis. "Like a reprieve kind of thing. People say the walk is like trudging through snow and hot coals all at the same time. It hurts to fall down. It hurts to keep walking. But it's a billion times better than being inside, and they fight to be the first out the door."

I stop talking, even though I haven't explained it very well and feel like I should try again. But then the inmates come into view, and my throat closes and I cannot say anything more.

It feels the same way it has ever since the first time Piper brought me here when I wasn't much older than Wills. There are only thirty-some of them doing the walk today. I know them all by name. I know what they're in for and when they'll get out. But then I notice something else. Or *the lack of something* would be more accurate. The gray skin. The stooped shoulders and slow shuffling feet. The faces crumpled and clenched in pain and defeat. Those details that I recall with a surprising amount of clarity are all . . . gone.

Am I remembering wrong? It doesn't seem possible. I know the reformatory walk like I know my own name.

I stare harder, wondering if they are just trying to be brave. But no. They are not skipping or filling their lungs with fresh air or holding their pale faces up to the sun. They are as miserable as you would expect locked-up teenagers to be, but they are not faded ghosts.

"Let's move it along," one of the guards yells. Another difference. Usually the guards are lazy and quiet. But the two out today seem tense and worried. They keep pushing the inmates, urging them to walk faster. It's like they want to get this over with.

The inmates are just rounding the corner, where they will once again be out of sight, when the bigger guard pushes the boy at the end of the line.

Grady Stonard. He shouldn't even be doing time. During any other year, his midsummer show would've been seen as nothing more than a harmless prank. He'd made the sky light up with brilliant flashes using an empty old squirt gun. I'd watched it from the middle of a field where I was just coming off a forget-me-not afternoon. Not a single person was hurt. Still it scared the shit out of everyone. They gave him six months, with the possibility of getting out in three for good behavior.

Seems like Grady's chances of getting out early aren't so great. When the guard pushes him, he stumbles forward a few feet and looks as if he's going down but catches himself at the last minute. Stooped over, he rests with his arms on his thighs. The guard comes up behind him again.

"Keep moving," he bellows, his hand out to push Grady once more.

But Grady is prepared this time. He spins and takes a swing at the guard, catching him in the nose. Blood sprays. Grady gets him a second time with a fist to the gut.

His fellow inmates have stopped to stare. I am ready to stand up and cheer.

Then the other guard comes in. He uses his stick and swings it like a baseball bat straight at Grady's head. Grady turns just in time to have it hit his ear. He falls.

I gasp and scramble to my feet, ready to throw myself into the fray. Foote's hand grips my arm, pulling me down beside him.

There is no one to hold back the other inmates though.

Seven of them rush the guards, while the rest hang back, probably too scared to join the fight. Still at seven to two, the odds should be in their favor. But the same soil that leeches strength from the inmates gives it—along with a propensity for cruelty—to the guards. They pull out their sticks, with their electrode tips, and even the odds very quickly. Two inmates go down almost immediately. But that still leaves five. Among them is Stasia Cole, the girl who had half the school howling at the moon last year, when they became werewolves. Arnie Stock crashed a party and put all the guests to sleep by humming a lullaby and then made mustaches grow on their faces when they were out. But their abilities faded as quickly as they'd bloomed and can't help them now. Stasia and Arnie fall. The last three run, with the guards chasing after them.

Eventually new guards come out. They could pick up the inmates who have been beaten to a pulp and put them on stretchers. Instead they grab their ankles and drag them across the yard one by one.

When it is finally over, Foote and I crawl away, back to the cover of the trees.

Foote pulls off his hat and runs his hands through his hair, scrubbing at his scalp. "Holy shit," he finally says. "I wasn't expecting that."

I look back at the reformatory. The place I thought I knew. It is still large and intimidating, like it always has been. Now, though, I notice that it seems to be sitting at an odd angle, like it has shifted off-balance. Like a good shove might be enough to push it right off the mountainside. Just looking at it makes me feel unsteady too, as if it's already crashing down.

"Yeah," I answer at last. "Neither was I."

DO YOU REALLY WANT TO HURT ME?

Seven Years Ago

"WOW," I SAID WHEN WE REACHED THE CLEARING where you had set up our picnic. "It's bee-yoo-ti-ful."

"Thank you." You gave a little curtsy, then gestured to the blanket laid out on the grass. "Please have a seat."

I carefully lowered myself onto the blanket and crossed my legs so that I didn't bump any of the dishes set there. Chance barked excitedly and leaped beside me. Grabbing him by the collar, I pulled him away. You had taken GG's best china—without permission. We'd both be dead if he accidentally broke something.

After getting Chance to lie down a few feet away, I took a moment to admire the elegant serving bowls and platters. I hated sitting at GG's table, knowing she'd scold me if I even breathed on them the wrong way. But here they were in the woods, in our territory, being used to hold all of our favorite treats. The serving bowl that GG usually used for her extra-sour sauerkraut was filled with butterscotch pudding. The platter on which GG placed slices of rare roast beef now held pizza bagels instead. And to finish it off, GG's giant crystal punch bowl was overflowing with a gigantic root beer float.

"This is amazing," I said as you took your seat across from me.

"It was nothing," you said with a shrug. "And besides, you deserve some credit too. You did an excellent job keeping GG distracted while I ransacked the china chest."

I made a face. "Don't remind me."

"What's wrong, Pollywog? Was she lecturing you again on the duties of a Gardner?"

"At first," I admitted slowly. "But then I told her she was a hypocrite. That she should've done her time in the reformatory like everyone else if she was so interested in duty."

"Oh, Sky." You sighed. "You have a singular gift for antagonizing GG."

"I don't know what that means." I hated when you used big words. You'd been doing it more and more since you'd moved up to the high school.

"You piss her off," you clarified.

"Well, she pisses me off too!" I felt angry all over again just remembering it. Normally I would have stomped away, but I'd promised you that I would keep GG distracted until you gave me the all-clear signal. So instead of fleeing, I'd opened my stupid mouth, determined to show GG I wasn't just a dumb kid. That I knew more than she thought I did.

"They say you created a duplicate of every single person in your class, using nothing more than a lock of the person's hair," I'd told GG. "It was like having an instant twin, except they were just a copy owned by the original. At first everyone thought it was fun. They had their duplicate do their homework and chores for them while they went out all night. But after a week of that, the duplicates wanted more and rebelled. After two weeks some of the duplicates went missing. Or maybe the originals were gone. Nobody really knew. Your friends asked you to get rid of the rest of the duplicates, but you said you couldn't, that they had to do it themselves. The duplicates were tied with rope and dropped into the Salt Spring. Some people say they couldn't drown and that they're still down there waiting to be found. And you were sent to the reformatory. But most people say you didn't go. That you sent your own duplicate instead, while you hid away and waited. And after she was finally released, you drowned her too."

GG grabbed me and pulled me close so that our eyes were only inches apart. "The correct term is doppelgänger. And I didn't drown her. She went into the water on her own and liked it so much she decided to stay there. But if you're so clever, Skylar, why don't you tell me: what would you do with a doppelgänger of your own? Would you get rid of her, or would you make her your best friend? Would you give her parts of yourself just to keep her from going away?" GG's fingernails dug into my skin as she gave me a little shake.

I jerked away, losing a few bits of skin in the process. "Maybe we would be friends. What's so bad about that?"

"Someday you'll find out," GG said, while she stared at me in this awful, knowing way. I shivered, suddenly afraid that GG was going to tell me that I was your doppelgänger. That she'd created me to be your shadow. I would deny it. Of course I would. Even if it did feel so terribly much like truth itself.

I never got the chance to hear what else GG was going to say, though, because you had appeared, whistling a happy tune that was the signal for "mission accomplished."

"Never mind GG," you said, bringing me back to our picnic. With a flourish, you handed me a spoon. "Where should we start?"

I tapped the spoon against my lips, taking my time deciding, trying to get into the spirit of the thing. "Ummm . . . How about the butterscotch pudding?"

"Excellent choice."

Together we dipped our spoons into the bowl, clinked them together in a silent toast, and then each took a dainty little bite. After that, though, we stopped pretending and tore into the feast. You even let me lick the pudding bowl since butterscotch pudding was my favorite.

When it was over, I lay on the grass moaning, my stomach painfully full. You packed the now empty dishes back into the picnic basket, and we started to walk home. Halfway there, I began to sweat and shake. Tears streamed from my eyes.

"Piper!" I cried, and then I fell down, unable to take another step.

Pain like I'd never felt before came in waves. I curled into a ball, trying to make myself small, wishing I could disappear entirely.

You took my hand in yours and gave it a tight squeeze. "It's okay, Sky. You're gonna be okay."

"No," I sobbed. "I'm dying. I am, I know I am, Piper."

You peeled my eyes open and then lowered yourself to the ground so that your nose was pressed against mine. "You're not dying. You're getting stronger. You're growing armor. And it hurts."

"I don't know what that means."

"Remember the dirt from the reformatory, Sky? Remember the plan? Well, today's the day."

"You put it in the food." I felt stupid for not guessing it sooner.

"Just a tiny bit. Next time it'll be more."

"Next time." I moaned the words and rolled away from you, hating you for doing this to me. Hating you for wanting to do it again. "Nooo."

Undeterred, you finger-combed my hair away from my face and then rubbed your hand against my back. "Do you want to know when I first got the idea? It was in English class. We read this poem. It's pretty long, but this is the good part."

"I'm gonna be sick," I moaned.

"Try not to throw up. The longer you can hold it in, the better it will be next time."

I cried then for real. Hot, angry tears of pain and anger and frustration. I cried, knowing that I would have to do this again. And as I cried, you recited the poem:

> *"There was a king reigned in the East:*
> *There, when kings will sit to feast,*

They get their fill before they think
With poisoned meat and poisoned drink.
He gathered all the springs to birth
From the many-venomed earth;
First a little, thence to more,
He sampled all her killing store;
And easy, smiling, seasoned sound,
Sate the king when healths went round.
They put arsenic in his meat
And stared aghast to watch him eat;
They poured strychnine in his cup
And shook to see him drink it up:
They shook, they stared as white's their shirt:
Them it was their poison hurt.
—I tell the tale that I heard told.
Mithridates, he died old."

Every time after that, when we had our feasts of dirt, you would recite that same poem for me. And when I told you that wasn't enough, you added a patient explanation of the plan. We were taking the reformatory poison now in small, controlled doses to build a resistance to it in case we ended up there later. The more people who had this immunity, the easier it would become to fight the reformatory from the inside.

I hated the explanation. I hated that poem. And I hated you. Every single time.

But I still went along with it. Resentful as hell but still a good little soldier.

Eventually I asked why you weren't getting sick too. You said it must affect everyone differently. But when we started sneaking the dirt into the school cafeteria food, everyone who ate it got sick. Everyone. Every time. But not you. Not once. It was like the reformatory dirt didn't affect you at all. But that couldn't be right.

Could it, Piper?

TWELVE

AS FOOTE AND I LEAVE THE REFORMATORY, PUSHING
the bent bicycle between us, I cast one look back at the main
building. For a second I see a face at the second-floor window. It
is Piper, staring out at me, wondering why I am walking away.

But then I blink, and she is gone.

I try to imagine her inside. I try to imagine one of the guards
manhandling her. I can't. She would kill them. Like Ozzy. Poor
Ozzy if he messed with Piper, thinking she was defenseless.

Suddenly I can hear Ozzy saying to me, "My mom says I was
a good boy until I went to work at the reformatory. She says she
would rather have starved than had me work there."

We were standing on the bleachers. I remember it suddenly. I
am lying on the bleachers with time fading in and out. Ozzy sits
a row above me. One of the stadium lights behind his head gives

him a halo. He looks so sad and lost. I try to tell him it's okay, but my tongue won't work.

"Course we wouldn't have starved. Just lived on charity like we always had. But if I worked at the reformatory, we could have a nice house with one of them big TVs. Mom said it wasn't worth it, 'specially since you only can get one station on it anyway. Maybe she was right. From the first day, it felt bad being there. And then later, when it started feeling good, it still felt bad. I wanna be good. I wanna stop telling you Piper's in there somewhere, 'cause she's not. Not really anyway. Not like you want her to be. I got into that locked room, Sky. It wasn't locked 'cause they were hiding Piper away. The roof had caved in. It was just a safety thing. Safety. 'Cause we wouldn't want the inmates to suffer, right?" Ozzy laughed bitterly and then abruptly stopped. "I tried to kiss Piper. I'd been looking for her for so long, and then there she was. Different but the same too. She pushed me away and I got mad. I told her, 'In here *I'm* the one who's in charge.' Then I kissed her again. I know that's a bad thing to do, but some of the guys there do worse. They cop feels and close doors and tell me to keep watch in case someone comes, but no one ever comes. No one who cares or would do anything to stop it anyway. But I never did that except once or twice. Don't look at me like that, Sky. I didn't ever do it again after that second time 'cause the girl started crying. Just these silent tears falling the whole time. The only thing I ever did after that was try to kiss Piper, but that—"

Somehow I found the strength to reach out and touch Ozzy's cheek. It was wet with tears. But my touch wasn't enough to release him. He had already been damned. As my hand fell away, he stood and climbed the bleachers until he was at the top. He was black against the bright lights. Then he jumped, and for a split second the air held him and it seemed like he could fly away and find a better place where he could be a better man. Of course, that didn't happen. I never heard him hit the ground though. Instead, I closed my eyes and made both of us disappear.

"So you want to maybe explain a few things to a newcomer?" Foote asks me.

I stare at him stupidly, still seeing Ozzy. "What?"

"I'm feeling a little lost here. I thought maybe you'd want to take pity on me and break things down."

"Okay," I say, and nod. Then I take a deep breath and let it all out. "I think Piper killed Ozzy. He kissed her, and she shouldn't have any powers in the reformatory, but Piper's never been like everyone else. I think she told him to jump." I don't mention to Foote that I can't figure out why Ozzy didn't jump earlier, why he waited until that moment when I was beside him. I leave that behind and move on to the next puzzle piece. "And I think Piper somehow made Jonathan's sister, LuAnn, believe she's Piper. And I think Piper is behind what happened in the yard today. I think she's planning it all. I think she's going to destroy the reformatory."

Foote stares at me with wide eyes. "Is that . . . is that even possible?"

"No, not really, but . . ." I hesitate. Wanting to trust Foote. No, needing to trust Foote. There is something about him and the way he looks at me with his true blue eyes that makes me not care if he's just another devil with a pretty face. It must be the way that Piper felt about Elton. But even knowing how that turned out for her, I can't help but want to tell Foote. To take a chance and let him see Piper's brilliance and bravery. And maybe I want him to see a bit of that in me too.

"Seven years ago Piper and I began collecting the dirt from the reformatory and sprinkling it into our food. At first it made me and a bunch of other kids really sick, but then we built up a tolerance to it. The plan was that when we ended up in the reformatory, we wouldn't be victims; it wouldn't suck us dry. Instead, we would be strong and turn the tables on them, and then . . ."

"And then what?" Foote prompts me.

I smile stupidly, feeling like the world's biggest idiot. "Then we destroy the reformatory. Don't ask me how. I don't know. I just remembered that little bit a few minutes ago, but the rest of it . . ." My throat closes. "I forget."

One of Foote's oversized hands comes toward my face and gently wipes a smudge of dirt away. I grab hold of the hand and then am stuck, uncertain what to do next, only knowing that I want Foote to touch me again.

I wonder what it would be like to kiss someone—not like I did with Ozzy, using my body for barter the way Piper had shown me. And not like I did with Elton, feeding off something that had never belonged to me—never been meant for me. But a kiss simply because I like a boy and he makes my whole body feel tense and waiting and excited and maybe even a tiny bit happy underneath all the layers of sadness and anger.

Again, I can't help but think of Piper and Elton. She loved him. He loved her. It was a secret their bodies chanted when they were in the same room. It always amazed me that nobody else could hear it. But Elton never really trusted her. Trusted their love. He always wondered if she was in his head, making him feel that way.

And even as all these thoughts pinball their way around my skull, Foote and I are drifting toward each other in slow motion. And I understand why Elton didn't trust this. It feels like being in the midst of a spell. A wonderful spell. Something too good to be true. Still, I don't fight it when my eyelids grow heavy and fall. Then, at last, his lips are on mine and we are kissing.

And it is . . . electric. Like sticking your finger into a light socket, which is something I did as a kid. The thing I remember most about it isn't the pain but the surprise. How could something just sitting there in the open have the ability to zap and possibly even kill you?

I pull away, stumbling backward, wiping my mouth with the back of my hand. It doesn't help. My lips still tingle. I want to be zapped again.

"I'm sorry," Foote says, clutching the bike still between us, his knuckles white.

"What's your power?" I ask, my voice shaking. "You're a newcomer; you shouldn't have one, but you do. Maybe you had it before you even came here."

Foote stares at me, his face draining of color.

"Are you making me like you? Are you making me feel this way?" I screech the words, feeling like a crazy person and not caring.

"No!" He looks appalled. "No. God no. Why would you think that?"

The fight suddenly goes out of me. I stare at my feet, ashamed.

Embarrassed. Finally, I force myself to look Foote in the eye and explain.

"My father had the ability to make anyone love or hate him. He made everyone love him. Everyone except me. He touched people's hearts. Piper and I mess with their heads. Growing up, I never knew what anyone truly thought or felt or believed. Myself included. There was always this doubt."

I watch as Foote's face changes from being hard and angry to confused and full of pity. And then I look away, focusing on the bike. I grab hold of the handlebars, pulling it from Foote.

"I'll take it from here," I tell Foote, already pushing the bike. "I think I need some time alone."

"Okay."

I hear Foote's voice behind me, but only barely because my feet are pounding against the ground, and I let gravity propel me down the hill.

I don't go home right away. Instead, I walk back to the water and watch the waves until they swallow the sun.

When I finally head home, I expect the house to be dark and quiet. Instead, Wills and Mom are both sitting in the main room. They jump to their feet when I walk in.

"Skylar, thank goodness," Mom says.

It is like the night when we found out Dad was dead. Mom had waited up for me then too.

"What happened?" I ask, knowing it can be nothing good.

Mom's hands twist together and she cracks her knuckles. "Well—"

Wills breaks in. "Piper is home. She came this afternoon. We played in the backyard."

I stare at Mom, waiting for her to shush Wills, to say he's confused. Instead she just shrugs. "She said she escaped. She said you would understand. We were waiting for you to come home, but she was so tired. I took her to Piper's room. She got into bed and fell asleep right away."

"It can't be," I say, even as my heart pounds like crazy and everything else in me goes still, concentrating on wishing that this might possibly be true.

"Well . . ." Mom sighs. "I'm not sure. At first I didn't think so, but she seems so certain and familiar in so many ways. You should go up and see her—well, see all of them and let me know if you think one of them might be Piper. And if you do, well then, she probably is."

"One of them?" I ask.

"It's hard to explain. They came together, but they act like one person and call themselves Piper. Singular." Mom shrugs again. "It's hard to separate them in my mind. It's almost like they truly are one and the same person."

"One and the same," I whisper to myself, not quite able to believe it.

"I thought this might be what you've been waiting for." Mom smiles uncertainly as if she's given me a gift but is uncertain whether or not I like it.

I stare at her, wondering when exactly she went off the deep end. How can she not know Piper? How can there be any doubt? I don't question her, though, because the idea that Piper may be only a few feet away, that she may be home, has me running up the stairs and down the hall until I reach her door. It is closed. I hesitate, feeling sick, wanting so badly for her to be there.

Then slowly, slowly, I ease the door open. The room is dark, but a wedge of light from the hall falls across the bed, illuminating the face of the girl sleeping there. A part of me is certain it will be LuAnn. But the hair across the pillow is the same dark auburn brown as Piper's. My heart leaps, and I rush forward to embrace my sister.

"Piper!" I cry.

The girl wakes up and rolls toward me, her eyes wide and scared and blank. She whimpers.

This is not Piper. This is not even a good imitation.

"Sky?" she asks in a high and whiny voice that is nothing like Piper's slightly husky one.

And then three other girls pop up from where they've been camped out on the floor. "Pollywog!" They greet me with bright smiles.

The one in the middle is LuAnn, but the others I can't immediately place.

"No," I respond shortly, and then I turn and walk out of the room, slamming the door behind me.

FLASHDANCE . . . WHAT A FEELING

Eight Years Ago

PIPER, WE TALK ABOUT ALL THE FOURTH YEARS AND the smaller years in between except for one. We never talk about eight years ago. The year of the lightning.

At the time it seemed like just another fourth year. Another close call. But now it seems like something else. It seems like the lightning left a dark line in our lives. Everything before that line was our lives as I'd always known them. After the lightning was when everything started to change. You changed. I couldn't see it then, but now it's so clear. After that day, you started trying to outrun the train and began coming up with all the crazy plans. Everything I loved about you was more intense. And the things I hated were that way too.

So, the year of the lightning. That's what everyone calls it even though it wasn't really lightning. It didn't come from the sky. There was no thunder or zigzag flash cutting through dark clouds.

Do you remember, Piper, when we first saw it? We were walking home from school and suddenly we saw these balls of light dancing in the trees.

"Fairies!" I said, reaching my arms out toward them.

You pulled me back. "Don't be stupid," you said.

I barely even heard you, because the fairies were laughing and singing, inviting me to come and play. I jerked away from you, and the handful of my jacket slipped easily from your grasp. You must not have been holding on that tightly; you must have thought that your harsh words would be enough to check me. And on any other day they would've—but not this one. Fourth-year magic was even more powerful than you.

As I ran toward them, the balls of light bounced away. Not far—just enough to keep out of my reach, just enough to keep me chasing them. You tackled me at some point. And we rolled in the dirt, scuffling, as the golden balls danced above our heads. Finally, you were on top of me, pinning my arms to keep me from hitting you.

"Look at those stupid things. Just look at them," you demanded. "Can't you see they're . . ."

Your face changed then, from anger to wonder. Releasing my hands, you grinned down at me. "Oh, Sky. They're fairies."

Then we were both chasing after them. Faster and stronger and getting that much closer to finally catching them because we were together.

The balls of light took us back toward school to the marsh

that had finally been drained and filled after Eddie Sit's giant mosquitoes had sprung from there the year before. There was talk of it being made into a football field, but in the meantime, a giant fence surrounded it. LuAnn was in the middle of the field, and the balls of light surrounded her. More of the balls kept arriving from every direction. And all of them were followed by two or three young people like us.

You swung yourself up and over the fence in one graceful move. I can still see that when I close my eyes. Even while enthralled by the fairies, I stopped for a moment and stared at you, amazed. The fairies raced ahead with you, and I scrambled over the fence, not wanting to be left behind. As I tried to fling myself over, not caring if I fell into the muck on the other side, my jacket zipper caught on the fence, holding me there.

"Piper, help!" I cried. "Wait for me!"

You didn't turn. I don't think you heard me. The ball of light was so close to you then, and you lunged forward and finally grabbed it.

It exploded in your arms, sending streaks of blue light that branched out toward all the other balls of light, exploding them one after another. Then there was a final blast of light and I blinked and the world went black.

Actually, I had only passed out. Before I did, though, there was one thing that I saw. Later I told myself it was just my imagination. Now I wonder.

When that ball of light exploded, you disappeared, Piper. Like it had swallowed you whole.

But when I woke up, you were there again. Not a scratch on

you. Everyone else who was as close as you died. But you didn't.

Piper, if you disappeared—where did you go? And how did you come back?

Were those balls of light truly fairies? Did they make you one of their own? Is that what changed you, Piper?

I wish I'd asked before. I wish I hadn't been too afraid of your answer.

THIRTEEN

I CAN'T SLEEP WITH THAT GAGGLE OF IMPOSTORS down the hall. I told Mom we should throw them out, but she convinced me to wait until morning.

"They all look so frail, like something's been whittling away at them. I think they've all come from the reformatory," she said.

If they've come from the reformatory, then I feel certain Piper must have sent them. But why send them with her name? Why not come herself? These are questions I have no answer for.

As soon as darkness begins to soften from black to blue with the promise of the sun's rising, I climb out of bed and throw some clothes on. In bare feet, I slip down the hall. I don't make it very far. A huddled figure leans against Piper's closed door. At first I think it is one of the girls pretending to be her, but when a floorboard creaks beneath my feet, the person who looks up at me is my own mother.

She puts a finger to her lips, indicating I should stay quiet, and then climbs to her feet and leads me downstairs and into the kitchen. Sitting at the table, I watch as she puts the kettle on and her hands tremble from the weight. Sun begins to peek through the window, lighting her up, and with it, I see her in a way I haven't in a long time. She looks tired and too thin. The dark hair that usually curls around her shoulders has threads of silver streaking through it. I remember then that even though Dad was a cheating bastard, she was devastated when he died. She cried for weeks. Maybe months. I stayed away. Let the promise of soon-to-be baby Wills comfort her.

Time does not easily age people in this town, but grief does. I know this, but I hadn't realized how deeply it had left its mark on my mom.

Mom steps out of the telling ray of sunlight and sits in the chair opposite mine. "So not one of them is Piper?" She sounds disappointed. But she looks at me, in this reproachful way, as if disappointed that I won't accept those girls as Piper replacements.

Last night I'd wanted to scream at her for letting me hope— for even a few short minutes—that Piper had returned. Now, though, I kind of get it. She wanted it to be Piper as much as I did. She wanted it so badly she was willing to believe a lie.

"You know they're not," I say.

"I suppose I did," Mom answers. "But I thought maybe she'd changed or somehow transformed to survive."

I'd had a similar thought at first, but I don't tell Mom this. Instead, I repeat, "They're not Piper."

Mom sighs one of her legendary sighs at the same time the kettle begins to howl. She gets up and pours water into two cups. "Cocoa or tea?"

"Cocoa," I answer.

"Good choice." Mom pulls two cocoa packets from the cupboard and empties them into the mugs. Sticking a spoon into each, she sets one in front of me. "Make sure to stir it up real good."

Our spoons clink as we chase little clumps of cocoa round our mugs. "Piper and I did this once," Mom says. "You were sick. Do you remember when almost the whole school came down with that strange stomach bug? There was total panic. All these children who had never before had so much as the sniffles were suddenly so sick they couldn't get out of bed. They all—you included—thought they were dying. But for the parents, much to our own shame, we weren't just worried about our sick children. We were worried about ourselves. So many of us had come here to avoid sickness, we knew what it truly was to be at death's door and we didn't want to be there again. We worried that whatever it was that kept us healthy wasn't working anymore. Between taking care of you and becoming a hypochondriac, I couldn't sleep. I came down here to put the kettle on, and Piper joined me. She said she couldn't sleep either.

"Then she sat there, exactly where you're sitting right now, and gave me one of those quintessentially Piper-type looks—like she could see straight through me. And she said, 'Don't worry. Everyone will be fine soon, and everything will go back to normal.' She sounded so certain. I believed her. I guess if I was a better mother, I would've asked how she knew. I didn't, though, because I had long ago given you two to each other, and you girls had in turn both come to see me as the nice lady you waved to on your way out the door."

I stand and push my untouched cup of cocoa across the table. "Give this to Wills. I've gotta go."

"He probably won't be up for a while. He's a bit under the weather, I'm afraid."

"What?" I stop in my tracks. I'd be less shocked to hear that Wills had flown out of his bedroom window. "What do you mean 'under the weather'?"

"It's just a cold, Sky. Nothing to worry about." Mom sounds calm, but I can hear the worry underneath it.

"People don't get colds here."

Mom shrugs. "That's what I'm trying to tell you. Things are changing. Wills isn't the first person to get a cold. From what I hear, it's been going around the last two weeks or so. I also heard that one of the old-timers is fighting a pretty nasty cough. They're afraid it might turn into pneumonia."

I want to deny it again. I want to tell her that things don't change here. But, of course, they do. They already have. People are getting sick. The Salt Spring is shrinking. The reformatory is crumbling. The inmates are fighting back. I have that same shaky feeling I had at the reformatory yesterday with Foote. It suddenly seems possible that things have already gone too far, that there will be no going back. Perhaps Gardnerville could have withstood Piper's and my tampering with the dirt, or Elton's pills helping everyone suppress their worst impulses. But the two of them together seem almost certainly catastrophic.

Maybe Piper has already figured out a way to deal with that. Maybe that's why LuAnn talked about an uprising instead of destroying the reformatory. Maybe Piper's plan has evolved.

"Really, Sky, don't look so worried. Wills is going to be fine."

"Yeah." I nod, feeling guilty that the worried expression Mom saw was for Piper instead of Wills.

"If anything, you should worry about me, having to take care of such a terrible patient."

As she smiles at me, I realize again how tired Mom looks. And scared. She came here because she was sick and dying. Gardnerville saved her. But what if Gardnerville can't save people anymore? Would Mom get sick again and even possibly . . . die?

I shake the thought away. I can only handle so many problems right now, and the one I've chosen to focus on is Piper. After I get her home, she can help me figure everything else out.

Still, instead of leaving the house with only my usual wave in Mom's general direction, I go to where she is still sitting at the kitchen table and give her a quick peck on the cheek before darting toward the door.

"Sky," Mom calls, with a hitch in her voice that breaks that short bit of my name into two. I turn back and see her hand held against her cheek as if I'd slapped her. It occurs to me then that I can't remember the last time I kissed her. I feel guilty about that for a minute, until I remind myself of all the times I walked into a room and she didn't see me because she only had eyes for Dad or Wills. Maybe she's thinking the same thing, because instead of saying her usual "See you later" or "Be safe," she simply whispers, "I'm sorry."

The automatic response of "It's okay" is on my tongue, but it doesn't get any further than that before I swallow it down. Because it's not okay.

I take off without a plan of what to do or where to go. I just know that I need to do something. Now. Or yesterday would be even better, because it suddenly feels like time is running out. I console myself with the fact that I can still clearly recall yesterday. It's an incredibly small victory, but I'll take it.

Eventually, I slow down and collect myself. A part of me wishes I could rewind and go to three days ago when there was nothing in my head except getting a fresh batch of forget-me-nots from Jonathan. It's not a particularly helpful desire right now, but it does give me a direction. I decide to head toward school. Maybe someone there will know something about the girls upstairs calling themselves Piper. I'm pretty sure I won't learn anything, but it is better than my other option, which is to try the reformatory again.

As I walk past the press box, it's impossible not to look up and wonder who is working it today and if there are any forget-me-nots still for sale. Probably not. And even if there were, I don't want them. Correction. I can't want them.

But I do.

Somehow I keep putting one foot in front of the other until the press box and pills are behind me, and the temptation to head up there has passed. Pivoting sharply, I head into the school.

I stand in the middle of the empty hallway for a few moments, lost and uncertain, knowing I'm just wasting time. The real answers are behind a locked door at the top of the hill; it's not like I can just go into the library and find a book with the names of those girls pretending to be Piper.

Oh.

As I take off down the hall toward the library, I wonder if I've always been this dumb, or if I can blame it on the forget-me-nots. Either way, the answer is depressing.

The library is empty. Not exactly a surprise in the middle of August.

All the yearbooks, going back fifty years at least, are lined up on a shelf near the librarian's desk, and I pull out the ones from the last four years and drop them on the closest table. I start looking for the girl sleeping in Piper's bed first. It isn't until I open the last yearbook—the one from four years ago—that I find her. She is on the first page. The first several pages are reserved for those who don't make it to graduation. Technically it's called the remembrance page, but everyone refers to it as the graveyard.

Her name is Lindsay Grove. She was fifteen years old and had just gotten her braces off. According to the yearbook, she perished on Piper's May Day. Someone has used a silver gel pen to scribble, *I love you, Lindsay. I always will.*

Turning the pages, I scan the rest of the pictures in the graveyard, looking for the other girls in Piper's room. Each person gets their own page. All of them have messages scribbled on them. Some just say, *Miss You*; others offer specific memories of the person—things that would have been written in that person's yearbook if they were still alive. None of the other girls are in the graveyard, and it's a weird relief to know there is only one supposedly dead girl pretending to be my sister.

Giving up on finding the other girls, whose faces I can only half remember at this point anyway, I flip to the student portraits that are taken at the beginning of the year, searching for Piper. She's not there. I turn the pages more frantically, not caring if they get torn. Finally I find the class picture they take in the gym with everyone stacked together on the risers. There are only around seventy kids, but I have to search for a moment, running my finger across the smiling faces until it lands on Piper. She is in the last row, arms crossed against her chest. There is something about the way she stands among her classmates, with them yet isolated. She is the only person who isn't looking at either the camera or a friend; instead her gaze is fixed somewhere to her left, far beyond what the camera captures.

I grab more yearbooks, going further back, trying to find more pictures of Piper. Now I remember how many times over the years she just happened to miss school on picture day. Looking at the yearbooks, it's almost like Piper never even existed. They didn't even include her name with a box that said "not pictured" like they did for the other kids who must have also missed picture day. It was like they were already punishing her for something she hadn't done yet.

I tear the page with Piper's class picture from the book and with a swipe of my arm send the yearbooks flying to the floor. It doesn't help. Clenching the stiff paper so tight that its edges bite into my skin, I flee the library.

Unmoored, I drift down empty hallways until I find myself standing in front of what was once Piper's locker. The middle school had an earlier dismissal, and this is the spot where I used to wait for her. Toward the end, when she was so wrapped up in Elton, I would stand here for hours after the high school had emptied out, waiting and waiting, but Piper would never come. I'd stomp home and glare in her direction, waiting for a guilty apology that hadn't even occurred to her. She'd forgotten me so completely that I could feel myself begin to disappear—as if I didn't exist without her.

"Well." A crisp voice interrupts my reverie. "Fancy meeting you here."

GG stands in the middle of the hallway, looking ready for battle.

I throw my hands up in mock surrender. "You found me."

"Unintentionally, I assure you. Quite frankly, it was my hope to avoid you for at least the next week, or however long it took me to overcome the urge to slap your face."

"Well, don't let me keep you." Turning on my heel, I march in the opposite direction.

Of course, GG follows me. "As it happens, your mother called me this morning. She was all in a tizzy, saying she was afraid you were going to do something stupid. I agreed there was a good possibility of that, but wondered what exactly made this different from any other day."

"Low blow."

"Oh, darling, if only that was the worst thing I could say about you. Your mother has enough to worry about without wondering if you're going to crave destruction on a grand scale the same way Piper did four years ago."

I stop and spin again to face her. "What is your problem? Do you think I need a fucking lecture right now?"

"No, I don't. But I've been storing this up for four years, waiting for a good time, and now that you have finally left your purple haze behind, I am seizing the moment." GG takes a deep breath and then abruptly switches topics. "We Gardners are a peculiar lot. My own mother used to say we were all cursed. I called her a superstitious old lady and told her our differences meant we were favored, not damned. I was so young then—don't look at me like it's so difficult to imagine, Skylar. I was indeed young once and I was much better at it than you. You know nothing and want to know even less. I, on the other hand, was full of conviction and contempt for everyone who wasn't me." GG stops mid-harangue, an odd smile on her face. "Funny, I'd forgotten that."

"Ha," I can't resist interjecting.

"Yes, Sky, you are not the only one who prefers to dispose of inconvenient memories. Try not to look so surprised, dear; it makes me wonder if there's anything left in your head at all. Anyway, it was Piper's poem—the one about things falling apart—that brought it back to me."

I know the line she means. It's the same one she recited at my retreating back the other day. Now it comes tumbling from my mouth before I can stop it. "'The best lack all conviction, while the worst / Are full of passionate intensity.'"

GG gives a low whistle of admiration. "My, my, my. Amazing, isn't it, the things that stick in your head, refusing to go away?"

I don't respond, because for a moment I am struck dumb with admiration for GG, stooped but strong. It's a nice change from my usual annoyance. But it's a little disorientating as well, to go from seeing her as someone standing in my way to someone who can show me the way.

"What should I do now?" I ask, certain she will have an opinion and for once actually wanting to hear it.

Instead of answering, GG turns and begins to stride down the hallway. "Well, come on," she calls back impatiently. I run to catch up and feel the old annoyance return. Of course, GG can't just give me a straight answer. It's going to be a whole thing.

My suspicions are confirmed as GG begins climbing up the stairs leading to the science labs.

"Sometimes," she explains as we walk, "the answer is not simple. As much as we both wish it was otherwise, and this is one of those times."

"And what do the labs have to do with that answer?"

"Oh, nothing," GG replies. "I just wanted to pop in and say hello to the quints while I'm here. They are my great-grandchildren as well, after all."

"I always wondered," I murmur in response.

GG snorts impatiently. "You could've just asked. It was never a big secret, and once they started producing all those pills, there was no doubt that they could be anything other than Gardners."

"What are you talking about?" I demand, as we reach the top of the stairs.

"Come now, Sky. Did you honestly believe those children were picking bouquets of forget-me-nots out of the fields and synthesizing them into your beloved purple pills?"

I shrug. "I hadn't really thought about it."

"Clearly."

"So, it's not the flowers then?"

"Mostly no."

"It's them."

"Mostly yes," GG confirms. "It's them."

I am braced for some big shock, but this makes too much sense to be a surprise. "Since you obviously disapprove of the pills, why don't you just tell them to stop?"

"Tell them." GG laughs with a distinct lack of amusement. Then she sweeps down the hall and into the science lab where the quints hold court.

When I walk into the lab, I find all five of them lined up, each one bent over a book. They don't look up when I enter, which is fine by me because it gives me a chance to study them.

They are completely identical in all ways, and I find myself searching for some small feature to distinguish one from the next. It is an impossible task. They are not just tiny but thin and reedy. Knobby knees hang out of baggy shorts, and their little feet barely touch the floor. They share the same white-blond hair styled in the same short cut, even though three out of five of them are girls. The style makes them look like evil little pixies.

Almost no one knows their individual names. No point, really, when you can't tell them apart. Most people call them the quints. Elton calls them his lab boys. Piper and I always called them the creeplings.

"Hello, dears," GG chirps in a rather sweet voice that I can't remember having ever heard before.

Several long moments pass until finally the one on the end

holds up a finger, signaling for us to wait.

"Seriously?" I mutter. GG shoots me a look that seems like it should be aimed at the quints.

As if reading my mind, GG says softly, "You are a spoiled idiot. They are temperamental geniuses."

It stings, but a moment later the hurt is allayed when GG presses her hand to my wrist and with it sends a secret that spreads through me like a healing balm. Having secrets literally handed to me is the only way I have gotten anything out of GG since I was three years old. That's when the whole family figured out what I could do. GG was the first one to take me aside. Kneeling down so that we were eye to eye, she softly explained that if I ever looked inside her head, she would cut my ears off, candy them, and make me eat them for dessert. All these years later, I have never found the guts to call her bluff. Or to eat her candied orange peels.

At any rate, this is the big secret: the quints have been making her special pills, called black-eyed Susans, that have saved her from complete blindness. She owes the quints a debt. And she pities them. But she does not love them.

I pull away from GG, unsure what to say about what she's just shown me, and look up to see that the quints have closed their books and are now watching us. It's disconcerting to have all of their eyes and attention on me. Then, even worse, they smile in a way that makes them look almost feral.

"Hello, Great-Grandmother and Half Sister." They speak in unison, in a strange monotone devoid of feeling.

"Hey, what's up?" I say.

As one, they look up to the ceiling and then back at me. "Nothing," they reply.

I laugh, but no one else does. They watch me expectantly, as if waiting for me to say something else. "I'm a big fan of the forget-me-nots," I tell them. "So good job on those."

I'm not sure what response I was expecting, but the huge smiles that overtake their tiny faces aren't it. "Do you find clarity in them?" they ask, for the first time looking interested in what I have to say.

"Um, well, I guess," I reply, uncertain.

They nod as if this answer confirms something. "They're meant to clear the mind of clutter, to allow it to focus in on what is truly important so that one forgets it not." They chuckle—the same tinkling titter—as one.

"I don't know if that's quite how it's worked for me."

Their brows furrow. "You don't disappear into darkness?"

"No, I do, I guess."

"And you don't reemerge from that same darkness, as weak as one reborn?"

"Ye-ah. That's about right."

"Ahhh." Their expressions clear and become pleased. "The clarity is there. At the center of the experience. The pill works."

The conversation is apparently over as they turn their attention back to GG, who has been avidly watching our exchange. I should be relieved to be out of the spotlight, but instead I step forward with a follow-up question while my heart pounds with the possibility that everything I've forgotten can be found again by listening to those tapes on Piper's dresser.

"Um, about that center—or, well, the notters call it the sweet spot—but anyway, would it be possible to record something, like on a tape, while in the middle of the darkness, and then not remember it later?"

They stare at me silently, and I think they're not going to answer when finally they nod as if coming to a decision. "Possible and probable. Yes. Forget-me-nots. The name was deliberately chosen."

"But I did forget." I can't help but nitpick. "Over and over again. It's just in the past few months that I started making these recordings, and I couldn't even remember doing it afterward."

They blink three times before responding, with more than a hint of condescension, "That is illogical. You cannot forget over and over again, without having first remembered over and over again. Therefore, the pills worked as intended."

"Wait a minute—" I start to say, but they cut me off, clapping their little hands, officially dismissing me. It's obvious they aren't willing to accept any criticism of their precious pills. Never mind that their carefully engineered "moment of clarity" is bookended on either side by being a drooling idiot.

"Your pills are by the door," they announce to GG in their freaky way.

"Wonderful. As always, I can't thank you enough," GG quickly replies.

They blink in unison but say nothing.

"And also, I wanted to say hello and see how you all are doing," GG adds. The quints remain unmoved, and GG, looking uncomfortable, clears her throat. If I weren't so creeped out myself, it would be funny. "So hello," she says at last.

"Hello," they respond.

"Would you mind if Skylar and I went into the lab next door for a chat?"

As one, they shrug and then flip their books open and begin to read once more.

GG exits, and this time I am right behind her without any prompting necessary.

HOPELESSLY DEVOTED TO YOU

Four Years Ago

IT'S FUNNY, BUT AS MUCH AS I THINK ABOUT THAT May Day four years ago, I spend almost as much time fixating on the night before. By the time the parade began, it felt as unstoppable as the train roaring across the trestle bridge. Too much steam had built up, and you could either let it out or let it explode.

I understand that.

That's why the night before bothers me. It feels like a moment when our whole lives might have swung in another direction. When if I had only been able to find the right words, disaster might have been averted.

Is that true, Piper? Was there something I could have said? Would it have fixed anything? Or were you already set on your course?

I guess it's silly to think I would've been able to change your mind once it was set. Maybe I'm not even really wishing that I had changed things. Maybe I'm just wishing that I'd at least tried. When you burst into my room with the news that Angie Walters was pregnant with Elton's baby, I could've tried to calm you down. I could've said, "Who cares about Elton—he's just a newcomer. A nobody." Instead I gasped like the injury was my own. In some ways it was. I felt insulted and outraged all the way down to my toes at the idea of Elton choosing someone else over you.

"It's not true," I'd said.

"He told me," you answered. "He told me himself."

I didn't say anything then because you started to cry. Not just a few tears, but great, heaving sobs that shook you off your feet, until you were on the floor, pounding it with your fists. It was a temper tantrum. A messy, dirty, undignified fit. And it went on and on.

It scared me. To see you broken like that. To know you could be broken. All the fourth-year horrors, they'd barely even fazed you, but this . . .

That's when I blurted it out.

"Piper, it's a fourth year."

I'd meant it as a warning, I think. Maybe as a distraction too. We both knew that every fourth-year disaster was the result of someone letting their emotions carry them away. But it wasn't meant as a call to action. That couldn't have been what I wanted to happen.

You looked up at me. Your eyelashes were wet with tears and they fluttered, like a butterfly working its way out of a cocoon.

You stared at me with an intensity that literally took my breath away.

"Yes." That's what you said.

"Piper." I drew the syllables of your name out slowly, part scolding, part warning. Like I was already trying to talk you off a ledge.

"This is my year."

"No."

"I can see it," you said, and you were smiling in this distant way, like you were already in the next day. Like it had already happened.

"Piper." Again I said your name, trying to bring you back.

You took my hands. "You should see it. Let me show you."

And that's exactly what you did. Without saying a word, you gave me every single detail of the final piece in your grand plan.

I'm pretty sure this wasn't the ending you'd originally imagined. Over the last few years, we'd taken dirt from the reformatory and used it to poison ourselves and others. You'd befriended Ozzy so we'd have an in at the reformatory. Those things made a crazy sort of sense. The last part of the plan had always been for you and me to end up in the reformatory, but not like this. This new part of the plan didn't fit. It felt improvised and angry. Sloppy too. But I couldn't say that to you. It was our secret by then. Our plan.

I didn't protest after that. I did my part the next morning. You didn't even have to ask. I was up and waiting to walk with you to the high school. And when we got there, I stood at the front doors and took the secrets of everyone who walked past.

Anyone who had been untrue—in thought or deed—would walk in the May Day parade that night.

Why did I go along so easily at that point? What if I'd refused to give you the names? What would you have done then?

It wouldn't have stopped you. You just would have chosen your victims a little more indiscriminatingly.

Still I could've stayed out of it, not made myself an accessory, which could have landed me in the reformatory with you.

But of course, that was exactly why I did it. This wasn't going to be like when you did two weeks for the Ms. Van Nuys debacle. No, this time I was going to the reformatory with you.

Just like always, Piper. I was afraid of being left behind.

You hadn't really given me the full plan, though, Piper. You left out the part about the trestle bridge and the train. You left out the part where this wasn't simply revenge or justice—it was suicide.

FOURTEEN

IT IS A RELIEF TO ESCAPE FROM THE QUINTS' LAB, BUT the feeling is short-lived because a moment later the ground rumbles beneath our feet and the whole building trembles around us. GG stumbles and I quickly grab for her, pulling her close while we wait for the shaking to stop. Even after it ends, we still stand there, frozen and afraid.

"Was that a fucking earthquake?" I whisper at last.

"Things fall apart," GG answers, and then adds as an afterthought, "Watch your language."

I step away from her. "Enough with the cryptic crap. What's going on? Is this the beginning of the end?"

"The beginning of the end?" GG gives a sharp bark of laughter. "That already happened when you and Piper put the dirt from the reformatory into food. The reformatory needs to feed, but you made the food tougher to eat. And at the same time Elton found a way to make teenagers stop losing their minds. That's great for our stress levels, at least as long as we keep pretending the pressure isn't constantly building, demanding an explosion. A delicate balance is what's kept Gardnerville running these many years. It couldn't last forever. I always knew that, but I'd never guessed it could all go wrong so quickly. Skylar, believe me when I tell you this: It's not the beginning of the end. It's the end of the end."

"What does that mean?" I demand. "Why can't you just explain things clearly?"

"I'll do you one better. I'll show you where it started." GG lunges at me, her fingers outstretched and then tangled in my hair and pressing against my skull.

I fall to my knees, clutching my head. The secrets sting me, an endless swarm of bees. Until finally they die down and then disappear, leaving me to pull the stingers from my skin.

My stomach rumbles, warning me I'm about to heave. I hold it in. Cold sweat drips from my forehead as I uncurl my body and force myself to my feet. My eyes meet GG's.

I thought we'd come to an understanding, reached some sort of détente where we both realized we were on the same side.

I was wrong.

"Lachman Gardner," I croak. "The founder of Gardnerville was also . . ." I can't say it. It's too absurd.

"Your father," GG finishes for me.

"Great," I say, and then I lean forward and puke all over her shoes.

After that GG disappears, muttering something about people with weak stomachs. She tells me to stay where I am, so as soon as she's out of sight I push myself to my feet. Between the earthquake and the regurgitation, I'm a little weak-kneed. Stumbling back into the quints' lab, I head toward the open windows at the far end of the room. The quints, meanwhile, take one look at me and immediately stand and exit the room in single file.

"You're not going to say good-bye?" I somehow find the strength to yell after them.

Big surprise, they don't respond.

They didn't even pack up their things. Books and beakers and piles of pills cover the tables. Only a few short days ago I would've filled my pockets with the purple ones and fled. It's tempting. To leave the puzzles and questions behind.

I am torn between an inescapable need to know and a wish to be left blissfully ignorant. It's similar to the way I view horror movies—peeking between my fingers, wanting to watch, but so terribly afraid of what I will see.

Leaning out the window, I feel the cold air of the science labs press against my back as it flees the room and gives way to the sticky wave of humidity. The fresh air clears my head a bit, enough to sort through the mix of information GG filled me with and try to put it into chronological order.

Lachman was a small-time con man who spent his whole life searching for something. He didn't know what that something was; he just figured he'd know it when he saw it. And when he found Gardnerville—he did.

Of course, it wasn't Gardnerville then. Back then our town

wasn't a place so much as an idea. It had no name. Or no official one anyway. Some people called it a sanctuary, because they had arrived stumbling up from the ravine, half starved, certain they were going to die alone in the wilderness. Only those who were lost found their way here; no one ever discovered this place while they were searching for it. Those who left did so knowing they would never return.

By the time Lachman arrived, a thriving village existed. It was rustic compared to the outside world, perhaps even a bit backward, but the people who lived here were content with their home. They welcomed Lachman, like they did all the lost who came upon their village, and he in turn smiled at them in the same way a wolf brought into a flock of sheep might.

Lachman was not stupid, and when he wished, he could be very charming. He had a gift for making people love or hate him. He decided to make them love him, to become one of them, because the more he saw of this strange place, the more he began to suspect that this was what he had spent his whole life seeking.

That thing wasn't fame or money or beautiful women. It was something so much grander than those fleeting pleasures that it shamed him to realize he'd spent so many years thinking so small. That thing was eternal youth and life everlasting.

It took a week for Lachman to realize that there wasn't one person who looked older than forty, and yet every single one of them had lived in the village for at least that many years. Quite a few may have been there for hundreds of years. They didn't exactly know; they'd stopped counting long ago. After another week, Lachman understood that if he continued to live there, he could live forever too. It was that simple. One more week passed, and by then Lachman had already decided: it wasn't enough.

He wanted more than this quiet life full of simple pleasures. But he couldn't leave and go back to his old life, where he would grow older and older, always knowing what he'd left behind. Unwilling to walk away, Lachman put to use all he knew of schemes and scams and confidence games. Slowly, yet steadily, he spread discontent through the village as thick as the butter upon his bread.

He did this with no more than a word or a look directed at what he'd decided should be the target of the village's ire—the vermin. The vermin, or as they'd been called rather more simply and with considerably less disgust prior to Lachman's arrival, the rats.

Before Lachman began referring to them as vermin, the villagers had seen the rats as generous landlords. Everyone knew the rats had been there first, that in many ways this place belonged to the rats and they were incredibly generous to share it for nothing more than the promise of a bit of food left out for them at night.

After Lachman changed them from rats to vermin, the people began to see things differently. Now the rats were a nuisance. And worse: a pestilence bringing sickness and disease. This was obvious after one of the odious vermin bit Lachman, and the poor man was laid up sick for days, so weak and feverish he couldn't get out of bed.

When Lachman finally felt strong again, he announced— with the greatest reluctance—that he would have to leave. He simply could not live in such a place where vermin were given more respect than people. The people of the village, who had seen so many other outsiders leave and usually only shook their heads at such foolishness, this time shook their heads for another reason. They would not, they could not, let Lachman leave. If they had taken more time to think things over, they might have asked themselves why they cared so much about Lachman. And they might have concluded that while he had brought excitement and color to their formerly dull lives, he had also taken away the simple joys they'd once cherished. But they did not, could not, take that time, because Lachman did everything but pack his bags and demand, "It's them or me."

It was decided—by a unanimous show of hands—that the rats would be the ones to leave.

But getting rid of them proved more difficult than Lachman had anticipated. He poisoned them and watched them die, but the next day they were back again. He caged them, then drowned them, but the next day they were back again. Other men might've been discouraged, but Lachman simply saw it as an opportunity.

The simple shacks in the village were not to his taste, and he'd been working out how to introduce the idea of building something a little grander. There was a spot set up in the mountains where the villagers went when they were seeking an extra bit of peace. It overlooked the entire valley. A man who lived in a house built upon that spot would be the king of everything spread below him.

So it was that the rats were poisoned once more, but this time Lachman had their bodies crushed, mixed with clay, and made into bricks. The bricks were brought up the mountain and a wall went up. The next day more rats arrived, more rats become bricks, and another wall went up. It went this way for days and weeks, until finally no more rats were left and a grand brick building jutted from the mountainside, foreign and dreadful.

The day Lachman moved in, it began to rain. The water that fell tasted salty. Like tears. Not a single person said it, but they all thought it.

This was the first misgiving.

After all the business of killing and building, there was at last a lull, and regret quickly settled in. Second thoughts were followed by third thoughts, but it was already too late. By the time the rain stopped, the Salt Spring had formed at the base of the mountain, and Lachman had moved back down to the valley. He complained that the villagers had built his new house poorly. They would try again, he said, but this time they would build something a little closer to the new town center; it wouldn't do for the founder of Gardnerville to live so far away.

Life continued in the place now known as Gardnerville. At first nothing really seemed different. New houses and other buildings were built; that was the most obvious change. Other things, like aging, weren't noticed until someone looked down and didn't recognize their own wrinkled hands. And it was only once people realized their youth was slipping away that they also noticed there were no more newcomers. Not a single person had stumbled upon their town since Lachman had arrived. It seemed that they would die, and Gardnerville with them, but Lachman wouldn't allow that.

Yes, he now realized there had been some flaws in his

vermin-removal plan. And yes, his tinkering may have resulted in killing the very thing he'd cherished about this place. But he was not ready to admit defeat, because while the residents of Gardnerville no longer looked youthful, they were still healthy. Most importantly—they were still alive. They were no longer living forever, but most people reached at least a century before they gave in to the need for an eternal rest. Lachman decided this was enough for him, and he thought it would be more than enough to make other people want to live here too.

Lachman set the young and able-bodied to work once more, this time digging into and through the mountain, until they came out on the other side.

It took time, years and then decades, and during that interval Lachman began to see signs of his own mortality creeping up on him. Suddenly a century did not seem like enough time to live; he wanted the immortality this place had first promised. His gaze settled on the empty brick edifice built into the mountainside. For so long he'd avoided looking at it. What he saw there scared him. That building made out of the dead rats had somehow come to life. It could not speak or move, but it radiated its intentions in a way that was unmistakable. It was hungry. Angry and betrayed too. It did not respond to his charm, except as something it could feed on. Lachman recognized that insatiable hunger; it was not so different from the thing that drove him. Although he'd once run from the building, now he saw an opportunity to give it something and get something from it in return.

Lachman married a sweet young girl, and a year later she gave birth to twins, a boy and a girl. On their second birthday,

Lachman pulled them from their beds and carried them up the mountain. The children's mother was frantic; she didn't know where her family had gone. A week later, Lachman and the little girl came back down the mountain and they were not the same after that.

The little girl seemed stuck at two for years afterward, but eventually, slowly, at half the speed of other children her age, she grew older. No one knew what the girl had seen in that house on the mountainside, but it must've been terrible. It was no surprise that she grew up with the ability to make other people see things too.

As for Lachman, his charm had changed. It was no longer soft and oozing, but a weapon similar to Cupid's arrows—he had access to all hearts and he pierced every single one. People now loved him without knowing why. They loved him without reason and without the will to do otherwise. Perhaps if they did not love him they might've wondered how it was he no longer seemed to age. Or they might have asked what exactly had happened to his son. Lachman would only say the boy was gone.

His wife died soon thereafter, some said of grief, although Lachman saw it as a betrayal, that her love for him wasn't enough to sustain her. By the time he married again, the tunnel through the mountain was complete and the trains were running into town, and his daughter from his first marriage now looked older than him and had begun to refer to herself as his grandmother.

Fourth years were also an accepted part of life. The first one occurred a few years after Lachman's son was lost. It wasn't called a fourth year then, of course. That came later, after a pattern emerged. Then it was just called madness when a young boy, upset about something so unimportant that years later even he couldn't remember what it had been, started screaming. Those closest to him lost their lives. Others, at a farther distance, became completely deaf.

The town was shocked. Lachman was relieved. The building needed to be fed again, and now he had a volunteer. Lachman decreed that the building set into the mountainside would become a reformatory for young troubled souls like the poor screaming boy. They would be sent there until it was deemed safe for them to become part of society again.

That was how Gardnerville became the place we know today.

Lachman Gardner—my father—created it.

I am suddenly certain of something else: if Piper succeeds in destroying the reformatory, she will be taking all of Gardnerville down too.

"I wasn't expecting to see you here."

I jump as Elton's voice carries across the room.

Slowly, I turn to face him. "I came to see the quints."

"I didn't know you were friends."

Elton stands in the doorway with Foote at his back. I stare at Foote for a moment, looking for some sign that he is on my side and not getting ready to double-cross me. His face is flat and he doesn't meet my eyes. I focus on Elton again. "We're not friends. We're family."

He gives me his bright, blank politician smile. "Sky, I'm worried about you. I've said it before and I'll say it again: if there is anything you need, you can come right to me for it."

"Yeah, as long as that thing is purple and round and makes the whole world go gray." I cross the room, ready to kick his silver legs out from under him if that's what it takes to get away. He is stronger and steadier than I've given him credit for, though. His hands grip my shoulders and he propels me backward step by step, until my spine is pressed against the lab table with the pile of purple pills.

"Have a pill. Take a few extra for later too. It may not seem like it right now, but it's for your own good. We've talked about that before. Maybe you've forgotten."

"I remember more than you think." I lean forward, close enough to kiss Elton, and then I whisper, "I remember the night Piper didn't come home. She said you slept under the stars together beside the depot. You proposed to her there. Even though you didn't have a ring and she was too young. You told her you loved her. Couldn't live without her. The next morning, you were woken up by the train tearing through town."

Elton's face goes red and his hands clench my shoulders harder. "That's a story. It didn't happen."

I smile then. "Really? 'Cause Piper never told me that. You did. Just now."

He releases me and takes two steps back. "It didn't happen," he says again, but less certain and with something else under his words. He reaches down to rub his knee and to avoid my eyes and to remind himself to be strong like steel. But that touch only increases the something else, because the something else is longing. Not longing for his lost limbs. Longing for the softer man who'd believed in love. And Piper.

"Take the pills and get out." His voice is hard.

"Which pills?" I ask. Spinning away, I move toward another table, where pills as red as cherries are stacked in neat rows. "Scarlet runners?" Grabbing a handful, I fling them at Elton and move to the next table. "Or maybe some of these pretty-in-pink foxgloves. I've heard they give heart to those who lack courage." I chuck another handful at Elton and then walk to the last table, where only a few yellow pills lie scattered across an open note-book. I pick one up and pretend to be stumped. "This one must be new, but it kind of looks like a . . . a sunflower."

I walk toward Elton with slow, deliberate steps. "I wonder what would happen if I took this pill. Or better yet . . . what if the whole town took this pill? Would we wake up singing a happy good-morning song, spend our whole day skipping everywhere we went, and fall asleep with a smile on our lips?"

Elton's eyes have narrowed to two angry slits, and his mouth is a hard, flat line. "You think because you pulled something out of my head that you know the whole story. You don't, though. You don't know the half of it."

"Well, why don't you tell me about it?"

Leaning down, Elton picks one of the purple pills off the floor. He looks at it for a moment, removes an invisible bit of dirt, and then stands and holds it out to me. "Take the pill and I'll tell you anything you want."

You'd think at this point, being so close to the truth, I wouldn't even be tempted. Oh, how I wish that were true.

Elton knows it too. He can see the struggle on my face. "Do the smart thing, Skylar."

My hand itches to smack the pill out of his hand, but I swallow the impulse. "You take it."

Elton blinks at me and then brings the pill to his lips. It's an amazing bluff, a fake-out. . . . But then I see it on his tongue just before he closes his mouth.

"Spit it out! Are you crazy?"

With a gurgling cough, Elton spits the pill back out onto the floor.

"Why'd you do that?" I demand.

"You told me to," he says, still staring at the saliva-covered pill oozing its purple coating all over the floor.

I reach forward to shake him, to make him meet my eyes, but I don't want to touch him again. He was right about me not knowing the whole story. Elton is a master manipulator. The whole pretending-to-take-the-pill stunt is him playing with me, trying to confuse me, making me think of Piper, reminding me how alike we are. He still doesn't get that I see that as a positive thing. Maybe it's time to drive the point home.

"You do what I tell you to now? Well, good." I point to the window. "Exit that way and try to grow some wings before you hit the ground."

Elton looks up from the pill at last. He blinks at me the same way he did before taking the pill and then turns toward the window. Oh, he's good. I'll give him that. He's playing chicken with me. Waiting for me to admit I've been bluffing and fold. I cross my arms over my chest as he uses a chair to clamber up toward the windowsill. One curved leg and then another steps up, and then he is crouched, framed inside the window. This is the part where I'm supposed to break. I can see the tension in his back and the trembling in his legs as he waits for me to—

Elton jumps. His silver legs, like pistons, push him up and out into the air, where he hangs for a moment—frozen—before falling. Foote pushes past me and then dives through the window after Elton. He doesn't hang in the air; he doesn't try to fly. He aims downward like he is racing to see who can reach the ground first.

Reflexively I put my hands over my ears, not wanting to hear the crash, the screams, the whatever comes next. For a full minute I hold that pose. Eyes closed. Ears covered. Trembling from head to toe. Then slowly I let my hands fall and open my eyes. I am in the science lab. There are pills everywhere. I wonder if I took one without knowing it. Maybe I imagined everything that just happened. That maybe happened. That couldn't have happened.

I slide my feet across the floor as if I am on ice and it might shatter beneath me. When I reach the window, I take a deep breath before leaning over the sill and peering down. Foote and Elton both lie there.

I stumble backward, crashing into the quints.

"Elton. Foote." The words fall from my mouth as a shaking finger points toward the window.

The quints nod. "We know," they say, watching me with their milky-white eyes.

"Well, you're the geniuses here. Do something. Fix them."

Their brows furrow, and something that looks like pity slides across their faces. "We don't fix things that are broken. We just try and find ways to make it hurt less."

"Of course." I push through them, and they quickly scatter. Then I am taking the stairs two at a time and my sandals are skidding on the slick floors as I run down the empty hallways. I push the front doors open with a bang and the humid air gives me its usual big wet kiss hello, but I barely notice because Elton is sitting up, rubbing his head like it aches, but otherwise he looks fine. His hair isn't even messed up. There isn't a single ding on his metal legs.

I look past him, my chest expanding with a dangerous kind of hope—that is quickly deflated.

Foote lies still and twisted.

I turn away so fast it makes me dizzy. The too-blue sky swirls above me. Then a hand grips my arm.

"Come with me," Elton says.

I go without argument. He'll probably funnel a pile of forget-me-nots down my throat.

Just ten minutes ago that seemed like something terrible, but at the moment I can't quite remember why.

PLEASE, PLEASE, PLEASE, LET ME GET WHAT I WANT

Eight Years Ago

I MUST HAVE BEEN UNCONSCIOUS FOR ONLY A few moments after the fairy orbs exploded, because when I opened my eyes and the world reappeared in front of me, it was full of smoke and chaos. The air smelled like rotten eggs. I tried breathing through my mouth, but it had a matching sulfurous taste that coated my tongue. Pulling my shirt up so that it covered my nose, I headed toward where I had last seen you.

You weren't there.

That was when I first felt afraid. Truly afraid.

"Piper!" I screamed your name. "Piper!" The sound coming from my mouth was shrill and crackly. It made my throat ache. But I couldn't stop yelling as I stumbled across the field, sometimes tripping over bodies. Beyond a quick glance to make sure they were not you, I tried not to look at them. They were frozen in the poses they'd been in at the moment of the explosion—eyes wide, mouths smiling, and arms stretched out, reaching toward something wonderful.

I circled around and around in the field, every time making the circle a little smaller, until finally I was at the center. LuAnn was curled up, a ball of misery, sobbing into her hands.

I stood over her for a moment, trying to hate her for what she'd done. But I couldn't, not even with you missing—or worse. Crouching down, I tapped her shoulder.

She shuddered. "Is . . . is it time to go?"

"No, I'm not from the reformatory," I corrected her.

Finally, she glanced up at me. Already she looked like a different girl. "Oh. They'll be here soon then."

"Yeah," I quietly agreed. There was no use in denying it. Then I asked, "Have you seen Piper?"

LuAnn's hand went to her mouth. "I'm not sure I know her. Did she touch one?"

I nodded.

"You're one of the Gardners, aren't you?" LuAnn said, recognizing me. "Is Piper your friend?"

"She's my sister." I spit the words out.

I hated her then. Just a little bit.

Tears filled her eyes. "I'm sorry. I'm so, so sorry. That's right. I knew that. It's just that everything is so fuzzy right now. I don't even know why I did it. I really don't." She began sobbing again, and her face fell back into her hands.

Standing, I looked over the field. The smoke had cleared, but the last of the sun was gone and it was a dark night. I decided to circle the field again, but already I knew you weren't there. Except you had to be there. You couldn't have just disappeared. I marched back to the spot I'd last seen you, while giving myself a little pep talk. "Piper is alive. She is fine. She did not disappear. She will be lying right there, and when I finally find her, she'll open up her eyes and say, 'There you are, Pollywog. What took you so long?'"

And amazingly enough, that is exactly what happened.

You were right at the spot I expected you to be. The same spot I'd already gone over four or five times. Your eyes fluttered open as I threw myself onto the grass beside you. Then you said the exact words I'd imagined, as if I'd put them into your mouth.

I never told you any of this, Piper. It was like I wished you back into existence. And I knew you wouldn't like that.

"I feel funny," you said as we were walking home.

"Funny how?" I asked, worried.

You hugged your arms to yourself and then held them out, wiggling your fingers in front of your face. "I feel funny like I'm not all here. Like something is missing. I feel . . . I feel like a ghost."

I laughed, or tried to anyway, but it sounded hollow and false.

"That bad, huh?" Piper laughed too. Hers sounded a little closer to the real thing.

"You're fine. You'll see when we get home. You look the same as always. You *are* the same as always."

"Okay, yeah." Piper stopped wiggling her fingers and let them fall to her side. "The same. I still feel like a ghost, though." She laughed. "Maybe I've always been a ghost."

A horn sounded behind us then, and we had to jump to opposite sides of the street to let the reformatory car carrying LuAnn up the hill pass by. With the car between us, I couldn't see you, and for a moment I worried that you had disappeared again. That maybe you really were a ghost. But then the car passed and you were still standing there, and Chance came running down the road with one of his "so happy to see you" barks.

You never mentioned the ghost thing again, and we never spoke of that night. We never even put it on tape. It was like we thought if we could just forget it, then maybe it had never happened at all.

FIFTEEN

"DAMN YOU, ELTON!" I SCREAM THE WORDS EVEN though he is long gone and even though it upsets my precarious balance and sends me spinning underwater once more. As I cough and sputter and gasp for air, the life jacket that Elton strapped me into like a straitjacket, with my arms pinned to my sides, pushes me to the surface and onto my back again. I kick a few times, gently—too much will send me spinning again—and study the ceiling of the pool room.

It pains me to do so, but I have to admit it: Elton is an evil genius. The pool is the worst place he could've put me. There is no place in town, including the reformatory, where I would feel so completely out of my element.

Even worse, the longer I'm in here, the harder it becomes to stop myself from thinking about Jonathan dying in this same place . . . at Elton's hands. The fight between them keeps replaying.

Distantly, I remember hearing Elton say, "Take her to the locker room and get her cleaned up, Foote. But don't let her leave. I'm gonna fish Jonathan out, and then we're gonna see if Skylar can make a dead man talk."

Now I can't help but wonder if Elton is disposing of Foote in the same callous way that he got rid of Jonathan.

Tears fill my eyes and I quickly blink them away. More liquid is the last thing I need right now.

"Swim lesson's over."

I jerk toward the unmistakable sound of Foote's voice, and it sends me into another underwater spin, but this time something snags the back of my life jacket, pulling me up and then out of the water. I try to tell Foote how happy I am to see him, especially to see him alive and well, but a thick wad of emotion clogs my throat. He bends down to where I lie at his feet, a weepy beached whale. Gently he unzips the jacket, helps me to my feet, and then wraps a towel around me. My arms are stiff after being pinned to my side for so long, but somehow I force them up and around Foote. My heart pounds harder than it should for a boy I barely know, risen from the dead. I can feel the grin stretching across my face.

He does not hug me back. Instead he gently pushes me away.

"What's going on?" I ask.

"Elton asked me to deliver you to the reformatory."

I stare at Foote, unwilling to comprehend. "Deliver?"

"I'm sorry," he says, and then he scoops me up as if I weigh nothing at all and carries me out of the pool room and into the hallway. Elton is waiting there, looking grim and determined.

"Be careful, Foote," he warns. "I know you think that you like her, but trust me, the Gardners are made out of nothing but smoke and mirrors." There is no mistaking the bitterness in his voice.

"If you're concerned, you're welcome to come along," Foote offers.

"You can handle it. Now get her away from me!" Elton snaps. It's then that I can see how afraid he is. Of me. Not wary like he's always been, but actually and truly—ready to pee his pants—terrified.

For a moment I'm tempted to apologize. To tell Elton that I didn't think he would actually jump out of that window. I am still not entirely sure why or how that happened. It doesn't seem possible that Piper could have gotten to both Ozzy and Elton. And even if she did, that leaves the question of why they'd wait until they were near me to try out their wings. Of course, the simpler answer is that I did it. I made them jump.

But that's impossible. Piper puts thoughts into people's heads and I take them out. That's how it's always been. Lately, though, lots of things are not the way they've always been.

As Foote carries me down the hall, I twist around to glance over his shoulder at Elton. He's already heading in the other direction at such a quick pace one might think he's running away from me. Elton thinks he does a good job of hiding his discomfort with the strange powers that rule this town, but his fear has always been obvious. Or it has to me, at least. It's actually amazing that he ever allowed Piper to get so close to him, maybe it's even a testament to how much he truly cared for her.

For this reason, I hope that Elton keeps going until he's on the train headed out of town, because I have a feeling that things are about to get a lot scarier around here and I'm not sure he can survive it.

The front doors bang shut behind Foote and me, hiding Elton from view. Once outside Foote finally sets me down, and together we survey the mostly empty parking lot.

"We're supposed to wait here for the reformatory van," Foote tells me.

"So where are we really going?" I ask, because somewhere during that short walk the sense of betrayal seeped away and I relaxed into Foote's arms. Without even reaching into his head, I finally decided once and for all that he was someone I would trust.

Foote's deep chuckle reverberates through my body. "Wherever you want to go."

"Home first," I answer immediately. "There's something I need."

"And then . . . ?"

"And then we'll see," I say. Though my plan extends beyond the next five minutes, I'm keeping it under wraps for the moment. I know Foote well enough by now to guess he won't go along with my idea to turn myself in at the reformatory. But it's the only smart thing to do. Gardnerville is such a small town there's no point in running, and even hiding wouldn't be effective for too long. More importantly, it's the move I've been destined to make. I've tried every way I can think of to look for Piper; now only the most obvious one is left: going into the reformatory to find her myself.

"Okay." Foote pulls some keys from his pockets, tosses them into the air, and catches them again. "How about we take Elton's car?"

It sounds like a fine idea to me, and moments later we are cruising down the road.

A block away from my house, we decide to ditch the Prius and walk the rest of the way together. We have only taken a few steps when the ground trembles beneath our feet. It's a smaller tremor than the earlier one, but I still grab hold of Foote's arm, and when the shaking is over, that grip slides lower so that we are holding hands.

Once I have hold of his hand, I can't stop myself from going a little further. My fingers find his chest, broad and amazingly whole, not a single rib bent the wrong way. Next I move to his shoulders. They're straight and even. It's not enough. I want more. So the examination continues. Rising onto my tiptoes to reach him, I explore the back of his neck, finding where his backbone begins. I've gone this far without being pushed away, and now my curiosity takes me even further. My arms wrap all the way around him, trapping his arms to his sides, while my fingers glide down his spine. I stop when I reach his lower back, where the waist of his pants creates a line I don't feel bold enough to cross.

"Well?" he asks. His voice rumbles from his chest, and it's only then that I realize my ear is practically pressed against it.

I take a step back, dragging my reluctant hands along with the rest of me.

"You're not dead," I say. "You're not even hurt."

"No, not anymore," he answers softly, his breath fanning my cheek.

"How? Why?"

"I don't know. I've always been lucky that way."

"Lucky," I repeat, remembering. "Like the lucky rabbit's foot that didn't work for the rabbit."

"That's me."

"So when you jumped out the window after Elton, you did it to save him. You absorbed the hurt, instead of him."

"Yeah," he admits softly. "Sort of like that."

"And you've always been that way, even before you came here?"

Foote nods. "I'd tell you the whole story, but it's a long one and I don't think we have the time."

"Yeah, okay," I agree, containing my curiosity.

We continue toward my house, this time hand in hand, which leads me to marvel at the comfort that comes from having another person's fingers intertwined with your own.

It ends too soon. When we reach the front porch, Foote gently extracts his hand. "Go get what you need. I'll stay out here and keep watch."

I reluctantly agree and then slip inside the unusually silent house.

"Mom? Wills?" I call. No one answers. Worried, I run up the stairs to Piper's room, wondering if the impostors are still there, but the room is empty and the bed neatly made, as if they'd never been there at all. For some reason this makes me even more uneasy.

Ignoring the urge to run through the house searching for Mom and Wills, I turn toward Piper's dresser, to get what I'd come back home for in the first place. But the piles of cassette tapes are gone. Did I move them? It's possible, but I seem to remember seeing them here. For whatever that's worth.

I close my eyes, trying to grab hold of some solid recollection, when I hear a screech from outside. I fly down the stairs and, hearing a second shriek, follow it out the door that leads to the backyard. Our yard stretches out into a rolling lawn with a scattering at trees at the very back of the property, and in the shadow of those trees is where I finally catch sight of Mom, Wills, and the four girls who think they're Piper.

I sprint toward them, a sick feeling in my stomach, despite by now having recognized the screams as sounds of joy rather than distress. As I get closer, I at last see the source of their excitement.

They're playing a game in which they throw shiny filaments into the air, attempting to snag them on the tree branches. From the number of tinsel-like strands in the treetops, undulating outward like some strange insect infestation, they have been at it for a while.

Wills runs among the girls, yelling along with them, not quite understanding the game but enjoying it just the same. Mom sits on the grass, her head cradled in her hands as if upset about something. It is only when I stop beside her that I realize the origin of the twinkling threads.

I run at the girls to stop them. But it is too late. Much too late.

The cassettes that I was searching for only moments ago have all been ripped apart and unraveled. Not a single one has survived.

It's funny—all those memories I worked so hard to forget, and now when it's too late, I'm finally realizing what I lost.

"Why?" I demand, directing most of my fury LuAnn's way. "Why would you do this?"

She hands me the plastic shell of one of the cassettes. In the transfer, a few broken strands of the tape get caught by the wind. "The past is gone. Let it go."

Just like that my anger crumbles, replaced by the deep, aching sorrow that's been my constant companion these past four years. "I can't. I've tried and tried, but it keeps coming back."

"It's time to go," LuAnn replies, looking past me.

I turn, expecting to see Foote, but instead it's ten guards from the reformatory bearing down on us. I expect LuAnn and the other girls to flee, but, forever unpredictable, they practically skip toward the guards. In moments they are handcuffed and led away.

That's when the six remaining guards turn their attention to me. I think about taking a swing at them. Or running. I'd planned to turn myself in, but now that the moment is here, I'm not ready.

"Skylar." Mom's voice breaks through my mental chaos. She holds Wills in her arms with what looks to be an iron grip. Our gazes lock. I don't need to seize her secrets to know what she's thinking. It's right there on her face. She's afraid. Not just for Wills, but for me too.

Turning to the guards, I put my hands in the air. "Okay," I say. "Take me away." I don't let them cuff me, though, not in front of Wills. When the first guard pulls a pair of handcuffs from his belt, I growl in a soft undertone, "Put those away." To my surprise, he does it without hesitation.

The rest of them surround me on all sides, but no one touches me. They all share the same wary expression, like they're escorting a ticking time bomb. I almost tell them not to worry, that I've seen enough people hurt for no good reason. Then I remember they're taking me to a place designed to slowly kill the best parts of me. Maybe we're not enemies, but we're not exactly gonna become good friends either.

As we walk, I search for Foote, hoping for some sign that he got away, but when we reach the van, my hopes are dashed. He's seated in the very back and looks like a mess. His face has been beaten bloody and they have him trussed up tight with both his wrists and ankles cuffed. Pushing past the guards, I climb in beside him.

"You okay?" I ask.

"I'm sorry," Foote answers. "They came in so fast. I tried to warn you—"

"Shhh," I interrupt. "I know. It's okay. But why are they taking you too?"

If possible, Foote slumps even lower in his seat. "Elton never really trusted me. He was constantly testing me. Today I finally flunked out."

"If it helps, Elton doesn't trust anyone."

Foote shrugs. "He had reason not to trust me. When we met,

he told me he'd never met a backstabber who could do it without ever lifting a knife, and he said that if I ever crossed him, he'd make me sorry."

"Typical Elton macho bullshit." I shake my head. "What does that even mean?"

"It means that I killed someone," Foote admits in a low voice.

"What? No way. I don't believe that." No response from Foote, who stares down at his knees. I slide my hand into his, the same way it had been during the walk to my house. "You said before that you'd tell me about your past when we had some time. Here we are with nothing to do but sit back and wait."

"It's not a nice story."

"Perfect. Not-nice stories are the only types I know."

"Okay." Foote takes a deep breath, as the van begins to reverse down my driveway. "Here I go then, telling you everything."

"You don't have to," I interrupt, understanding more than most people how difficult it can be to remember. Trying to lighten the mood, I add, "We could sing 'Ninety-nine Bottles of Beer' to pass the time instead."

"Anything but that." Foote laughs and I join him. Then he starts speaking again, and all the mirth fades from his voice. "I don't know what happened to my mom. Or my dad either. The man who raised me said he was my uncle, but he was a con man, gambler, and professional liar, so I was never really sure that we shared any blood at all. Anyway, he told me that my mom didn't want me 'cause I was a freak. He told me he was the only person in the whole world who was able to put up with me, and I'd better pray that nothing ever happened to him, 'cause I'd be a goner without him. Every morning he'd ask me, 'You got my back?' and every morning I'd tell him that I did. And then we'd get in his van, leave behind whatever motel or apartment we'd been staying at, and go find some suckers.

"My uncle made his money getting people to bet against him. Sometimes he'd have a partner, usually a girlfriend, who'd set it up for him. She'd gather a crowd out in a field or at the edge of a parking lot or in a deserted building. He liked to have around twenty-five to fifty people to make it worth his while, but when times were tough he'd settle for just five or six guys willing to pay. By the time I was ten, getting people wasn't a problem. Instead of us going into towns and explaining what he was about, people already knew and were waiting to see him. Sometimes he had to turn people away because we were attracting too much attention. There were just too many people who wanted to see 'the man who couldn't be shot' for themselves."

"This can't be good," I say, unable to hold the words back, because I already have an idea of what is coming next.

"It's not," Foote confirms. "He had this rickety delivery van with an ancient claw-foot bathtub in the back of it. When we got to the site, I'd take off my shirt and pants so they didn't get messed up and then lie down in the tub. It was always cold, even on a hot Alabama August afternoon. He'd blast heavy metal from the car stereo, cranking the volume as high as it could go so that no one would be able to hear me scream. It was all I could hear too; there was no hint or sound I could detect from the outside to give me warning. To brace myself. I just had to lie there and wait. That was the worst part—the waiting. I knew, though, from one of his chattier girlfriends, how it all went on the outside.

"Uncle Gage had a little platform he'd build. He'd stack bales of hay behind it with bull's-eyes pinned on them. Then he'd start his spiel, egging the crowd on, asking who dared to try and hit him. Telling them to step up and try their luck. Usually, the first one took the longest to convince. In the early days, he'd sometimes put a ringer in the crowd, to take the first shot and get things moving. It was anywhere from twenty-five to a hundred dollars for a chance at bat, depending how bad the crowd wanted it. Then the shooter would stand on this box set up about ten feet away. Gage's girl would give the guy a bow and arrow and he'd get five tries. If they all went wide, Uncle Gage'd let the shooter move the box up for half of what he paid the first time. They usually hit him then. Sometimes a few times. They'd see the arrow heading straight toward him and then it would just . . . disappear.

"After that first arrow, everyone wanted to watch it again. Everyone wanted to hold the bow and see what the trick was. If it was a bigger crowd, I'd usually pass out before it was over and not wake up until Uncle Gage started pulling the arrows out of me. That's when I started smoking. He'd light me one after another and tell me to practice blowing smoke rings while he worked."

"Foote," I whisper, not knowing what else to say.

"It's okay," he says. "I mean, it isn't, but it was a long time ago and I survived. Right?"

"How long ago?" I ask.

"I was twelve the last time. Uncle Gage felt like we'd over-worked the Southeast, so we went west. And it was amazing. In places we'd never been before, these huge crowds were turning out. Word was spreading online—there was even a shaky video that someone had made. I think it went to Uncle Gage's head. In New Mexico, when five hundred people showed up, instead of turning most of them away, he told them to stay and try their luck. When they ran out of arrows, he asked who had a gun. Turns out, a lot of them did. It took me three weeks before I could walk again, and I was coughing up bullets for even longer than that."

Lost for words, I squeezed Foote's hand.

"Uncle Gage made almost ten grand in that one day, and he decided to do it again once we got to California, but this time he wanted to double that number. He probably would've too. I'd never seen a crowd so big. That was Uncle Gage's mistake. Well, that and parking on a hill. It made it real easy to put the car into neutral and let it roll away. Once I got some distance, I hot-wired it—a little something I'd looked up online a few days earlier."

Foote pauses.

"Uncle Gage was still lucky in a way, I guess. Whoever shot that first arrow had a hell of an aim. It went straight into his eye socket. He died almost instantly."

"He deserved worse."

"Yeah, probably. I mean, it wasn't like I'd never thought about running before I finally did. For years, I wanted to get away. I even snuck out one night when I was ten, but after an hour in the dark by myself with nowhere to go, I got scared and went back. I guess that would've been the better way to do it, instead of leaving him thinking he was safe and then ending up with an arrow hanging out of his face."

"He deserved worse," I say again, this time with a snarl.

I feel Foote's head, which has been resting against mine, nod.

"It was the right choice," I tell him, knowing he doesn't quite believe it and wanting to say it again and again until he does. Foote shudders, and I lean my body into his, trying to give him some small comfort. Wishing things were different. Then my gaze drifts out the window, and I realize we are at the base of the hill that leads up to the reformatory. Not much time before we're there. A terrible panicky feeling pushes against my chest. To keep us both distracted, I ask Foote another question.

"So what happened next?"

"At first things were pretty good. Some social workers got me into school and found me a family with a bunch of other foster kids to live with. It wasn't perfect, but it was better than anything I'd ever known."

"At first," I say.

"What?"

"You said that at first it was okay, which means that later it wasn't."

"Yeah," Foote agrees. "Later it wasn't."

"But you were happy for a while."

"Yeah," he says again, this time in a lower voice.

"So was it worth it? What I mean is . . ." I take a deep breath as I struggle to put my thoughts into words. "Is it worth having something good when it's just gonna be taken away? When it's only temporary and later you're left wondering if you imagined it anyway?"

Beside me, Foote is silent. Then he takes a deep breath of his own. "One of the other foster kids was a little girl named Amy. A month after I moved in, they had her first birthday party. Over the years I was there, I got to see her grow up. She was a little behind for a kid her age. *F*'s were especially tricky for her, so she called me Doot. She loved being held, and every time I sat down to eat or watch TV or do homework, she'd crawl onto my lap and plant herself there."

When I asked him about the good being taken away, I was thinking of Piper. But now it is the thought of Wills that makes my throat tighten.

"Okay," I say, meaning "that's enough." But Foote isn't done.

"I had just turned seventeen when the fire happened. It was the middle of the night. I woke to hear this huge boom and I felt the whole house shuddering. Then I heard Amy scream. I jumped out of bed to help her, but couldn't get any farther. I was . . . burning. I didn't even realize it at the time—couldn't make sense of it—but my whole body was on fire. I was in a coma for two weeks, and when I woke up, the first thing I asked was if Amy was okay. They said she was, but that everybody else was in the hospital, too, and in pretty bad shape. It was some sort of gas explosion. This fireball just ripped through the house. They'd had to dig through the rubble for hours to find all of us. Amy was the last to be found. No one expected her to be alive, but when they found her, she was sleeping peacefully, not a hair out of place, not a single bruise."

"So it was okay," I say, surprised at how relieved I feel.

"That's what I thought—just my usual mix of bad luck/good luck. But then this guy showed up at the hospital and told me that he'd been looking all over for me. At first I thought he'd wandered in from the psych ward, 'cause he told me how he was the owner of a magical train. 'People from all over the world want a seat on this train,' he said. 'Some would even kill to ride.' I asked why, and he told me about Gardnerville. I called him a liar. 'Look it up,' he said. Once he'd had to sell people on the place, but now the internet did all the selling for him. He said I could start out by helping a friend of his on the other side. If things there went well, expansion was almost certain, and I'd be in a good place to move up within their organization.

"I thought he was crazy, but I looked it up anyway. The things I read were insane, but kind of awesome too. And in some weird way, Gardnerville almost felt familiar. Like I'd been there before. Ten days later I boarded the train."

"And Elton was the friend on the other side?" I guess.

"Yeah," Foote confirms. "I gave him my protection."

"Your protection," I say, and then I remember not being able to breathe after taking too many forget-me-nots and the bicycle crash. "And you gave it to me too, didn't you?" I ask, but I don't wait for an answer. I press my warm lips against Foote's. After a moment of hesitation, he kisses me back.

My eyes drift closed as the kiss becomes more than just a mix of gratitude and sympathy. In a way the kiss becomes about nothing at all. Except Foote. And me. Right now, that's enough to make my head spin and my heart pound. It's enough to make me simply forget about everything else. Even Foote's deep pool of secrets has gone quiet—except for one small whisper that gently sighs *yes*.

Or maybe that one is coming from me.

Either way, like all good—no, great—things, it ends too quickly.

The van door rumbles open, and a pair of guards smirk at us. "Welcome to your new home, lovebirds," one of them says.

"Sorry you can't carry her over the threshold, Romeo," the second one adds.

They laugh loudly at their own wit, but the amusement never quite reaches their eyes.

Ignoring them, I help Foote climb out of the van. Then there is nothing to do but stand in front of the gates as they slowly creak open and the dread mounts higher and higher.

"This way," Guard One finally says, and we step forward, passing through the gates, officially on the grounds of the reformatory.

I look over at Foote. Our eyes meet and we share wry smiles.

"Thanks," I tell him. "For everything."

His smile turns into a frown. "That sounds like a good-bye. I'm pretty sure they're taking us to the same place, and this may be kind of cheesy, but there's nobody I'd rather be locked up with."

My throat tightens and I have to look away to blink tears from my eyes.

"Let's move," my goon says.

Still not wanting him to touch me, I immediately follow orders.

"Sky—" Foote calls from behind me, sounding hurt and . . . betrayed.

Without stopping, I look back over my shoulder at him. "It's the reformatory," I attempt to explain. "You don't understand, you won't . . ." I swallow hard, trying to keep my own fear at bay. "The reformatory is where luck runs out. Even yours."

"Heh," Guard One says, in a way that sounds more wistful than cruel.

Foote keeps looking at me, as if expecting me to say something more.

"I'm sorry," I add, even though I know it's not what he's looking for. I am though. I am so very sorry for each and every one of us.

IF YOU LEAVE

Four Years Ago

"YOU SHOULD LEAVE."

That's what you told me, that May Day morning on our way to school.

"Leave?" I asked. Not like I didn't know what you meant, but like I'd never even heard the word before.

I've learned with Wills that sometimes explaining a simple word can be difficult. "What's hope?" he'll ask me. "What's forever? What's normal? What's disappear? What's Tang?"

I usually tell him to go ask Mom. That last one, though, I figured I could handle in the time it took me to finish stirring his drink together. But even Tang was tough. I had to explain astronauts and outer space. Wills asked if we could order a spaceship and go there too. I told him it was too far away. Much farther than the end of our driveway. Farther than Main Street. Even farther than where the train tracks disappeared into the mountain. He squinted at me, trying to process it, and then he stared up into the sky. I have to admit, I found myself looking up too. Turns out trying to imagine something that far away, trying to imagine myself somewhere beyond everything I knew . . . that was a concept I struggled with as well.

Your May Day morning was bright and clear, Piper. The type of day that seemed so perfect, nothing could ruin it. But you did ruin it, with that one simple word.

I kept walking beside you, even though it felt like the ground was being pulled out from beneath my feet. "Leave?" I asked again.

You ruffled my hair and laughed, like I was being funny. "Yes, leave. You know, just get on the train and . . ." Your arm shot straight out, indicating the trajectory of the train. "Go. And don't pretend you've never thought about it before."

"Just because I've thought about it doesn't mean I would do it. I don't do every little thing that comes into my head. And anyway, I can't leave—what about all the plans?"

"Oh, that." You waved your hand in this dismissive way. As if it wasn't something we'd spent the last three years working on. As if we hadn't poisoned ourselves and half the town as part of the plan. As if you hadn't let Ozzy feel you up, to have eyes inside the reformatory. You acted like I was referring to a childhood game that we'd both outgrown a long time ago.

"Sky, can you just be serious for a minute?" You gave me one of those lowered-brows, disappointed looks that always cut right through me. You'd think I'd become immune to it, but nope—it got me every time. And this was no exception.

"I was being serious," I muttered.

You switched tactics, disarming me with a sunny smile. "Just forget that, okay? So back to the topic of leaving. I wonder if it's even worth you finishing school first. . . ."

"What?" I stopped in my tracks, staring at you.

"Drama queen, chill out. I'm not saying you should leave tomorrow. You'd probably want to wait a few months at least."

"Piper, no," I said.

You steamrollered right over me, as if I hadn't even spoken. "One of us needs to see the rest of the world. Represent and report back. And I think it would be really exciting for you, Pollywog. I think you would do great out there. And it's what you always wanted."

"No, that's a lie. I never wanted to leave."

"No," you corrected me. "That's the truth. Remember how you cried after seeing *The Wizard of Oz* the first time? Well, you don't really remember it, 'cause I made it up. You loved the movie. The whole thing from beginning to end. You insisted on watching it every time it came on. When it wasn't on, you acted it out with a pair of Mom's borrowed heels. "'There's no place like home. There's no place like home. There's no place like home.'" You stopped to click your heels together, imitating me imitating Dorothy. 'Why did she have to say it three times anyway?' you continued. I think she was trying to convince herself. I think Dorothy really wanted to stay in Oz, but thought going home was the right thing to do. I couldn't let you have such a lame role model. That's when I told you the story.

We were watching the movie together and when it got to that part, I turned it off. When you asked me why, I lied and said I didn't want you crying again like the last time. You didn't even question it, Sky. You believed me."

My hands were held in your tight grip by the end. Your eyes were locked on me. "I always believed you," I whispered.

"Then believe me now," you said, matching my hushed tone. "You should go."

I jerked my hands away and focused my gaze on my shoelaces. "We'll both go. We can leave right now, if you want."

"Oh, Sky," you sighed. "I wish I could, but that's not my part to play. But you, I think you'd thrive out there, and eventually you'd forget this place and wonder why you ever wanted to stay."

"Stop." I finally looked back up at you, not trying to hide the tears streaming from my eyes. "Just stop. I'd never forget you. Not ever. We're one and the same, remember?"

With a sad smile, you brought your hand up, and I pressed my palm against yours.

"Okay, you win," you said. "Remember me. But do it the right way. Remember it all. The good, the bad, and the ugly. I'd rather be forgotten than remembered the wrong way."

I promised that I would remember you the right way. It had seemed like an easy promise to keep. It wasn't, though, and I've broken it a million times without even meaning to.

Sometimes, Piper, it's like I can't remember or forget you—all at the same time.

SIXTEEN

THE NIGHT OF PIPER'S PARADE, LONG AFTER ALL THE
survivors had been dried off and returned to their beds, I stood
outside the gates of the reformatory, searching for some sign of
my sister.

Mom had been shocked when I walked in the front door.

"Piper's at the reformatory," I told her.

It's hard to remember exactly what happened after that.
Those first few months without Piper are so hazy. Then I started
taking the forget-me-nots to keep things fuzzy. I took them to
forget . . . about Piper.

Missing her hurt too much. I'd wanted to wipe her from my
brain.

I hadn't been successful. Of course I hadn't. I couldn't erase

Piper without erasing myself.

Now as I pass through the reformatory's oversized front doorway and enter the too-dark interior, something roars in my ears,
like I swallowed the ocean. My heart beats fast, and even though
I keep trying to breathe in, none of the air seems to be making
it to my lungs.

Panic. Something inside me whispers the word.

I can't be here. I can't. I turn to leave, but the door has already
closed.

From a distance I can hear the guards talking to Foote. They
have his wallet and are pawing through it. One of them holds up
a bit of pink material. They all laugh too loudly as the guard flaps
it in front of Foote's passive face.

One of the other guards grabs it, his thick, grubby fingers
smoothing it out. I think it must be from that little girl Foote had
been talking about. Amy. A memento to remember her by. But
then the guard points to the embroidered letters. "Who's SLG?"
he asks.

"I am," I say, not even realizing the words are coming out of
my mouth until everyone turns to stare. My hand reaches out,
taking the piece of fabric, recognizing it as soon as the pads of
my fingers make contact with the worn material. It's the missing
piece from my baby blanket from when the little boy in the carriage was carried away by the birds.

"Holy shit," I murmur, suddenly certain that Foote is that
little boy. And even more certain that we are connected in some
powerful way. It would explain why he's the first person I've ever
met who can tell when I'm poking through the secrets in his

head. It might even be the reason behind his odd lucky streak. But when I turn toward Foote to tell him, he is already gone.

In fact, everyone is gone and they've left me standing here. I realize then that no one has touched me or tried to take any of my things away. They walk past me, almost as if they've forgotten I'm here. Even when I stare right at one of the guards, he doesn't seem to see me.

This would be the perfect time to look for Piper. I could go room by room, until I find the locked one that Ozzy mentioned. Or . . .

I walk up to one of the guards and tap him on the arm. He jumps and then looks at me in surprise. It is only then that I recognize him as the man who Foote and I watched beat the crap out of the inmates during the walk. Right now, he doesn't look so dangerous. If anything, he looks drowsy, and the longer I stare at him, the more his lids seem to hang over his eyes, until only little slits are left.

"Take me to Piper"—that's what I was going to say. But instead, I hear myself say, "Um, give me a minute."

He nods, or maybe his chin just wobbles, but either way he seems prepared to wait. Which is good, because even though it's the moment of reckoning, I'm nowhere near ready for it.

I push my hand into my pocket and feel the broken cassette tape I stashed there. As my fingers wrap around it, I suddenly remember the recorder that goes with it. From what I recall, neither LuAnn nor any of the other girls had it, which mean that with any luck it's where I left it—buried on my bedroom floor beneath piles of last week's laundry. And if I'm royal-flush levels of lucky, then it will still hold the tape that was inside it the day I bought pills from Jonathan in the double-wide. Amazing that was only three days ago; it feels like it was a different lifetime.

I turn to the half-comatose guard. "I need to make a phone call," I tell him.

Immediately he turns and leads me into a back office. The walls are lined with filing cabinets, and in the center is a wooden desk with an old rotary-style phone sitting on it. I pick it up, stare at the heavy black receiver in my hand for a moment, and then start to dial. As the phone rings at the other end, I study the guard while he waits by the door, arms slack at his sides. It hits me then that he isn't there to watch me or hold me in place; he's simply waiting for his next order. From me.

I told Elton to jump. He did.

I told the guard not to touch me. He didn't.

And here inside the reformatory, where I should be weaker than ever, I feel strong. And unstoppable.

How though? All that reformatory dirt I ate must be part of it. But that doesn't explain how I have Piper's powers too all of a sudden.

I can still hear the guard's hidden thoughts too. I think. I reach out, testing my power. As if I'd split his gut open, his secrets fall out like the foulest entrails. That boy wasn't the first one he hit. He's beaten several inmates near to death. Is known for it. And enjoys it too. At least as long as he's here, inside these walls. At home, doubts creep in. He goes to the bar to drink them down. A couple times he tried some forget-me-nots. Nothing worked as well as taking extra shifts, though. When he's here, everything seems fine. Better than fine.

Take that thought, a voice whispers inside me. *Take them all. It'll be a gift and a curse and he deserves both. Take every thought from his head 'til it's empty and clean.*

I nod, agreeing, and then reach toward the guard again—

"Hello?" Wills's voice, sweet and squeaky, comes through the line. The whispery voice is gone along with the urge to hurt the guard. "Hello?" Wills says again. Unexpected tears spring to my eyes.

"Hey, buddy, can you get Mom? I need to talk to her." Setting the phone down, I look at the guard again. Greg is the name sewn onto his shirt, but he must be wearing someone else's uniform because the name I pull from his head is Paul. "Hey, Paul," I say. His eyes when they connect with mine look uncertain and a little scared. He thinks he's dreaming; that's how he's making sense of what's happening now. Usually, though, his dreams about this place are darker. If Wills hadn't answered the phone when he did, it's possible that he wouldn't be feeling or thinking anything at all ever again. I almost apologize to the guy, until I remember that I didn't do anything. I'd been about to, but I hadn't. It's more than he can say for his bad deeds. Still my voice is gentle when I tell him, "Cover your ears and hum. Okay?"

Without hesitation, he puts his hands over his ears, and a steady hum of "Row, Row, Row Your Boat" comes from behind his closed lips.

Turning my back to him, I pick up the phone once more. "Mom?"

"No, it's me," Wills answers.

"I told you to get Mom."

"But I wanted to talk to you."

I sigh. Amazing. I can make a guard inside the reformatory bend to my will, but not my little brother. I change my tone. "Please, Wills, it's important. And if you do this, I'll get you some candy the next time sweets come in on the train."

"Okay," he quickly agrees. There is quiet on the other end, and then, finally, Mom.

"Sky? Is that you? Are you okay?"

"I'm fine. That's what I wanted to call and tell you." I turn back and look at the humming guard, making certain he's still occupied. "And also, I need to ask you a favor. Could you go look in my room for that old tape recorder? You know what I'm talking about?"

"Yes, of course I do. You've been carrying it around with you for months now. Hold on a minute, and I'll go check."

I hear the phone thunk onto the table. I close my eyes, cross my fingers, and wait.

"Sky?" Mom comes back on the line.

"I'm here."

"I found it."

A mix of relief and panic wells up inside me. "Is there a tape in it?"

Something crinkles and clunks on the other side, and then Mom says, "Yes. It's labeled, 'Don't You (Forget About Me).' Oh, I loved that song. You know it broke my heart when you and Piper recorded over all my old mix tapes."

"Well, they were just sitting up in the attic."

"That doesn't mean they were free for you two to take. You could have at least asked me first."

"Mom!" I scrub a hand across my face, unable to believe we're fighting about this right now. "I'm sorry, I really am. Now please play the tape."

She sighs loudly, and then I hear the familiar whine of the tape starting. A moment later Piper's voice comes through the receiver.

"Skylar, if you're listening to this, then it means everything went the way I wanted it to."

I fall into a chair, and my eyes drift closed as her voice continues to play over the line. Every word is painful and precious. And when it is over, I don't try to stop the tears falling down my cheeks.

"Sky." Mom's voice comes on again. "Sky, are you there? Are you okay?"

I have to clear my throat a few times before I can talk. "Mom, if I don't come home, you need to talk with Wills and explain to him that he's not normal—" I stop and shake my head. "No. Wait. Don't say it like that. He shouldn't see it as a disability. Just tell him he's a Gardner and that comes with certain unique responsibilities. And abilities. Or maybe it would be better to explain about Piper and me first—"

"No, Skylar," Mom interrupts. "We don't need to have this discussion. Wills is not—"

"Yes, we do need to talk about this. That's what I'm trying to tell you. Wills needs to be prepared. I've already seen the signs of his power, okay? He's a Gardner, and we're twenty different types of messed up, and if he's gonna have any chance of fighting that, he needs to be ready."

"Skylar, for once just shut up and listen." A deep breath followed by a heavy sigh comes through the line. "Wills is not your father's child. There was another man. It was right after your father left. I was so desperately lonely and it just . . . happened. Wills isn't like you. No powers. He's just a little kid."

"Who—?" I start to ask but then stop, realizing it doesn't matter. "You're wrong. Wills does have power. I think he's kind of like Dad with the feelings. When I'm with him, I feel calm and just . . . better."

Mom doesn't say anything for several long seconds, and I wonder if my words are making her rethink Wills's parentage. "Oh, Sky, that's not a special power." Mom laughs sadly and then sighs again. "Or maybe it is."

"Oh," I answer, and then without another word, I gently rest the telephone receiver back in the cradle.

After that I simply sit there for a long while, let time pass, and absorb.

There are so few constants in Gardnerville. Most places, you know that whatever else might happen, in the morning the sun will rise. But Ezekiel Wood blew that to bits over twenty years ago, when he kept the whole town in darkness for six days straight. We're left to create our own constants, to find small things to cling to when all else is incomprehensible chaos.

For me, that was Piper. Four years ago, losing her rocked my world. But the truth about Piper that I just heard on that tape destroys it.

Now I remember why I took all those forget-me-nots. The only way to survive was to forget. It's tempting to try and forget again, but it's too late for that. I've already put this off for far too long.

I push myself to my feet, finally ready.

The stupid guard still stands there, humming as I walk right past him. Turning a corner, I run up the stone steps that lead to the second floor. At the top of the stairs I stop for a second, uncertain of which way to go. Should I continue up to the next floor, or search this one first? Ozzy once told me the place was a labyrinth, and from the looks of it, this was one thing he didn't lie about.

My decision is made for me when a group of girls come bounding toward me with outstretched arms.

"Sky!" They cry out my name from mouths stretched wide with smiles.

I take a step back, an automatic response. They all look a little insane.

They surround me, wind their arms through mine, and propel me forward, chattering nonstop about how happy they are to see me, asking if it's time. When I can take it no more, I shake them off.

"Is it time for what?" I demand. Then, as an afterthought, "And who the hell are you people?" As I ask the question, some of their faces begin to feel familiar. Felicia Davids, Georgia Armice . . .

But those are not the names they give me.

"We're Piper," they say together. "And it's time, Sky. It's finally time."

DON'T YOU (FORGET ABOUT ME)

Four Years Ago

SKYLAR, IF YOU'RE LISTENING TO THIS, THEN IT MEANS everything went the way I wanted it to. I know that may be difficult for you to accept—that I actually wanted to let the train catch me. But what you didn't understand from the first time I walked out on that track was that I was never trying to get away from it. I never wanted to win. I was just working up the courage to let it run me over.

Pollywog, I can see you shaking your head, not believing it. *Piper couldn't be suicidal.* That's what you're thinking. And you're right. Ending my life is the last thing I want.

Except.

My life. It's not right. It didn't begin like yours. It won't end like yours either.

I'm sorry if I'm not making sense. I guess I don't know

quite how to explain it. I've only begun to understand it myself. Although, that's not really true. I found out four years ago. It was one of those moments when everything in you goes *aha*, when so much that has seemed wrong has come right. Not right in a good way. I put the puzzle together. There was some satisfaction in that. But the picture it made . . . I didn't like that at all.

I think I'm still confusing you. Let me try again. Remember LuAnn's fairy balls? That was the day I found out. That was the day my life truly ended. That was the day I found out that I was only make-believe.

The fairy ball told me, just as I touched it. Or maybe in the moment after, when everything exploded into that brilliant light. I thought I was dead. It was an actual thought in my head. I could feel my whole body shattering, splitting, and separating, like I was a bomb going off.

This is it. The end.

Those were the exact words in my head. But then the fairy ball whispered to me. "I can't kill you. We're the same, you and me. Made of someone else's magic. That's us. We're one and the same."

Do you know what my response was, Pollywog? "Oh, wow. That makes a lot of sense."

Finally I understood why no one ever remembered me when I wasn't standing right in front of them. Do you know why I refused to get my picture taken for the yearbook? Because they always listed me as "unknown." My real existence was limited to family. You thought everyone stared at me because I was special. You were sort of right. I was always the new girl. I don't know when I began to resent that. When I started thinking of ways to make them remember me.

Do you think they'll remember me now, Pollywog? Do you think they'll know who led them onto that bridge? Do you think for the rest of their lives when they hear the train's whistle, they'll recall my name?

I don't know how long I was out after the fairy ball exploded. Eventually I heard you calling, demanding that I wake up. That I return. So I did.

I know you may find this difficult to believe, Sky. You'll say I imagined it. That it was a near-death experience. For someone who's lived their entire life here, you can be so prosaic at times. And tonight, if the train did what I thought it would, then you watched me disappear just like I did when the fairy ball exploded. Except I hope the train, made out of steel instead of magic, will ensure that you won't be able to put me back together again. If everything went right, then I winked out of existence like a star that had burned out a long time ago.

I can still hear you making excuses: "It was dark. Chaotic."

So let me remind you that this is not the first time you've seen this happen.

Remember when Chance was hit by the train when he was just a puppy? I know you think you do. You're probably looking at his missing leg right now as the number-one reason you'll never be able to forget. But Sky, for all your ability to see into everybody else's heads, you've never been much good at navigating your own.

"What do you mean?" I can hear you ask.

What I mean, exactly, is this: you remember things wrong.

Chance was hit by the train. He heard that piercing whistle, and although he'd heard it many times before, for some reason he decided to follow it. We raced after him on our bikes, screaming at him to come back. He'd never been a very obedient dog, though, and that day was no different. By the time we reached the tracks, the train was nearing the station and slowing. Chance started running alongside, eyeing those steel wheels like he was waiting for his moment to take a chunk out of one of them. The final car was about to glide past, when he made his move. It happened so fast. He went in for the wheel. A second later he was gone. There was no blood. No yelp of fear and pain and terror. Chance just disintegrated beneath the wheel. He was there and then he wasn't.

You couldn't accept it. We both saw the same thing. We both knew that the dog had been a gift from GG. The moment he disappeared, it became horribly obvious what had happened. GG up to her old tricks. Or maybe just trying to do something kind for her grandchildren. But either way, the result was the same. She made us see something that wasn't there. She gave us an illusion, and reality killed it.

I tried to explain this to you. I'd never known you to be so stubborn, so unwilling to hear me. You insisted that the train was moving slowly, that he'd slipped underneath. You wanted to search for him. He might be hurt, you kept saying.

It turned into a fight. I called you stupid. You said that I'd always been jealous that he liked you better. It was true. Chance had never taken to me. He slept on your bed but never mine. He would sit patiently, wagging his tail when you pulled him into a crushing hug, but bristled when I simply reached out to gently run my hand along his back.

You accused me of making him run after that train. Of putting the thought into his head.

I slapped you then. You were only seven years old, and I shouldn't have done it. But we were screaming at each other, with our faces red and our eyes glaring as hard as they could at the other. When you said that I'd made Chance do it, my hand snapped out and caught your cheek before I could even think to stop myself.

You gasped and then went silent. It wasn't until your hand crept up to touch the spot where I'd hit you that you started to cry.

I could've said I was sorry. The truth is, I was. But I was also still angry. And feeling betrayed that you would believe such a thing about me.

I ran away and left you standing there, sobbing.

I didn't want to go home, so I went into the woods behind Al's Grocery. Some kids were adding on another section to the fort, and I joined them. When it got dark, everyone started to head home. I was the last one to leave. Not because I was trying to avoid you. No, by then my anger had spent itself, and only regret remained. Finally, I thought about how sad you must be after losing Chance and then having to deal with us fighting on top of that. I wanted to make it up to you.

I started walking home slowly, waiting for the perfect idea to come to me. It finally did when I saw a pile of boxes sitting near the grocery Dumpster. I picked the cleanest-looking one, and practically skipped home. We would have a burial for Chance, I decided. All of his puppy toys would go in the box, then we would hold an elaborate funeral. Finally, we would figure out the perfect place to bury him and spend the rest of the day decorating his grave. It was, I decided, the perfect thing.

And it would've been too. I am almost certain of that.

If only Chance had stayed dead.

As I came up the driveway, the burial box tucked under my arm, I heard the sound of a dog barking inside the house. It was the excited, high-pitched bark Chance would use when you dangled a toy over his head and out of reach of his spring-loaded legs.

And when I opened the front door, that was exactly what I saw.

I stood there, staring at Chance, who, despite missing his front right leg, looked no worse for wear.

"Hey," I said.

You smiled up at me. "Look, Piper. Can you believe it? I found Chance lying in the field by the train station. He was in pretty bad shape, but GG helped me patch him back up."

I don't remember what I said then. Something like, "That's great." Or, "Wow."

Really, I was struggling to understand what had happened. The best I can figure is that you brought him back, Skylar. That you willed him back into existence.

Pollywog, I have to admit, that scares me more than a little bit. You hold on so tight. You want so badly for things to be a certain way that you just ignore it when they aren't.

Sometimes I wish I could be more like that. I wish I could forget what that fairy ball whispered to me.

When I met Elton, I thought that loving him, and having him love me, might be enough. I thought that if he and I got married and had babies and lived happily ever after, it would prove I was real. Remember when Elton and I started getting serious, when he asked me to go steady and we both giggled about him being so old-fashioned? I told you I needed to talk with GG, to get her blessing.

Really, though, I wanted to ask her if what I suspected was true. I wanted to know if at some point I might start to fade away, like a dream that gets fuzzy and worn over time.

GG said she was surprised it had taken me this long to ask. Then she spilled everything. I'd been Mom's idea. It was after that neighbor boy was taken by the birds. Dad was acting weird. He saw how upset Mom was that something had almost happened to you, and he was jealous. And resentful. Mom was starting to feel the same way, and some part of her knew it was Dad making her feel that way.

And you were inconsolable. You cried day and night. Even years later, Pollywog, you would talk about that boy. "John Paul will be back," you'd say in your little toddler lisp. "I told him to come back."

Sometimes, Sky, you can be scary.

I guess Dad thought so too, because one night Mom came into your room and found him holding a pillow over your face.

That's when she decided you needed someone to watch over and protect you. A dummy child to draw Dad's attention away from you. The two of them—Mom and GG—dreamed me into existence. GG took a lock of your hair and braided it together and left it in her spare room. The next day I was sitting there, a fully formed four-year-old who was more mature than her age and who drew every eye to herself wherever she went.

GG said that none of her pretend people had ever lasted as long as me, and that she was fairly certain the only reason I still existed was . . . you. You had given me so much more than that lock of hair. Without knowing it, you shared bits of yourself—including your power—and in doing so made me more than just imaginary.

So, that's what I am.

By now, I hope you aren't still shaking your head. By now, even you must admit this is the truth. That it makes sense in a Gardnerville kind of way. But that doesn't mean you will accept me being gone. Oh, Sky, I know how stubborn you are. Now you are saying, "Who cares what you are? Why does it change anything?"

Skylar, did you ever suspect that—like you—I could hear secrets sometimes? Probably not. You didn't want to know. It made sense that I put thoughts in and you took them out. Two connected but separate powers. It would be messier if we could each do both of those things. We could though.

And that day, talking with GG, I saw the hidden thought that she didn't say aloud. You'd shared so much with me—given me so much of yourself—that I could take the rest. I could be the real girl, and you would be the shadow.

I wish I hadn't found that secret.

I wish I could say it wasn't tempting.

But it was. And it still is.

It is tempting enough that I often start thinking of all the things I've done for you. All the times I've shielded you from Dad. I've even tried to keep you safe from the reformatory. And that's when I think that maybe you owe me. Maybe it's my turn to be shielded and kept safe.

But I wouldn't hurt you for anything, Pollywog.

That's why things have to change.

I am asking you to let me go.

Remember me, or don't—if it's easier that way.

But whatever you do, when the train finds me, please don't pretend it didn't happen. Please, let me go.

SEVENTEEN

THE PIPERS LOOK AT ME WITH EXPECTANT EYES,
waiting to hear my words of wisdom.

"Ummm," I say.

They nod eagerly in response, wanting more.

I rub my tired eyes. Just when I think I have a handle on this,
everything shifts again.

"Is there somewhere I can sit alone for a minute?" I ask at
the same moment a drop of water hits my head. I look up to see
a hole in the ceiling above us that penetrates the two floors over
us as well.

"Shouldn't someone fix that?" I ask, as the girls take my
hands and lead me to a door at the end of the hallway.

"They do," one of the girls says. "But it just falls apart again.
The whole building's like that."

"'Things fall apart,'" I whisper to myself. "'The centre cannot hold.'"

"Your room," the second girl says, as she swings the door open.

"Great, thanks." I force myself to smile at them before stepping inside and closing the door in their faces. The room is spare. A table with a drawer. A wooden chair by the window. When I sit on the edge of the bed, it creaks loudly in protest. I close my eyes for a moment, trying to focus. Trying to decide what to do next. Nothing comes to me. Except the thought that perhaps I should crawl under the bed.

I open my eyes. The walls are the color of GG's oatmeal, which makes me hungry. And sad. Then the sun comes streaming through the grime-covered window, revealing a wedge of dust motes that Piper used to call fairy dust. I feel my lips twitch, as if trying to smile at the memory. Distantly, I know that I am building myself up toward finally saying good-bye. To letting Piper go.

And then Piper herself strides through the wall, as if even the bricks that compose it are unable to refuse her. She takes a few steps toward me, until she stands in the wedge of sunshine. The dust motes dance around her and the sun shines straight through her. She leaves no shadow. The bits of dust are more substantial.

I sigh heavily, and then slap my hand over my mouth, afraid that I will blow her away.

Piper laughs then. "Pollywog, haven't you grown up at all?"

"Piper." I finally allow myself to say it then, as I rush toward her with my arms open, half expecting her to slip right through them. But she doesn't. Something—not Piper exactly—but something cold and hot at the same time hugs me back. I step out of the embrace quickly, less relieved than I expected to be.

"You certainly took your time getting here," Piper says.

"I did?" I ask stupidly.

Piper rolls her eyes. "Yes. We've been waiting."

"I've been waiting too!" I interrupt. "Well, waiting and trying to figure out if you were actually in here."

"Please. Just because I'm stuck up here doesn't mean I have no idea what's going on below. You haven't been waiting. You've been hiding."

"I wasn't!" I can hear the little-sister whine in my voice, but can't quite conquer it.

"Calm down, Pollywog. It worked out fine. This is a town that bides its time. Nothing was going to happen until another fourth year rolled around again. I assumed you knew that. But when we came into August and you still hadn't made your move, I decided it was time to take action. That's why I sent LuAnn to shake you up a bit. And when you still didn't come, I had to give up three more."

"But Piper, I don't even know what my move was supposed to be. Why couldn't they have told me?"

"Pollywog, if you can't say anything smart, just shut up and let me do the talking. Okay?"

I gulp and nod.

"Thank you. So, I know you'd love to do some catching up and all that fun stuff, but the girls are all worked up about getting the plan rolling, and it's pretty high on my to-do list as well.

How about we get that going first, and then we'll kumbaya and braid hair and tell stories all night long."

As the novelty of seeing Piper fades away, I can't help but notice there's something off about the way she's talking. Not the sound or pitch of her voice, but the cadence. She's talking faster and the words sound harsher than I remember. But this is Piper, I remind myself. Piper taking charge and leading the way once more.

I nod again.

"Here's the plan. First we need to get rid of the guards. We'll send them off the roof—make an example of them. Then we round up every person under eighteen and find them nice rooms here. They'll be freaked out, but we won't keep them too long."

"No-oh," I say, amazed to hear the word tumbling from my mouth. Piper seems amused.

"What is it, Pollywog? Feeling left out?"

I shake my head. "That's not the plan. You said--you wanted . . ." My tongue twists as my half-wrecked brain races and sweats, trying to pull the exact memory into place. In my mind, I see the wheels of the tape recorder turn and then, at last, I am able to locate it. "You wanted to bring the reformatory down. Destroy it. That's what you said. It's evil. It's wrong. You said that too. You can't just kill all those guards the same way you did Ozzy."

"Please." Piper smirks at me. "I had nothing to do with Ozzy. In fact, I'm annoyed with you for making him jump like that. He was one of the few who actually saw me all the time and remembered me too. It was only that way for those who loved me, you know, and he truly did."

"That's not possible," I say, although it's what I already suspected. I was with Ozzy when he jumped. And he'd been talking about the terrible things he'd done to the inmates here, and I'd been so angry just thinking about it. . . .

"Pollywog, where did you go? Are you daydreaming or just stalling?"

"No." I say it louder this time. I always hated that nickname. I never protested because there had been affection behind it, even if it was also used to remind me of my place. But now it is nothing but condescension. "I'm not stalling. I'm making a new plan. A different plan. It's a simple one too. We're just going to leave this place and never come back."

Piper takes two steps toward me and then shoves me with both hands, which seems to penetrate my chest. I flop back onto the bed and she stands above me. "Don't be stupid. We can't just leave. The rats need to be fed."

"The rats?" I can't help but look around. Nothing is there, but I now have that itchy feeling of something crawling over me.

"You can't see them," Piper explains impatiently. "They're in the walls, the air, in everything. They are this place. They run it. They rule it."

"Not anymore," I say, trying to sound more certain than I feel. "That's the way Lachman did things, but we don't have to continue it. We can just leave and they can starve."

Piper gives my cheek a quick little tap-tap-tap with the tips of her fingers. "Think, Skylar. Just try and think what the consequence of that might be and how it would affect everyone out there."

"It would be the end of Gardnerville," I say. It's true. I already know it. It doesn't seem like a tragedy to me. "I don't care. We could leave. Like you always wanted. We could see the world. Maybe it would even be good for us."

Piper turns away from me then. She wraps her arms around herself and shivers. "You could leave. I can't. Before I couldn't exist outside this town and now . . ." She looks my way and our eyes meet for an instant and I see the old Piper there. Not this strange ghostly version of her, but the Piper that I grew up with.

"Why, Skylar?" Tears fill her eyes. "Why couldn't you just let that train carry me away? It's what I wanted—to choose when I would disappear. But you couldn't let me go, and you plucked me from the air and brought me here on the back of another girl. What's even worse, though, is that you left me. Left me with the rats. And they took me in and gave me what they could to replace what I'd lost. They made me one of them. That part was easy; I was already half rat, you could say, and that's what I'd been trying to escape. If you had only let me go, I'd already be gone. I'm here, though, broken and patched back together with too many pieces missing, but I'm here and this time . . . I'm not leaving without a fight."

And scary Piper is back.

I hold my hands up, surrender style. "I don't want a fight. All I've ever wanted is for you to come home."

In a blink, she is softer again. "You should leave. Take that boy you like and don't look back."

"I can't just go home and pretend this never happened."

"Of course you can't. You need to leave this whole town. Leave me and the little Pipers and the rats to work everything out, and you won't have to worry about it, because you'll be gone. Isn't that what you always wanted? To leave this place? To see the wonders of the world?"

No, it's what you wanted. That's what I should say. But we are one and the same, so maybe a part of me wanted it too. And for a second, I can feel what it would be like to leave.

My hand tucked securely inside Foote's larger hand, our feet walking in step together, out of the room and away from the cold of the reformatory, until we are standing on the platform of the train depot, boarding a train. I look at him and ask, "What are we doing?" He doesn't answer. He can't. His eyes are vacant and he seems to be lost inside some sort of dream. I know the dream. It's a dream of all the places the train could take us. I am having the same dream. And it's lovely. I am happy to remain lost in it all the way through the tunnel and then to whatever else lies beyond it, but the blast of the train's whistle shakes me awake.

Except it's not a train whistle. It's the buzz of the reformatory gates in front of me. I was ready to walk through and leave the reformatory as easily as I'd entered. And Foote too. He stands beside me, just as I'd imagined him, sleepy-eyed and lost.

Piper did this. Even now I can feel her in my head. We were one and the same after all. What she wanted, I wanted. But it had never worked the other way around.

I'd forgotten that too.

I shake Foote, softly at first and then as hard as I can until his eyes flutter open.

"Who are you?" he asks.

"Foote, it's me, Skylar." I stare at him, trying to figure out if he's still half asleep. He seems totally aware now, even looking around. "Foote, are you okay?"

He turns to me with a funny squint on his face. "Foote. That's my name, right? It's weird, but it feels familiar."

The reformatory shouldn't be working this quickly. And even if it has, memory loss is not one of the side effects. I wonder if Elton slipped him something, but that would've kicked in long ago.

I pull the broken tape from my pocket, using it as a touchstone that might trigger another memory.

I RAN (SO FAR AWAY) the label reads.

Then, finally, the last piece falls into place. Now it makes sense that over the course of four long years I never once remembered the truth of Piper's origin. And I also know the source of Foote's sudden memory loss.

It's me.

I forget things. I've always forgotten things. The more I take from others, the more I lose of myself.

After everything I've done today, I should be the one who doesn't remember her own name. But Foote protected me from that; he took it and, in doing so, lost himself.

"Go," I tell Foote, pushing him through the gates. "Run."

He takes a few steps and then stops, turning back to me. "Aren't you coming too?"

"I have to do something," I tell him. "I'm not sure what, but I gotta do it."

"Okay, that sort of makes sense," Foote says kindly, but it's clear he's now just humoring the crazy girl.

And even though it's not the best time, I don't know if I'll get another, so I quickly add, "You probably don't remember this, but you were right. You told me you felt like you were from here, and it's true—you were. My mom knew your mom. We were friends. Well, we were babies, so we didn't really have friends, but we shared a carriage and that's how you got lost. Or taken. It was a fourth year and these birds took you from the carriage and carried you out over the mountains."

Foote stares at me.

"It probably doesn't make sense right now, but it will later. Just remember it, okay?"

"Yeah, okay," he answers, and this time there's no kindly condescension.

"Now go!" I reach toward Foote to give him another push when it occurs to me that I have no idea what's going to happen next and I may never see him again. Grabbing hold of his shirt, I pull him down a bit and then stand on my tiptoes to meet him halfway so that I can give him a big wet kiss to remember me by . . . I hope.

He kisses me back—briefly—before I pull away.

A goofy smile fills his face. "That was nice." The smile dims as he squints at me. "What was your name again?"

I don't want to tell him only to have him forget it again; my heart might break if I have to say it more than once. So instead I channel the dangerous dame from *The Maltese Falcon*. "What would you do if I didn't tell you? Something wild and unpredictable?"

Foote grins, quickly getting the reference, but he doesn't respond as I expected with Spade's answer of "I might." Instead he plucks two of the best lines from the movie and links them together all while doing the best Bogart impression I've ever heard. "You're good, you're very good. The, uh, stuff that dreams are made of." The gates buzz again, getting ready to close and reminding me that this is maybe not the best time to flirt. I leap back, not wanting Foote to get caught on the wrong side of the gates. "Go," I urge him once more.

He stumbles back a few steps, his brow furrowed in confusion. The gates slide shut between us.

"Run," I remind him, before turning away.

"Wait," Foote calls. I stop. "Do I . . . We're friends, right? That didn't end when we were babies?"

A choking, aching laugh escapes me. "Yeah, we're friends."

Foote nods. "Well, good lu—"

I quickly cut him off. "Don't say it. You've given me enough luck already."

He stares at me, as if trying to figure me out, but with a shake of his head says, "Here's looking at you, kid."

"Wrong movie," I answer. "That's *Casablanca*."

He shrugs and then pulls his hat down low so that it covers his eyes. "The endings are similar, though. He doesn't get the girl either time." As Foote turns and finally begins to walk away, I stifle the urge to tell him to pretend that Brigid and Spade find the Maltese falcon they'd been searching for and live happily ever after. Except I suddenly recall that when Spade says the line about "the stuff that dreams are made of" he's referring to the

Maltese falcon . . . which in the end he finds out is a fake. I can't help but think of Piper then and all the time I've spent searching for her. Even when I finally found her, she wasn't what I'd been looking for. It's looking more and more like I'm not gonna get the girl I'd wanted either.

That's not an ending I'll accept, though, and that's why I watch Foote walk away until he disappears from view, and then with even more dread than the last time, I brace myself to reenter the reformatory.

I RAN (SO FAR AWAY)

Four Years Ago

I CAN'T FORGET YOU, PIPER. BUT SOMETIMES, I CAN'T really remember you either.

I could keep blaming the forget-me-nots. I could say they help me live with things too painful to remember.

But that's a lie.

The truth is I've always had holes in my memory. Every time I took a secret, I lost something of my own. Not always immediately. Sometimes not until weeks later. It was never anything big. I'd forget what we had for dinner the night before. Once I couldn't remember what color the sky was. Then it got worse. One day I couldn't remember how to get home from school. After that I started to avoid the secrets that clung to everyone I met. It was like trying not to scratch a mosquito bite. It called and you automatically reached toward it, needing to relieve the itch. Slowly, over time, I made a habit of not scratching, of looking away until the urge passed. Except sometimes there was no helping it. Some secrets slipped through the cracks.

When I went to GG, hoping she could explain my memory loss, she called it yin and yang, and said that I would notice the effects of it more and more the older I got. This is the way she explained it to me: She made people see things so lifelike they became real, and, in doing so, bit by bit she lost the ability to see, until she was almost completely blind. Daddy made everyone love him but eventually couldn't feel that emotion himself. And I messed with the minds of everyone around me and slowly lost little pieces of my own.

You knew how it was for me, Piper. Better than anyone. You said we needed to tell our stories, to keep them. Mom had a pile of mix tapes that we slowly recorded over. Each tape was titled with the name of her favorite song in the mix. Years earlier Dad had made Mom put the tapes away; he hated anything that gave her joy that didn't originate from him.

When we found them, she told us she didn't care if we recorded over them. "It's just my old eighties music from when I was a kid," she'd said dismissively, like she didn't care. But sometimes when we played them back, bits of music played between pauses, and if Mom was anywhere nearby she'd start to quietly sing along.

In some ways, I think those songs were Mom's story. You never knew this, Piper, but sometimes I'd listen to the songs on the tapes before we recorded over them. I thought maybe I'd understand Mom better. You would've laughed at me. And you would've been a little bit mad, too, that I still cared enough to try.

Now I am watching the tiny wheels turn round and round as I tell our story set to Mom's soundtrack.

I started taking the forget-me-nots to forget that I'd forgotten. I wanted to forget to remember. But people don't work that way. We are constantly searching, wanting to fill in the empty places. Wanting answers. The more I forgot, the further I got from the truth, the harder I searched for it. When I started looking for answers, I always started at the same place: your May Day.

When I close my eyes, I am there again. At the bridge watching you run with the train on your heels and Elton determined to save you. He almost had you. Your fingertips touched his. Too late. The train was too swift and unforgiving. It didn't run you over though. You weren't ground to a pulp beneath its wheels of steel. The second the train touched you, you disappeared. You vanished and left Elton clutching only air. If I were him, I'd have stood there gaping while the train ran me down. Not Elton, though. He threw himself over the bridge. Not quick enough to save his legs. The train kept those as a souvenir. But he kept his life.

I wonder what you would think of him now, Piper. Would you love the person he's turned into? He hardly ever mentions you. Acts like you never existed at all. But every time he looks at me, I can feel him thinking about you. It's not even a secret I have to take.

Elton had a close-up of you becoming nothing. I saw it from

a distance. Even so, I knew exactly what I'd seen and yet . . . That night, I scrambled down the bank and into the Salt Spring, screaming your name the whole time. Chance found me then; he barked at me from the shore, warning me to come back. He hated the springwater—I knew that—but I was desperate.

"Come on, Chance," I called to him, patting my legs. "Come here, boy. I need you to find Piper."

He came then, whimpering the whole time; he swam out toward me and then, with my encouragement, kept going farther out until I couldn't see him anymore. "Good boy. Find Piper. Good boy." I kept calling, until I couldn't even hear his paddling. That was the last I ever saw of Chance. I think I sent him into the spring not truly hoping he'd find you but as a trade. An offering. Take my dog. Give me back my sister.

I stood there, waist deep in the water, waiting. Finally someone came swimming toward me out of the darkness. I could feel the panic in the way she chopped at the water. It was nothing at all like the calm and deliberate way you swam. Still, I was certain it was you. It had to be you. I grabbed you, pulling you from the water. You struggled, screamed.

"Piper, it's me," I yelled.

You stopped and looked at me. It wasn't you. It was just a girl. Someone we went to school with. I couldn't even recall her name. "You did this, didn't you?" she asked.

I shook my head, denying it. Not to escape the punishment or the guilt, but because this was yours. Your fourth year. Your place in our twisted history. I couldn't take that away from you.

"No," I said. "It was Piper."

She swiped the water from her face, then leaned in closer. "Who the hell is Piper?"

I dove into her head then, digging through it, looking for any bit of you. But she really had no idea who you were. Not your name or your face . . . or anything.

I released her and she fell back into the water. "You're Piper," I said, even though I knew she wasn't. Even though by then I had a terrible feeling that you were more than simply gone . . . that perhaps you had never existed at all. But I wasn't ready to let you go. I would never be ready to let you go. I needed you to be there then. I wanted her to be you. I made her into you. I didn't mean to.

Or maybe I did.

Reaching into the water, I pulled her back up. I still had the lock of hair you'd given to Elton. It felt like fate, seeing it there clutched in my fist. I grabbed hold of her hand and pressed the tress into her palm, until her fingers closed around it, making it her own.

I looked up to see that the water had filled with boats and searchlights. Rescue. And retribution. I stood there in the water, growing cold, watching. No one looked my way. They rescued some, they pulled others from the water too late. A few were gone, never to be seen again.

And the girl I'd called Piper was packed into the reformatory van. I watched them lead her away. She didn't struggle. Instead she walked, head held high and proud. As they pushed her into the van, she looked back at me. Our eyes met, held. The door slammed between us, but we didn't break eye contact. She pressed her hand to the glass window, and as the van began to move away, I watched her lips form the words *One and the same*.

I raced after it. I couldn't let them take you away. I ran all the way up to the reformatory. I begged them to take me too.

When it became clear that they wouldn't, I went home.

Mom and Dad were waiting up. Mom threw her arms around me, did the whole thank-God-you're-alive thing. Then she asked what happened.

"It was Piper," I said.

Mom just nodded, like she'd already guessed. Dad frowned and puffed out his chest. Then he did the strangest thing. He wrapped his arms around me and gave me a gigantic, smothering hug. His hand smoothed my hair and his breath was warm in my ear, shushing me as if I were crying. I stood stiff and still in his embrace, waiting for it to be over. He was clumsy, trying to force his way into my heart. When his lips brushed my cheek, I pushed him away.

He looked shocked and then angry and then shocked some more. He came at me again, arms held out, this time ready to strangle me with his love.

Maybe that was when I realized how much you had stood between us. You had shielded me from him. This horrible monster of a man who could make anyone love him but could no longer feel that emotion himself.

I'd wanted you to kill him for a long time, Piper. Even before I was old enough to realize that the time he spent in your bedroom wasn't right. You couldn't do it. You loved him. You hated him too. But in this instance love conquered all—including hate.

I could do it, though. I should've done it a lot sooner.

I told him he should take a walk. I wished you'd sent him off the bridge with the others. Except I wanted him to jump off a higher bridge. I wanted him to fall farther and feel death rushing toward him with no way to avoid it.

Dad left easily. He kissed me on the cheek and for a moment he looked sad. I told him to write. He did. The same day he jumped, he put a postcard in the mail with a picture of the Golden Gate Bridge on it.

After he left, I went up to my room. That was when I found the tape you'd left. It was labeled DON'T YOU (FORGET ABOUT ME). I listened to it once. You said some terrible things, Piper. I can't quite recall what they were right now, but I know it was awful, because I recall the way I had to keep pausing the tape to catch my breath.

I made myself forget, Piper. Before the pills ever arrived, I reached into my head and extracted my own secrets. I didn't destroy them. I hid them in a safe place for later. But when later came, I'd forgotten where I'd put them. I'd forgotten they'd existed at all.

Here's the funny thing: I thought it would be easier that way.

EIGHTEEN

AS I ENTER THE ROOM WHERE I LAST SAW PIPER, THE
tape I listened to from her is at the forefront of my mind, along
with the other ones I'd recorded and then done my best to
forget—they have finally all come back to me.

Now I understand why everyone calls me the Pied Piper.
They think the last fourth year was mine. To them, Piper never
existed. Only the people who loved her remember her. Me, GG,
Elton, Ozzy, and maybe Mom, too. It's a shockingly short list.

Walking over to the window, I look down at the empty train
tracks below. I run my finger along the glass, tracing the bridge.
I stop at the exact spot where the train struck Piper. The place
where she disappeared. The moment that I lost her. Or the best
parts anyway. The bits of herself that she'd built around what
everyone else had imagined for her. The Piper in the reformatory

is somebody else, Piper's ghost reanimated by my hand and then reimagined by the rats.

Slowly, I turn in a half circle, scanning the room, waiting for Piper to reappear. I can't leave her here. I can't take her out. I can't be part of her plan to fill the reformatory with the innocent. It makes Elton's way of doing things look positively democratic.

And then there's Piper's original plan—destroy the reformatory and everything it stands for. I never really took the plan seriously, and so I never really thought about the consequences. Now, though, I do. What would happen to the old-timers? To the people like Mom who came here because they were sick? To Piper? So many people would be saved, and so many others would be lost.

"The best lack all conviction." That was another line from that damn poem. If that's true, then I must be the greatest fucking person on the planet 'cause I still have no damn clue what to do.

"Oh, Skylar, how many times must I tell you to leave?" I whirl to face Piper, and in the same moment the ground rumbles beneath my feet, like it did earlier—except a million times worse. It's followed by a horrible cracking noise, like thunder. I run back to the window just in time to see the earth split. Huge chasms appear, snaking every which way for miles in every direction.

This isn't some random event. I know because there are secrets screaming through the air, coming at me from all directions, demanding to be heard. It's not Piper or anything with a human voice.

It's the rats.

Things have been unbalanced for too long, and now a resolution must be found. They must be fed or released.

"Make them stop!" I scream at Piper.

She laughs. "I can't and I wouldn't if I could."

Another tremor rips through the earth, this time shaking me right off my feet. I lie there for a moment, stunned, until the sound of distant screams reaches me. Pushing myself to my feet, I race back to the window and then peer down to watch Gardnerville get ripped apart.

The worst of it is the trestle bridge. The giant span buckles beneath its own weight, making the metal holding it together scream in agony. As it collapses, bits of split wood spray out. I rub my eyes, unable to believe it could be so easily destroyed.

I spin around to glare at Piper. "You finally beat the bridge. Don't even try and tell me that wasn't you."

"It might have been my suggestion," Piper admits with a shrug.

Finally, the earth stops its endless shivering. I fall to my knees, relieved there's nothing more to see. Piper kneels beside me and gently strokes my back.

"There, that wasn't so bad, was it?"

"Not so bad?" I scramble to my feet, wanting to get as far from her as possible. "It's the worst thing I've ever seen."

"Really?" Piper coldly replies. "Worse than watching the train overtake me?"

"Yes," I choke out.

"So much for sisterly love." Piper glides over to the window and looks down. "I've been upstaged by the appetizer. By the time you see the entrée, I fear I'll have completely fallen off your list of horrors."

I force myself to take one step and then another, until I am at Piper's side, looking out the window once more. At first I am relieved to see no further destruction. No more chaos. It looks like people are already getting out and cleaning things up.

But the longer I look, the more undeniable it becomes that everyone is moving in the same direction; they even seem to be forming a line . . . almost like a parade.

I watch a moment longer, as the head of the growing chain takes a turn that can lead only one place.

It's exactly the way LuAnn had described it: "We'll call it the uprising. It's the way Gardnerville was always meant to be, everyone gathered together in the reformatory." That was the plan. Days ago, she came right out and told me exactly what was going on. And like an idiot, I stood there thinking, This poor crazy girl, who knows what she's blabbering about?

"You're really bringing them here," I say, still struggling to believe it.

"Yes," Piper agrees. "I really am."

"No," I answer, vehemently disagreeing with Piper for the first time in my life. "You're not."

And then we proceed to fight over the fate of Gardnerville in the way that other siblings might squabble over a cherished toy, tugging it back and forth, each of us declaring that it's "mine."

The difference here, of course, is that the fate of every person in this town is at stake.

DON'T STOP BELIEVIN'

This Year

AUGUST WAS ALMOST ALWAYS TOO HOT AND
sticky for parades, or any other type of activity more strenuous
than lifting a glass of ice-cold lemonade to your lips. And the
August of this year in particular was one of the hottest anyone
could remember. Despite this, toward the end of one especially
steamy late-summer evening, a parade began to wind its way
through town.

All the young people were a part of it. Their feet lifted and
fell in an odd way, as if they were following the beat of some hidden drummer. Or perhaps it was more like they were being held
in the sway of a snake charmer's flute, playing a tune only they
could hear.

The adults, left out of the parade, watched their children walk
along the route with a sense of distant alarm. Something about

this whole thing felt wrong, but every time they took a sip of cold water, the feeling faded away. It must be the heat, they thought.

By the time the parade began to march up the hillside toward the reformatory, every child eighteen or younger was a part of it.

You probably think you know what happened that day, but you couldn't possibly understand it all. So I'm recording it for you, Wills. I'm using this last tape for my last Gardnerville story.

I used to do these recordings for Piper. It was her idea. All the good ones always were. She said that if we didn't tell our stories, other people would and they'd get it all wrong. Really, though, Piper wanted me to remember, and I think also she wanted me to see things the way she wished for them to be, even if that wasn't quite the way things truly were.

Now, Wills, I'm trying to remember things the right way, especially the things I'd rather forget.

Like Mom.

Before she died—weeks before, actually, when she was growing weaker but could still get around and we still had hope that she might make it—Mom said something I can't get out of my head. She was reminiscing about the time after she'd come to Gardnerville. She said that for the first couple of months she was here, she felt like she was inside a waking dream and kept waiting to return to reality. Now, though, she said, it was her life before Gardnerville that seemed like a dream: hazy and fuzzy and as substantial as a soap bubble.

I can't imagine ever feeling that way about Gardnerville. Sitting here on our old front porch, it seems impossible to think of this place as nothing more than a memory. But I guess it will become that way for everyone. The little kids like you will grow up without any substantial memories of the fourth years, and they'll never experience one, so it will feel like a story. Like someone else's dream. And for everyone else, I guess eventually time won't be counted in fours. The fear and anticipation won't go away immediately, but after a few uneventful fourth years, everyone will relax and then, soon thereafter, they'll forget.

Trust me on that, Wills. That's how it will happen. The Gardnerville where you were born and where I grew up is already gone. Funny how it never felt temporary, even when Piper and I were already beginning to destroy it. I never thought anything would really change. I believed that things would stay the way they'd always been.

And then Mom died.

Well, first she gave me this tape. All these years, she'd had one smuggled away, unable to give it up. The first song on the tape has this line about a girl who takes a midnight train. Mom said she listened to it, rewinding it and playing it again and again, for the entire train ride here. She gave the tape to me only after I promised not to record over that one song. Someday, Wills, I'll give you this tape, and that song will be the first thing you hear on it. Maybe it'll help you feel closer to Mom. To remember her and how much she loved you. I sure hope so.

I wish I could give you more of her than just that, Wills. And I hope you know that I didn't want to let her go. We'd already lost so much.

But she told me straight out, "I was lucky to have a wonderful extension on life. Now it's over and that's okay. It's time."

"No." That's what I said to her. "No. You can't. I won't let you." "I think you already tried that once," Mom reminded me. "It didn't work out so well."

That was when I was finally able to kiss her and say good-bye.

I guess that was also when I really and truly realized Gardnerville was gone. I walked through town. Buildings were boarded up. Milly had passed away too, and her empty restaurant already looked dusty and forgotten. And then I somehow ended up at GG's. When I told her about Mom, she said it would be her turn next. And I reminded her that I had fifty bucks with the bookie on her living another hundred years.

I still think it's possible for GG to make it that long—just out of sheer stubbornness.

Sometimes we talk about our father, Lachman. It's still mind-bending to remember that GG is technically my sister. I think that's part of what has allowed us to finally understand each other a little bit better. Well, that and the way everything ended on that horrible August day.

We haven't discussed it that much—hardly at all really—but GG did mention it once. She said, with this tone of voice she uses when announcing facts that cannot be argued against, "It had to be done."

I wish I shared her certainty; maybe then I could stop replaying that day and wondering if it could have worked out another way.

Wills, I can almost see you squirming as you listen to this, waiting for me to get to the good part. The action. If you were at my elbow right now, you'd be demanding, "Tell me what happened to the reformatory. And Piper. And the rats."

Have you ever tried to wrestle a ghost, Wills? It was no surprise, really, that Piper fought dirty. She'd knee me in the kidney
and then when I attempted to return the favor she'd become
smoke. My fist would waft straight through her.

In between taking swings at the air, I tried to reason with her.
"Piper, what are you doing?" I'd say. "This isn't what you wanted.
We wanted to keep everyone safe from the reformatory, and now
you're trying to pack it fuller than ever."

I don't think she even heard me. It didn't feel like Piper was
even in there anymore. Her movements were somehow both skit-
tish and sly, and her eyes had gone black and beady. She had been
overtaken by the rats. She, they—whatever it was—jerked my
feet out from under me and laughed when I crashed to the floor.
A corner of the bed met my skull, and a bright flash of light was
followed by darkness.

I couldn't have been out for more than five or ten minutes.
I came to with a throbbing headache, and immediately searched
the room for Piper. For the moment, though, it seemed I was
alone. I dragged my aching body to the window and peered
down.

The parade marched ever closer to the reformatory, and the
gates were beginning to squeal open in anticipation of admitting
its newest inmates. The steepness of the hill had slowed them
down considerably; parts of the line were barely moving forward
at all. Still, many of them were close enough now that I could recognize the faces of sleepwalking classmates, some of them hand
in hand with their younger siblings, pulling one another along.

LuAnn and the other three Pipers led the way. I recognized one of the girls as the one who'd come crawling from the water on May Day, the one I'd used to keep Piper alive. I did that, Wills. In that moment I finally recognized the wrongs I had done. I accepted my part in the terrible uprising we were all caught within.

It felt like a new low, but then my focus shifted to the two big football players lumbering directly behind the false Pipers, each with a child slung over his shoulders. My heart nearly stopped when I realized one of them was you, Wills.

I spun around and ran from the room. My feet felt like they were made of cement, holding me back. I forced them to move faster, taking the stairs two or three at a time. You would not pass through those gates. I wouldn't allow it.

I burst through the front doors of the reformatory, nearly losing my footing as I sped toward the opening in the gates.

Without my bird's-eye view, it wasn't as easy to pick you out of the growing crowd of people patiently waiting for the gates to open and allow them in. I swayed, uncertain. And angry. And scared. And so many other things. All the emotions that had been tied into those forgotten memories filled me up and then overflowed.

You need to help them, said a voice inside my head. It sounded like me, and yet not like me at all. *And the best way to help them*, the voice continued, *is to do what you do best. Go into their heads, but this time don't stop with peeping; this time, take. Make them forget. You know better than most that forgetting is a sort of kindness. A mercy. Be merciful. Not that they'll remember. They'll forget, the same way they forgot Piper. Now it's their turn to be forgotten. See how they like it. It's no less than they deserve.*

I nodded in agreement, feeling more certain than I had in days. More certain than I'd ever felt in my entire life. *Yes,* everything inside me said, *this is right. This is what I was meant to do.*

Catching sight of the Pipers, I advanced toward them, ready to rip every thought from their heads. *Yes, yes, yes.* The voice inside cheered me on. *Start with them and then go down the line, until every single one has been wiped clean.* My gaze traveled over the parade of people coming my way. All of those heads stuffed full of ideas and memories and observations, soon to be scrubbed clean.

LuAnn stepped forward, holding her hands out, willingly giving herself to me. I reached toward her and as I did, you, Wills, came into view again.

"No," I mumbled aloud as the voice inside my head screamed at me to grab hold of LuAnn. *NOW!* it demanded.

Wills, I don't know how I beat the fourth-year madness, because that is what those voices surely were. They were all the way inside me—I had given myself to them completely—and then . . . they weren't.

"Wills!" I screamed, tearing you away from the football player and pulling you into my arms. You lay heavy and limp, but the steady rise and fall of your small chest reassured me that you were okay.

Slowly I sank to my knees and laid you on the ground. I peered down at your little face, streaked with peanut butter. The parade must have caught you in the middle of eating your afternoon snack. Finding a tissue in my pocket, I gently wiped your face clean. Then I gave your shoulder a shake. "Wills." I stroked your hair. "Come on, Wills, it's time to wake up."

You stirred and your eyelids fluttered. "Sky?" you said in a groggy voice.

I cried then. Giant tears rolled down my face, and as each one fell you reached up with your chubby little hand and scrubbed it away.

"Did you have a nightmare?" you asked, still confused by where we were and what was happening.

You weren't the only one asking that question. All around us the parade was breaking apart as the sleepwalkers woke from their strange dreams.

Just like that, I'd foiled Piper's plan. There would be no fourth-year event, nor any fresh meat for the rats. The cycle needed to repeat or else unravel. Unwittingly, I had undone it all. And in doing so, I lost her for the last time . . . and Gardnerville too.

In some ways, it felt like the same thing. Piper was Gardnerville. Gardnerville was Piper.

A terrible rumbling noise came from the reformatory. I looked up at the gray and dark and crumbling structure. Then I searched every window until finally I saw Piper staring back at me. She brought her hand up and pressed it against the glass.

One and the same. I watched her lips form the words.

This time I didn't say them with her.

Standing and leaving you behind, Wills, I marched toward the heavy front door of the reformatory. I was expecting another fight, but it gave way with only the slightest touch from my fingertips, swinging open and hitting the wall on the other side with enough force to make the whole building shake.

A moment later the inmates began to escape from the darkness of the reformatory and into the dying light of the day. Single file they staggered out, one after another, with the guards themselves leading the way. Bits of brick fell from the building, slowly at first and then, as the parade reversed itself and wound down the road and all the way into town, the tumbling debris increased to a steady cascade. When the last person exited, the whole building trembled.

I stumbled backward, afraid of being crushed in the inevitable collapse. Again, I couldn't help but search for some sign of Piper still standing in the window. There was too much dust in the air, though, for me to see farther than a few feet in front of me. I thought I could leave her there. I thought that finally I was able to let her go.

Instead, I found myself taking tentative steps forward again, straight into the air thick with the dust of crumbling bricks. The door had swung closed once more. I slammed my hand against it, but wasn't surprised when it stayed shut; the weight of the sagging bricks above had pinned it tight. It seemed unlikely it would ever open again.

The reformatory felt like a tomb then. A final resting place for Piper. It was the last thing she would've wanted, to be trapped inside.

I threw myself at the door, screaming at it to open. It creaked but didn't budge. Then from the other side, I could hear someone pounding against it. Someone who wanted out as badly as I wanted to get in.

BAM. BAM. BAM.

Frantic and desperate, I kicked at the door, pleading with it softly to please please please just open.

An avalanche of bricks came tumbling down. Covering my head, I retreated a few steps, and as I did so, the door flew open.

A river of black, at least a foot deep, rushed out. The current split around me, flowing over my feet as if it were one body, except now I could see that it was made up of rats. Hundreds. Thousands. Perhaps there was no number large enough to contain all those rats.

Later I would hear how they scurried over the feet of those leaving the reformatory. They became their own parade, going all the way into the center of town to the corner of Main and State where the May Queen had once disappeared. Then the rats scattered in every direction.

The children caught up in the parade dispersed slower, less certain where they belonged now. But they would have time to figure it out, along with everyone else as they realized the Gardnerville they'd known was gone.

It would take days, weeks, for the full impact of that to be understood. As the old-timers passed away one after another. As those who'd come here to escape illness succumbed to their cancers and diseases once more. As those still alive made the decision whether to stay or to go.

Even with no train running, lots of people were talking about leaving. They hesitated only out of fear of what was out there on the other side. And of course, without the train, the journey was that much more difficult.

The first few to leave loaded their belongings into rowboats to cross the Salt Spring. But the water grew increasingly shallow every day without the reformatory to feed it, and the boats began to run aground. These days, those wanting to get to the tunnel have to slog through six inches of mud. It's drying up quickly, though, and my guess is that by the time we've said all our good-byes, the water and mud will be gone, leaving only a fine sprinkling of salt behind.

Not everyone is leaving, though. A smaller, more vocal group is insisting on staying and finding a way to make life here work once more. Surprisingly, Elton is leading that group. He insists that there is still something special about Gardnerville.

Despite all our differences, I can't help but hope he is right.

As for me, I did see Piper one final time. When the last of the reformatory crumbled to the ground, she came skipping through the bits of rubble until she was right in front of me, and then we were wrapped in each other's arms.

The rats were gone. This at last was truly Piper.

"Remember." She whispered just that one word, and then she was gone, leaving me holding nothing but air.

Sometimes I think I shouldn't have let her go, that I should have found a way to make her stay. But there is no place for imaginary girls in this new Gardnerville. And there is no place for me, either. A girl who knows everyone's old secrets, but has no idea what currently hides in their hearts and never again will. The world is shockingly quiet now, and sometimes I wonder how everyone else manages to go through day after day with only the thoughts in their own head to keep them company.

At least I have you and Foote to go along with me and keep my thoughts from driving me crazy. And in return we'll be there to remind Foote that he can no longer absorb bullets or my lingering memory problems. Perhaps we'll find him a new name too, now that he is no longer lucky.

Along the way, he wants to find his mother. And I want to see a big city. One like we've seen on the posters at Milly's, full of neon signs and buildings that crowd out the sky. Piper said there must be magic there. I disagreed then, but now I'm not so certain.

I've done some research, and they say most of the big cities are full of rats, and ours are now nowhere to be seen. I can't help but wonder, if we see the ones from Gardnerville, will we recognize them as our own?

The truth is, Wills, I'll be looking for Gardnerville everywhere we go, hoping to find it again. You keep asking me, Wills, why we have to leave. You cry and plead for us to stay. Sometimes it's all I can do not to join in.

But we have to go, Wills. If we didn't then I'd be here, always trying to forget the way things ended, always hoping for a better outcome.

Forgetting the past doesn't change it, and if we want a better ending we'll have to go out and create it for ourselves somewhere on the other side of the mountain. Until then we have our stories. I'll tell them to you as many times as you want. Then you'll repeat them to all the new friends you'll make. Most people will think you're making them up. They might even call you a liar, and then, Wills, there's only one thing you can say.

Say it with me now, Wills. Once like it's our curse. A second time as if it's a relief. And finally like it's nothing but the plain and simple truth. Let's say it now, so we both remember.

There's no place like home.

There's no place like home.

There's no place like home.

ACKNOWLEDGMENTS

THANK YOU TO MY BRILLIANT EDITOR, ERICA SUSSMAN, whose questions and comments have become an indispensable touchstone that I continuously come back to as I cut, tweak, and rewrite my way from the sloppy first draft to the final polished pages.

Thank you also to Stephanie Stein, the epically awesome Epic Reads Tea Time pairing of Margot and Aubry, and everyone else at HarperCollins in editing, design, marketing, and sales who all put so much work into launching this book.

Thank you a hundred million times to Alexandra Machinist. Two books in and I am still pinching myself, unable to believe my luck in having you as an agent.

Robert Brunschmid aka Bob, Bobbeo, and most recently Zumba Bobby (quite possibly my favorite incarnation yet). Thank you so much for all your help and advice in the months and weeks leading up to the launch of *Another Little Piece*. You are absolutely amazing and I feel so lucky to have you in my corner.

I often make fun of my decision to pursue not one but two impractical degrees, but I would not trade the experiences from my theater major days at Niagara University or the time spent pursuing an MFA in film and television production at Chapman University for anything. Thank you to all my classmates and teachers at NU and Chapman who taught and shared so much with me.

To all the wonderful writing friends I've made since beginning this journey, especially: all the Lucky 13s, the Class of 2K13, my Wednesday-night writing-group peeps, and my amazing longtime crit partner, Alyson Greene.

And finally to all of my family and friends, you know who you are and also (hopefully) know how much I love and cherish each and every one of you.

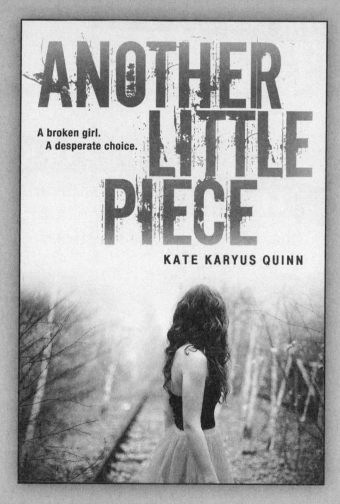